W9-CEZ-781

Covenant at Coldwater

John Osier

St. Luke's Press
Memphis

Library of Congress Cataloging in Publication Data

Osier, John, 1938–
  Covenant at Coldwater.

  I. Title.
PS3565.S55C6 1984   813'.54   83-19264
ISBN 0-918518-28-8 (pbk.)

The people, places and events described here are purely fictional and have no resemblance to actual places, events and/or people, living or dead.

ISBN 0-918518-28-8 (pbk.)

To Barbara

For in this limbo we must forever dwell,
Shut out alike from Heaven and Earth and Hell.

"The City of Dreadful Night"

James Thompson

THE events recounted here occurred in the spring of 1977 in North Mississippi. They were first related to me one evening several years ago over a bottle of Jack Daniels by an old friend and former newspaper associate who is referred to in the book as George Burke, although that is not his real name. Nor are any of the other people involved given their real names. In the place of Burke's actual town, I have drawn a composite from two or three different North Mississippi towns and borrowed the name of a real one, in order to protect Burke's fellow citizens.

Shortly before his death two years ago, George Burke gave me his papers and files concerning the following events but without any photographs. All of those, for reasons that will be made clear, he had long since destroyed.

—John Osier

CHAPTER 1

THREADING their way through the dark pines, they came to the ditch where the old Studebaker lay rusting and desolate. Vines snaked through the windows. The wheels and engine had been stripped away; the empty windshield gaped at them forlornly. A lone door hung from one hinge at a crazy angle.

They eyed the wreck somberly—the thin boy with hair the color of pale Scotch whiskey and the stocky boy who tossed his head to keep the wild, black hair out of his eyes. The ditch was a dim tangle of vines, and both wondered if a cottonmouth might be down there coiled in the cool of the car.

"It'll be dark soon," Scott said. "Maybe we better wait."

His companion looked at him and shook his head. He whipped the hair out of his eyes and, clutching the hacksaw, started down into the ditch.

Scott kicked a clod of earth onto the Studebaker. He did not like this place. It was too silent, too dismal. Beyond the pines he could see the fruit jars winking in the fading sunlight and he saw something else: at the edge of the trees an open grave waiting for its possessor, he guessed. But there was no funeral party in the little graveyard; it was deserted, and beyond it stretched the big swamp.

Bobby was at the bottom of the ditch now, his dark head bent to examine the hinge on the car door. Then the saw he had taken from his father's toolbox rasped against

9

the hinge, breaking the stillness.

Scott climbed reluctantly down and smelled it immediately above the odor of damp earth—a reek like human sweat, yet also something else that reminded him of sickness, a faint, sweetish odor of decay. Wrinkling his nose, he peered inside the car but saw only a nest of yellow jackets under the dashboard.

The sawing stopped abruptly. Bobby was staring at a thicket of creepers at the far end of the ditch. His brown face had gone pale and there was a pinched look about his nostrils. Following his gaze Scott could see nothing, but the air seemed suddenly chill as though a cold, invisible mist had drifted in from the swamp.

They stared at each other.

The vines rustled. They turned and saw them trembling. Bobby whirled and began scrabbling up the face of the ditch. Scott clawed his way up the clay and heard a thrashing sound from the vines.

They reached the top together and, without looking back, bolted into the pines. They dodged through the trees, running until they were exhausted and at last collapsed into a mound of clean-smelling pine needles. For a long time they listened to the sound of their own panting. In Bobby's dilated pupils, Scott saw his own face tight and drawn.

"What was it?" he gasped.

"Hush!" Bobby stared back in the direction of the ditch. Both of them strained to listen. But Scott heard only a faint breeze soughing in the tops of the pines.

"You didn't see anything?" Bobby said at last.

"No. Did you?" They rose and brushed off the pine needles.

Bobby shook his head. He cast another look in the direction of the ditch. Then they started toward home.

"Something was sure in those vines," Bobby said. "I reckon a fox might have a den in there." He smiled, but his eyes were uneasy.

Scott seized the thought. "Yeah. From the smell it must have killed something." They trudged on in silence and reached a newly planted cotton field. As they were

10

stepping between the rows, Bobby suddenly stopped.

"The saw," he said. "I left the saw!"

Behind them the sun was sinking below the pines. In front of them the dying light reflected off the town's water tower less than a mile away. They were both silent awhile.

"I got to go back," Bobby said finally. His voice sounded queer.

Scott stared at him. "You sure you left it down at the ditch?"

Bobby nodded miserably. His dark eyes slid away from Scott's blue ones. He squinted in the direction of the water tower, then back toward the gloomy pines.

"I've got to get it. Pa will whip me. He'll whip me good."

Scott scuffed the toe of his sneaker into the dry dirt, raising a little puff of dust. "It's too late. Wait until tomorrow."

Bobby gave him a look of despair. "I can't. He'll miss it tonight and know I took it. He told me never to touch his tools." Bobby's voice was pleading. "Are you coming with me?"

Scott did not answer. He studied the mound of dirt where the tiny green cotton stalks were just beginning to break the surface. He studied the ground for a long time.

When he looked up at last, Bobby had already started walking slowly back toward the pines.

Then the pines swallowed him. Scott stood alone in the field in the fading sunlight staring at the place where Bobby had entered.

He felt alone and vaguely guilty.

He tried to tell himself it was not his fault Bobby had left the hacksaw. And he had not asked Bobby to swipe it out of his fathers's toolbox to begin with. And selling the car door for scrap had not been his idea either. But the guilty feeling remained. His friend had asked for his help and he had denied it because he was afraid. Afraid of what? A noise in some vines?

At school tomorrow Bobby might tell everybody how he had gone back to the ditch and found a possum in the

11

vines. Scott afraid of a possum! All the kids would laugh at him. The sun had vanished and he could feel the earth cooling beneath his feet. He kicked up a tender cotton shoot.

"All right," he muttered. First he started walking toward the pines, then broke into a trot.

"Bobby!" he shouted. "Wait up!"

But Bobby did not reply. Somewhere ahead of him a dove mourned in the dying light.

FROM the swamp he could hear the frogs calling. A faint mist rose out of the ditch. He stood twenty yards from the ditch and called again. He thought he could hear his heart pounding in his chest.

Bobby might be hiding behind a tree waiting to jump out at him. Scott headed slowly toward the ditch. It was dim down here in daylight; now it was almost dark. He thought of supper and how his parents would be angry with him. Bobby was probably not even down here anyway. As soon as he had gotten out of Scott's sight, he could have circled around and gone back to town. Right now he might be home eating his hot supper.

Scott shivered. With the sun gone, a chill rose on the mist from the ditch. He was only a few feet away now. He approached the edge with a sensation that his feet were suddenly going to swivel around like weather vanes and spin him off in the opposite direction.

Maybe Bobby had fallen and hit his head on the car. A picture of him lying crumpled at the bottom of the ditch flashed through Scott's brain.

Or maybe *something* behind those tentacled vines had gotten him.

He realized he was panting now. His knees felt rubbery. Once again he called in a voice that sounded feeble to his own ears. No reply. Soon it would be pitch black.

Wiping his palms on his jeans, he took a sudden deep breath and rushed to the rim of the ditch.

Bobby was not down there.

12

Behind him he heard a noise and spun around. He could see nothing, but he heard a swishing noise as though something were plowing through the pine needles.

"Bobby!" he yelled. "This isn't funny."

He strained his eyes into the darkness. The noise was closer. It was like somebody sweeping slowly with a broom.

He began edging to his right; the sound stopped, then shifted direction with him. He turned and fled in the opposite direction. A night heron screamed and his heart jumped like a hooked fish.

Clearing the pines, he stumbled over a raw mound of red clay and sprawled on his belly whimpering. Then he was on his feet again. He darted through a maze of glass jars. Behind him came a shuffling sound and a sickly odor clogged his nostrils. Suddenly he was up to his knees in mud; all around him frogs sang and ahead of him lightning bugs flickered over the swamp.

FRED Loomis pulled up to the Gates' house shortly after nine. He parked the patrol car and walked up to the front door of the big ranch-style house. Sam Gates owned his own insurance agency and Loomis had his life insurance policy with him. Sam met him at the door.

"Sorry to get you out like this, Fred," he apologized. "I've been looking all over for him. His mother is frantic." His voice was calm, but his eyes revealed his own anxiety. "I don't know where the hell he could be."

Lucy Gates stood in the hallway. "He's never done this before," she said. "He's always home by supper."

Loomis' eyes behind the steel-rimmed glasses quickly took in the plush carpet and expensive living room furniture beyond her before lighting on her tense face.

"I'm sure it's gonna be all right," he soothed. "You saw him right after school?"

"Yes. He came home and left right away again. He said he and Bobby Bowen were going to try and collect some scrap iron." She rubbed her temples. She was a good deal

13

younger than her husband. "I've called Bobby's mother several times and he hasn't shown up either."

"Did Scott give you any idea where they might be going?"

She shook her head.

"Well, I'll have a look around town. Try not to worry too much. They'll probably turn up before long, hungry as hounds."

Sam went with him out to the car. "You don't suppose they've run away do you?"

"Don't know, Sam. Let me look around and get back to you."

He got into the car and pulled away leaving Sam standing on the sidewalk beneath the street lamp.

He had driven half a block when he saw Will Lawton's little Triumph coming down the street with Sharon Gates in the passenger seat. She waved at him as he passed. She did not know yet that her step-brother was unaccounted for, Loomis thought.

He drove over to the Bowen house on Depot Street. It was a four-room house in a run-down neighborhood. Bowen, a brakeman for the Southern, every once in awhile went on a drunken spree. A couple of months ago a neighbor had reported in the middle of the night a gunshot coming from Bowen's house. When Loomis had arrived to investigate, Bowen was sitting in a chair in the middle of the kitchen cradling a shotgun. There were a lot of holes in the floor and an almost empty fifth of rye on the kitchen table.

"Damn rats," Bowen had growled. "Think they can take over the whole damn house. I'm gonna blast 'em all."

Loomis had prevailed on him to get an exterminator.

Angie Bowen answered the door. She was a thin, faded woman who worked at the shirt factory. Bobby was her only child.

"Who is it?" a man's voice yelled over the noise of the TV.

"Sheriff Loomis." She slipped her fingers through her stringy hair and invited him inside.

Hank Bowen, a short, paunchy man with big shoulders

14

and almost no neck, got up from his chair in front of the TV and eyed Loomis without enthusiasm.

They had not seen Bobby since breakfast. They did not know exactly how he spent his afternoons since they both worked and Bobby was old enough to look out for himself, but from now on they knew exactly where and how he was going to spend his time after school.

"He gonna hep his Grandpa at the gas station," Bowen said and thrust his head out from his heavy shoulders like a turtle for emphasis. "He ain't gonna have no time to call his own."

"What do you think could have happened to him?" Angie Bowen said.

Loomis told her they would probably turn up soon.

"Lord, I hope they didn't get into that swamp," she said.

Loomis scratched his head and avoided her eyes. That was a possibility that had occurred to him and he had immediately tried to put it out of his mind.

As if reading his thoughts, Angie Bowen gnawed her bottom lip and turned away. She hurried out of the room.

"That kid ain't been nothin' but trouble since he was born," Bowen said. "When he gets back, I'm gonna skin the hide off him."

After he left Bowen, Loomis drove downtown. The picture show had let out and Tatum's Rexall, which served as the bus station, was dark. The town closed down early. He turned down a side street and stopped in front of an old crumbling brick building with Holman's Feed and Merchantile in peeling letters on the dirty glass window. He got out and walked to the side of the building. The ground sloped down toward the rear of the building, and he came to a basement door with a tiny glass pane. It was dark inside. He rapped loudly on the door, waited a few seconds, then rapped again. A few yards away stood a heap of twisted, rusting metal higher than his head.

Finally a light came on, and he waited nearly a minute and a face peered at him through the pane. The lock turned and the door opened a couple of inches.

"What is it?" the old man said.

15

"Can I talk to you a minute, Mr. Sheed?"

"I can't stop you, can I?" Sheed grumbled. "I reckon you better come in."

Sheed led him through a labyrinth of battered chairs, old curio cabinets, dusty wardrobes, sagging sofas, and rusty stoves. Loomis was startled by a dim, bespectacled figure that suddenly appeared in front of him and turned out to be his reflection in a full-length mirror. Along the walls rose stacks of old newspapers bound with string in bundles. At the end of the maze they entered a small room lit by a forty-watt bulb dangling on a long cord from the ceiling. It contained a table, two wooden chairs, a small refrigerator with a hot plate on top of it. There was a shelf containing canned goods and in one corner a metal cot with the blankets in disarray. Sheed sat in one of the chairs and Loomis remained standing and gazed at the small window high in the wall that gave Sheed a view of the sidewalk and, he imagined, people's ankles. The place smelled of mice.

Sheed rubbed his veined nose with his fingers and squinted at Loomis. "I don't suppose you came to buy something." He was wearing a greasy dressing gown.

He had a sharp nose that seemed to dwarf his other features. His small eyes were squeezed too close to it and his sunken mouth was a mere period to its exclamation point.

"Did two boys come by selling scrap today?" Loomis asked.

"No."

Loomis heard a skittering sound in the other room. It sounded like a mouse or maybe a rat.

"Nobody tried to sell me scrap today. Why do you want to know?"

Loomis told him.

"Sometimes they bring a few pounds of scrap iron around. They in some kind of trouble, are they?" He sucked his lips judiciously, making smacking sounds.

"I just told you they're missing. I didn't say they were in trouble."

"Same thing." He cocked his head and eyed Loomis

16

shrewdly. "If they weren't in trouble, I don't guess would be disturbing a man, rousing him out of a sou. sleep."

"Well, I can find my own way out," Loomis said.

"No. I got to lock up after you. Lots of people would mind you waking 'em, but I don't hold it against you. You're just doing your job." Sheed rose and for the first time Loomis noticed the big bulge in the pocket of his robe.

"You got a license for that thing?"

"Don't need one as long as I keep it here."

Muttering under his breath, Sheed led Loomis back through the labyrinth. Suddenly he turned. "See that roll top desk over there," he said, his eyes glittering. In the dimness Loomis could barely make out the humped shape. "A real antique. I'd give you a good price on it. Come back tomorrow and look it over. An heirloom for your office." He smiled, but it came over as a leer.

Loomis shook his head and listened to the skittering close beside him. It sounded bigger than a mouse. He wondered why Sheed lived this way. The old man hardly ever went out and did not believe in banks. He was rumored to have thousands of dollars stashed somewhere down here. Maybe he had a safe, although Loomis had not seen one.

At the door Sheed turned again. "You come back tomorrow. I'll give you a good buy. Yessir!"

Loomis was glad to get back outside in the fresh air. He heard the lock snap and heard Sheed shuffling back to his interrupted slumber.

Back at the car Loomis decided to alert the highway patrol after he checked once more with the parents. He was sliding into the seat when Thelma Howe, the dispatcher broke in on the radio with the news that Scott Gates had returned home.

"What about the Bowen boy?" Loomis asked.

Thelma told him Scott had been picked up by a driver on the old swamp road and he had been alone.

"Well, does he know where Bobby is?"

"His mother says no."

17

Loomis slung the microphone back on its clamp, shoved the car in gear, and headed back to the Gates' house.

ON either side of the road dead trees loomed like grotesque totem poles in the headlight beams. The road ran for several miles through the swamp. Every Thursday night Dave Stewart drove this stretch of road on his way to and from his night course at the University forty-five miles away.

Over the car radio Lena Horne was singing "Stormy Weather." In the darkness he let the rich, feline voice wash over him like a soothing wave.

He was weary of these weekly trips, but the semester would end in another month and, if he could finish his thesis this summer and get his Masters Degree, he might have a shot at a college teaching job in the fall. He had already begun applying to several community colleges, but without any great hope because of the tightness of the teaching market, particularly in History.

The car ran in and out of a patch of mist; then out of the corner of his eye he caught a blob of white in the swamp. He had gone a hundred yards before what it was registered in his brain. He hit the brakes, skidded to a stop, then backed the Pinto up.

Fifty feet from the road the boy was hip-deep in stagnant water. As Dave watched, the boy slipped and nearly went under. He struggled to regain his feet and thrashed forward again and slipped again. This time he almost did not rise.

Dave got out and pulled off his shoes. He turned up his pant legs, hesitated a moment, then waded into the water. It was colder than he had expected and the mud oozed between his toes through the socks and sucked at his ankles. He almost went under himself before he reached the exhausted boy and pulled him forward until he could get an arm around him. They floundered together toward the road bank, and Dave was panting and sweating with

18

exertion by the time he dragged himself and the youngster up on the shoulder.

Shivering, the boy sat down abruptly, his back against the car door. His face was scratched and streaked with mud and his blond hair matted and filthy. His teeth began chattering. Dave took off his one decent sport coat and hung it over the thin shoulders.

"Come on," he said. "Get in."

As they drove, the boy huddled against the door and stared dully through the windshield.

"Do you live in town?"

"Yes."

"What's your name?"

No reply. They rode half-a-mile in silence then suddenly sobs. After awhile he wiped his eyes with the back of his hand. "Scott," he said.

At the outskirts of town, Dave pulled into the all-night service station.

"I thought you might want to wash up before you go home."

Scott got out of the car. A few minutes later he returned, his hair still matted, but his face and arms reasonably clean.

He directed Dave through the darkened business section and down a street of well-kept houses. A scent of honeysuckle hung over the manicured lawns.

"There!" The boy pointed.

They stopped in front of a ranch-style house with two silver maples flanking the sidewalk to the front door. Before they reached the porch, the door opened and a girl appeared. She rushed out and hugged Scott.

"Are you all right?" she murmured.

She looked at Dave, her gray eyes questioning. A man and another woman appeared.

"Scotty," the woman cried. She clutched the boy's shoulders. "Where on earth have you been?" she demanded.

The girl was studying Dave. The porch light gleamed on her long, chestnut hair. He had seen her around town with Will Lawton, but he did not know her name. He

19

guessed she must be Scott's sister.

"Where did you find him?" she said.

"Out on the swamp road."

Driving into town, instinct had warned him not to question Scott until he had calmed down. He was certain the boy had experienced some sort of trauma. He did not want to say anything more in front of Scott. But the others were staring at him now.

He had taken off his filthy socks in the car and had not put his shoes on again. He and Scott looked like they had sauntered in from a frog-gigging. He wiggled his toes self-consciously.

The girl suddenly smiled. "I've seen you before," she said.

"Yes. I'm Dave Stewart."

The man held out his hand. "Sam Gates. We're grateful to you for bringing Scott home."

Gates looked to be in his late forties. He was a chunky man with a square jaw and thinning silver hair. He introduced his wife, who gave Dave a quick, almost curt nod, then hustled Scott inside.

"What happened?" Gates said. "Exactly where did you say you found him?"

"His feet must be freezing, Daddy," the girl said.

"I'm forgetting my manners," Gates said. "Please. Come in."

He started to make an excuse, but he knew Gates was anxious for details and he followed him into the hallway. Gates ushered him into the living room and motioned him into a chair. Dave told him where and how he came across Scott. "I didn't question him, but I got the idea something happened out there he wasn't ready to discuss with a stranger."

Gates frowned. "I'd better go see about him. Excuse me."

The girl came in with two cups of steaming coffee and handed Dave one. She was tall and pretty with high delicate cheekbones.

"Don't you teach at the high school?" she said.

"Yes." He took a sip of the coffee and nearly scalded

20

his tongue.

"I'm Sharon Gates." She sat on the sofa. "We've had the Sheriff out looking for him. He's never pulled anything like this before. We've all been pretty worried." She sipped her coffee and made a face. "Poor Mrs. Bowen. Bobby still hasn't turned up. Scott won't say anything except that he doesn't know where he is."

"Who is Bobby?"

A car had pulled up outside and a knock sounded on the front door.

"Excuse me." She rose and went to the door. She returned, followed by Sam and Lucy Gates and the Sheriff. Gates introduced Loomis to Dave.

To the Sheriff Dave recounted again how he had happened on Scott.

"I'd like to talk to him a minute," Loomis said to Lucy Gates.

"He doesn't know where Bobby is. Can't it wait until tomorrow?"

"I'm afraid not."

She returned with Scott, who was clean now, and in his pajamas.

Loomis asked when he had last seen Bobby. The boy stared at the thick carpet a moment. "When he went back to get the hacksaw." He looked at Loomis. "He forgot it. We were using it on some junk."

"Then what happened?"

"I didn't want to go. But after he left, I decided to go after him."

"And you couldn't find him?"

The boy shook his head.

"Why did you go into the swamp?"

Scott stared silently at the rug again.

"You've been asked a question," Sam Gates said.

"It's all right, Scott," Loomis said. "Take your time."

Scott looked at Loomis in mute appeal.

"Go on, son," Loomis prodded gently. "I know you had your reasons."

When Scott spoke again, it was so low Dave could hardly hear him.

21

"Somebody chased me."

"Who?"

"I don't know," he mumbled.

"Did you see him?"

"No."

"Then what makes you think somebody was chasing you?" Gates said.

"I heard him. Bobby and I both saw something—anyway, heard something behind the vines in the ditch. We took off and that's why he left the hacksaw. Then I went back and it was dark and I couldn't see," his voice trembled. "But he would have caught me if I hadn't gone into the swamp."

"That's enough." Lucy Gates glared at her husband and the Sheriff.

"One other thing and I'm through," Loomis said. "Could maybe Bobby have been playing a trick on you. Could he have been the one chasing you?"

Scott looked at him. "No sir, it wasn't Bobby."

"How do you know?"

"The smell," he said.

WHEN Loomis got to his office at the courthouse, it was nearly midnight. The Bowen boy had still not turned up and, if he did not show up by morning, there would have to be a full-scale search. Thelma Howe had a pot of coffee plugged in and he poured himself a cup.

"Get Holly and Clyde Lee and tell 'em to meet me down on the swamp road by the old nigger graveyard in twenty minutes. And call Bowen and tell him if he wants to come with us, Holly will pick him up." He eyed her over the rim of the cup. She was a plain, middle-aged woman, who favored big blond wigs and cowboy boots. "Also get the highway patrol and give 'em a description."

"Do you think it's bad?"

"If he's in that swamp, it is."

He remembered the two hunters who had gone in there for ducks a while back. They never came out again. The

22

Gates boy had been lucky. Loomis was not sure how much of Scott's story was real and how much imagination, but he knew the boy was bright and something or somebody had frightened him badly to send him into the swamp.

GRIM dreams flitted like bats through his sleep. Scott awoke with sweat beading his forehead and stared at the patch of moonlight on the wall. The branches of the silver maple tossed in the breeze and with the dancing leaves formed phantoms; a one-legged scarecrow roistered across the wall, and a huge spider danced a slow and sinister quadrille.

He twisted in bed and pulled the pillow over his head to shut out the pictures. Except for his own breathing, the house was silent. The entire town slept. But whatever had chased him into the swamp was not asleep. That kind never slept at night. They prowled the woods and dark alleys, their eyes burning and their mad hearts hammering with joy of darkness and the hunt; and when day came, they hid in some dank cellar, crumbling loft, or dim thicket to await the night again.

He groaned. He knew they did not believe him about what had happened down there at the ditch. The only other person who could tell them was Bobby, but Bobby was gone. And Scott knew he would not be back anymore.

CHAPTER 2

THE four men stood in the gray dawn peering down at the abandoned car. Earlier they had inspected the ditch by flashlight and found the hacksaw. Now they had returned for a closer look.

Loomis wiped his glasses with a handkerchief, carefully adjusted them on the bridge of his nose, then eased himself down into the ditch. The two deputies and Bowen remained above and watched him. Before Scott had gone to bed, he had told Loomis about the smell and rustling in the vines. Loomis smelled only the fresh dew and the tang of pine needles.

Studying the soft earth, he could trace the boys' footprints clearly in the early light. He walked over to the thicket of vines and could see some of them were broken and crushed. But there were no tracks.

He turned away and walked over to the Studebaker. The upholstery had rotted, and springs poked through the seats like rusty spikes. Under the dash some sleeping yellowjackets clung to their nest.

The three men gazed down at him bleary-eyed. They were scratched, dirty, and exhausted from combing miles of woods and fields along the edge of the bottoms.

Finally, Loomis climbed out of the ditch. He stood awhile looking thoughtfully at the thick vines.

"We're going to need some more help," he said at last. "And we can all use some food." He turned to his younger

24

deputy. "Clyde Lee, you stay here and don't let anybody go messin' in that ditch, hear? We'll bring you back something."

As they began to walk toward the cars, Bowen stopped and stared at the hacksaw in his hand. His large nose and tiny eyes combined with his short neck to give him a mole-like appearance. Loomis half-expected him to start sniffing the hacksaw.

He gripped Bowen's arm. "You need to get some sleep."

"I can't go home without Bobby." His eyes were glazed and staring.

Holly took Bowen's other arm. They led him away to the cars parked beyond the graveyard. Years ago, Loomis recalled, there had been a tiny wooden church, but it had burned to the ground, and the graveyard was seldom used anymore.

But at the edge of the trees near the ditch, Loomis noticed a new grave. Like most of the others it had no headstone, only a card inserted in a metal holder and enclosed by a fruit jar. While Holly took Bowen on ahead, Loomis stooped to read the card. Printed neatly in blue ink was the name Louis Biggs. He had known Biggs, a powerfully built Negro several years younger than he was. He wondered what Biggs had died of.

He started toward the car again, then saw it close to his foot—a stub of brown candle. He picked it up and the wick left a char streak on his fingers. Tossing the candle away, he shook his head. Probably some kids, he thought, burning a candle in the graveyard for some kind of initiation rite.

After they dropped Bowen off at his house, they drove on to the courthouse. The stores were still closed, but there was traffic on the streets now. When they got out of the car, Holly said, "You reckon we'll find the kid?"

Loomis looked up at his deputy who stood a gangling six-five. Holly was one quarter Choctaw Indian. His nose was broken, and his eyes were black and looked fierce between cheekbones that seemed to jut outside his skin. His skin was the color of tobacco juice.

"Your guess is as good as mine."

25

In his office he poured a cup of coffee from a fresh pot Thelma had made.

"Call the Civil Air Patrol," he told her. "Get Charlie Joiner and tell him we need to fly over every foot of those bottoms. And check with the Highway Patrol and see if they've come up with anything."

He ordered Holly to go downtown and round up some volunteers for a search party. Then he helped himself to another cup of coffee despite doctor's orders that he should lay off the stuff. At eight-fifteen he left the court-house and drove over to the high school.

DAVE Stewart was talking about the 1912 Presidential election when Simmons, the principal, appeared and beckoned him out into the hallway.

Loomis was there, his eyes red-rimmed and a gray stubble sprouting on his jaw. "I'm asking senior boys to volunteer to look for Bobby Bowen. I hope you don't mind me interrupting your class."

Dave nodded.

Loomis entered the class amid murmuring. Through the town grapevine many students had already heard about Bobby. They became quiet when Loomis began speaking. When he had finished, most of the boys raised their hands immediately to volunteer. A few looked around, then raised their hands.

"Two things," Loomis said. "First, each of you needs to get an O.K. from your parents. The second thing is nobody wanders off on his own. You'll stay together and take orders from either me or one of my deputies. I don't want to be hunting one of you next."

After the boys left, Dave let the girls out earlier than usual. He was sorting out his notes at the lectern when he looked up and saw the girl. During the past few weeks they had gotten into the habit of casual conversation. Her name was Marie Villiers; she had transferred from another school over the Christmas holidays.

"Are you going with them?" She wore tight jeans and

26

a white blouse that emphasized her high, firm breasts.

"I don't know. Not until after school anyway."

"Then you'll be here at three?"

"Probably."

"Could I see you then? I need to talk to you about something."

"A problem?"

She nodded, her eyes on his.

Although she was a good student, he had the impression that she was not particularly interested in her school work. She was dark, perhaps there was some Negro blood there, yet her features, except for the full, sensual mouth, were white. With her raven hair and sloe eyes she could have her pick of most of the boys, but he could not recall seeing her with any of them. He suspected she was probably dating some college boy. He looked away from those darkly hypnotic eyes and reminded himself that she was only eighteen.

"What kind of problem, Marie?"

"Personal." She gave him a slight smile.

"I'll be glad to listen, but I don't know how much help I'll be." He had gathered his notes, and they walked out into the hall together.

"I appreciate it," she said. "I'll see you then."

He watched her walk away down the hall, then noticed he had company. Hobart, the math instructor, was standing in the doorway across the hall staring after her. They exchanged glances. Hobart shook his head, gave a low whistle and winked. He was a dapper man about forty with thinning hair and a small mustache. He wore a tweed jacket, and Dave remembered that he had left his own jacket at the Gates' house last night. He would have to remember to go by for it after school.

BENT over the sewing machine, Angie Bowen stitched a sleeve onto a shirt. She had come to work because she had to keep her mind occupied, and because she could not afford to miss a day's salary. But so far this morning

27

she had made numerous mistakes.

Dear Christ, she thought, don't let Bobby be in the swamp. Scott Gates had been found and that gave her hope, but also more alarm that Bobby was not with him. Why couldn't it have been Bobby who turned up instead of Scott?

When Hank had come home this morning without him, she had hated him. She had left him sleeping like he did after one of his drunks. Suddenly she realized she had not gathered enough material in the sleeve. She ripped out the stitches. Dear God, let my boy be all right. She ripped some of the material, flung it down, got up, and rushed down the row of machines past the motionless faces of her co-workers staring after her. She reached the refuge of the restroom just before the hot tears blinded her.

AT recess Scott's classmates sought him out.

"Did you see any snakes?"

"How about quicksand?"

"My Pa says there are still panthers in there."

He shook his head and felt sick at his stomach. His mother had wanted to keep him home, but he had been checked by Doctor Cornelia, and she had said it was all right to come to school. He had not realized everybody would be talking about nothing else except what had happened last night.

After recess when he went to geography class and saw Bobby's empty desk directly in front of him, he was afraid he might break down. He could not let Wendy see him crying or the rest of the kids. He stared at the colored map in the book in front of him. It was of Brazil and the Amazon River. He imagined himself in a canoe paddling down the Amazon beneath overhanging vines. Wendy was in the canoe with him, and suddenly it hit a snag and overturned. They reached shore, but Wendy got caught in quicksand, and he had to save her fast. He saw himself stretching out a long branch to her, but it not quite reaching. The only way to save her would be to plunge

28

into the quicksand himself. Even in his daydream he realized he was scared. He gripped the geography book tightly and stared at the empty desk in front of him.

HOLLY stood at the edge of the swamp and looked at the assembled search party. Counting the high school boys there were almost fifty people. Some of them were wearing hip boots for the swamp. Some were joking and swapping stories; others were sober-faced and silent. Duncan Rainey, the local bootlegger, had brought some of his cronies and customers and his bloodhound, Walter. Loomis was bringing an article of the boy's clothing, but if Bobby were in the swamp, Walter would not be much use, Holly thought.

George Burke, the local newspaper editor, stood to one side adjusting the lens on his expensive German camera. He might run a big spread in his weekly, *The Progress*, and Holly wondered whether to try and get his picture taken.

Everybody was waiting for Loomis to appear and give orders on how the search was to be conducted. Holly noticed that Bowen was not among the crowd. There was a general murmur, and he looked up to see Loomis striding toward them from the woods. He looked tired and older, Holly thought. With his heart condition he should ease up and leave the actual search to others. If they found the Bowen kid alive, the credit would go to Loomis even if he, Holly, did most of the work. But Holly had plans. He had already made up his mind to run against Loomis in the next election, if the older man did not retire.

The crowd formed a semi-circle around Loomis and became silent. Quickly he divided them into three groups.

"Rainey, you and Walter cover the woods," he said. "The rest of us will take the swamp. I don't need to tell you to watch out for quicksand and snakes." Then he passed a shirt that belonged to Bobby to Rainey Duncan. The crowd eyed the shirt somberly. Seeing the faded blue

29

shirt made some of them suddenly aware that they were hunting a boy who at that moment might be at the bottom of a sinkhole.

THE buses were rumbling past the window when Marie entered the room. Dave sat on the edge of his desk and motioned her to a desk in front of him. She put her purse on the floor and crossed her legs.

"I've learned a lot in this course," she said, fixing her dark eyes on him. "I'm glad I've got you for a teacher."

"I appreciate the compliment."

The last yellow school bus rolled by leaving a wake of silence. Her eyes did not leave his and, under the intensity of her gaze, he looked away. He picked up a BIC pen and fiddled with the cap, aware that his stomach was tight and his tongue felt dry.

She's just another student, he told himself, but that was a lie. She was beautiful and at this moment she seemed more desirable than any woman he had ever seen. What the hell is wrong with me? he thought. If he was not careful he could get himself into a sticky situation. The silence hung between them; her eyes remained riveted on his.

"You mentioned something you needed to see me about."

"Do I embarrass you?" she murmured.

"I'm flattered you think I'm a good teacher."

"It's not flattery." Her voice was husky. He noticed her irises seemed nearly indistinguishable from her pupils. His palms were moist; he could hear the whirring of the electric clock on the wall. Her eyes were drawing him. He stood up, and she rose, her hand touching his, caressingly. The touch was like electricity; her arms came up around his neck; her face swam in front of him. They kissed, her mouth opening, her tongue flicking against his. The blood thudded in his brain, and he felt as giddy as a kid playing spin-the-bottle for the first time. When they broke the kiss, she looked at him intently, a trace of

30

mockery twisting her lips.

"You're going to tell me that wasn't supposed to happen." Her voice was ironic.

He nodded, not trusting himself to speak.

"Why?" she breathed.

He realized he was holding her wrists and released them.

"I think you liked it," she said. "I know you did."

He started to say something, but she anticipated him.

"But you're going to say 'that's not the point.'" She licked her bottom lip. "But I say it is the point." She touched his hand again. "The whole point."

Maybe she was right. For the first time since Kay's death, he had felt the undeniable urge and an almost certainty that he could make it. Yet she was only a girl, and she was his student. He felt a sudden disgust with himself.

He stepped back from her. If she had a crush on him, he was taking advantage of her; and, if she was one of those who needed to gratify her vanity by seducing the teacher, she had come damn close to success.

She regarded him with open amusement now. "What makes you think I couldn't teach *you* things?" she said. "Many things you know nothing about. Nothing!" He was startled by the sudden vehemence in her voice.

She bent and picked up her purse. As she did, he saw she was not wearing a bra, and he glimpsed the smooth breasts and a strange little object dangling between them from a cord around her neck.

She caught his glance as she straightened up. Her eyes went suddenly flat. Her hand flew to the top button of her blouse to make sure it was secure. They gazed at each other in silence for a few moments, then she gave him a demure little smile.

"I've got to go. Bye."

From the window he watched her walk across the parking lot, get into a blue Volkswagen and drive away.

He visualized those lovely breasts again and smiled ruefully. Had she been momentarily upset because he had too obviously relished the view she had provided him, or

31

because he had discovered that strange little bag—it looked like leather—and would guess she was superstitious? He wondered what kind of charm it was supposed to contain—eye of newt? Maybe the bag itself was a goat's scrotum.

He shook his head, knowing he was thinking glib thoughts at her expense because her kiss had shaken him and, for a moment, he had wanted her with an intensity he had never experienced, not even with his wife Kay.

A POLICE car was waiting at the curb for Scott when he got out of school. Loomis had gotten permission from Lucy Gates to pick him up. His friends watched him get into the car with open envy on their faces.

Clyde Lee eased the car away from the curb and drove through town at a sedate thirty-miles-per-hour. He was worn out with fatigue. He had driven backroads he had not known existed until a few hours ago, stopping at tumbledown shacks, some raised high on stilts because of river floods, asking the same question and receiving the same answer from whites and blacks. Nobody had seen the Bowen boy. It was as if the bottoms had swallowed him. Once as a kid he had read a comic book about a pilot who crashed into a swamp and after years of rotting in a sinkhole had clambered out of the mud as a vegetable mutation and roamed the countryside and prowled the bottoms, seizing the unwary. Maybe something like that had snatched the Bowen kid. His lips lifted from his teeth mirthlessly. He must be even more tired than he felt. When he reached the highway outside town, he opened the throttle to seventy-five. He wished he could go to bed and sleep for several days. He looked over at the boy beside him. Most kids would be excited riding in a police car, but Scott was silent and barely bothered to look at the scenery.

"You want me to turn on the siren?"

The boy looked at him. "What?"

"I say, you want me to turn on the siren?"

32

Scott shook his head.

When they reached the old graveyard, Loomis was waiting. When he saw the ditch again, the sick feeling returned to the pit of his stomach, and Scott felt like running. He did not want to look, but his eyes turned to the dark tangle of vines at the far end. He showed Loomis where they had been standing when they first smelled and heard whatever had been behind the vines. Then slowly he and Loomis retraced the flight to the edge of the cotton field, and he pointed out the spot where he had last seen Bobby vanish into the pines. Loomis followed a route back toward the ditch, then another, then another, trying to guess the way Bobby had taken, but he found nothing, not even a footprint.

After they returned once more to the ditch, the Sheriff asked him to point out where he had first heard his pursuer and to retrace his flight into the swamp. But he could not remember exactly; he could only remember stumbling over a grave. Loomis searched the graveyard again for footprints, but found none, not even Scott's.

They gazed out at the swamp that stretched as far as they could see. In the late afternoon it seemed quiet and peaceful, almost beautiful. Scott turned away. Deep shadows fell over the graveyard; some of the fruit jars reflected the setting sun.

At last Loomis said: "Okay, son." His boots and pants were coated with mud, and his eyes were red. "I promised your mother I'd bring you home personally."

As they stepped between the graves on the way to the car, something stirred in the back of Scott's mind like a fish he had for a second hooked then lost.

He stopped. He had a feeling it was important and tried to call it back.

Loomis looked at him. "What is it, boy?"

"Nothing," he said. The best thing was to try not to think about it and maybe it would surface again.

But all the way home in the patrol car his mind worried at it. If only he could remember what it was, then maybe Loomis would believe him. He had seen the blue eyes slowly turn sceptical behind the glasses when they had not found a single track in the graveyard to back up his story.

His hands clenched into fists and he gazed out the windshield with a feeling of despair.

CHAPTER 3

IN the twilight he sat on the side steps of the ramshackle old house where he rented an upstairs room and watched Mrs. Anson's tortoise shell cat stalk a bluejay. The cat sprang, but the jay sailed up onto a tree limb and began screaming. The cat padded off into the high grass behind the garage.

Dave rose and looked at the deserted street. He wondered if they had found Bobby. Many people had gone down to the swamp in a kind of carnival spirit. Maybe that is why he had not gone himself, or maybe it was just because he was too lazy.

Just as he started to go inside, the car pulled into the driveway. The driver waved and got out. He walked over to her and they exchanged greetings. She was wearing a gray pant suit that matched her eyes.

"How's Scott?" he asked.

"The doctor says he's fine physically. He went to school today."

"Any word on Bobby?"

Her eyes clouded. "No. All day I kept telling myself he'll turn up, but now—"

Overhead the jay chattered at them, then suddenly flew away.

"Did the Sheriff find any signs of somebody else down there?"

"I don't think so. He took Scotty down there after

35

school this afternoon, but I take it they didn't turn up anything." She gave him a frank look. "Sometimes Scotty's imagination runs away with him."

"You think this was one of the times?"

She looked away. "I just don't know."

A lightning bug winked under the big oak in the front yard. He studied the girl's profile in the gloom.

"I almost forgot." She opened the car door. "You left this last night." She pulled out his jacket on a hanger. "I had it dry cleaned. I hope they did a good job."

"How did you know where I lived?" He took the jacket.

"Oh, I asked around." She smiled. "Actually, I asked Jenny Rikard."

Jenny was a bank teller he had dated a few times, but he had not seen her in over a month. "How did you know about Jenny?"

"Everybody knows everything about everybody else in this town. Don't you know that?"

He thought about the episode with Marie this afternoon. "Everything, you say?"

"Got a guilty conscience?"

"Doesn't everybody?"

"I guess that depends on what you've been doing, Mr. Stewart."

"Dave. I suppose it does."

"O.K., Dave. Anyway *you* shouldn't have a guilty conscience. Scott says you went into the swamp yourself and pulled him out."

"I'm a hero, all right."

"A barefoot hero—with cheeks of tan."

They grinned at each other. He realized he liked her. She was an attractive, sensible girl and seemed to lack pretense—she was, he thought, a lot like Kay.

Her smile faded and her eyes were serious again.

"Anyway, we're grateful for what you did last night."

They stood close in the gathering dusk—he could see the pulse beating in the hollow of her throat.

"Well," she said, "I'd better be getting home. They're probably waiting supper on me, and I don't need the

36

Sheriff out looking for me."

She started to get into the car, and he touched her wrist. She turned.

"Would you have supper with me?"

She looked at his eyes, a quick, searching look. "I'd have to go home for a minute."

"Do you like hamburgers?"

"My favorite."

He followed her home in the Pinto and waited while she went inside. A few minutes later she came back out. When she got into the car, she smelled of perfume and her own woman's scent, subtle and exciting, and her chestnut hair gleamed.

As the name implied, Mutt's Place across the street from the railroad depot was not elegant, but it served the best hamburgers in town, and the biggest. They ordered two each and ate ravenously.

"How did you wind up in this hick town?" she asked between bites.

"With the teaching market so tight, I was lucky to get this job. I think the only reason I got it was they needed a baseball coach too, and I played a little in college."

"What position?"

"Third base and outfield." He lowered his voice confidentially. "I don't usually tell this, but I once set a school record."

"Tell me," she whispered, leaning toward him, her eyes wide in mock admiration.

"Most errors by a third baseman in a single game. I believe it still stands. That's when they switched me to the outfield. They figured I could do less damage out there, I guess."

She sipped her Coke and traced a wet ring on the formica table top with a forefinger.

"Why are you still here if you don't like the town?"

She shrugged. "It's not that bad. And I guess I'm a Daddy's girl. We became even closer after my mother died. We sort of looked after each other. Then he married Lucy and Scott came along and I became—well more like a motherly aunt to Scott than a half-sister

37

because of the difference in our ages. And maybe because Lucy had taken my father I was trying to compete with her for Scotty's affections. You might say get revenge." She smiled at him. "How's that for a psychology minor?"

"Anyway, Dad and I are still close. After I graduated from college last year, he needed a secretary and wanted me to help him with the business. I had a Liberal Arts Degree and there's not an overwhelming demand for them nowadays, so I guess I took the line of least resistance. I know, you're thinking I'm afraid to go out on my own. Maybe I am. I've lived here all my life."

"I thought Will Lawton might have something to do with your staying here."

She looked at him over the rim of her Coke glass. "How do you know about him?"

"Like you said. Everybody knows everything about—"

"Seriously."

"I've seen you together."

"I've seen you too," she said. "It seems we've been noticing each other."

"Yeah. But I thought you and Lawton—" He did not finish.

"A lot of people think that. We've known each other since grade school. He was three years ahead of me."

They finished their hamburgers and he motioned for the check.

"Do you like movies?"

"Yes."

"Do you know what's playing?"

"It so happens I do. But—"

"But?"

"I'm afraid I wouldn't be very good company."

"Scott or Lawton?"

She stared at him frankly. "Mainly Scott."

"Do you think he would like to come? It might take his mind off last night."

"That's nice of you. But you shouldn't have to take Scott to humor me."

"You know what the Chinese say about being responsible for somebody if you once rescue them?"

38

"Yes. You're supposed to look out for them from then on."

"I want to take both of you—if you want it. If you don't, you don't have to say anything more."

Her eyes regarded him warmly. "You're a nice man, Mr. Stewart."

"Dave." He picked up the check from the table and they both rose.

THE moon, a pale crescent, lay high in the midnight sky and the highway unreeled like a silver ribbon beneath the Pinto's hood. Scott was asleep in the back seat. They had seen a Peter Sellers comedy and a John Wayne western, and at intermission he and Scott had gone to the concession stand and bought hot dogs, popcorn, and tall cups full of ice and Dr. Pepper, but mostly ice.

Sharon had groaned when they returned with the food. "I'm going to look like the Goodyear blimp and it'll be your fault." But she ate her share. When they left the drive-in, Scott was already asleep.

Now they rode in easy silence until Dave broke it. "Do you think he enjoyed it?"

"Yes. So did I." She sat halfway between him and the door. "I appreciate your bringing him."

"Maybe I took him just to bribe you," he murmured.

"Did you?"

"You'll never be sure."

"I am already." Her face was turned toward him; the moonlight curved against her cheek, concaving the jaw, and her eyes wide and soft studied him intently. For the second time that day he felt a sudden tightness in his belly. With Marie it had been lust. His hands tightened around the steering wheel. Ahead the lights of town rose out of the darkness to meet them.

When they pulled up in front of the silver maples, she reached back and shook the boy gently. His head snapped up, his eyes staring.

"We're home," she said.

39

His face relaxed, but the haunted look in his eyes remained. Until now the story of a phantom pursuer had seemed to Dave the product of Scott's imagination, but suddenly he was wondering if the two boys might actually have run into a maniac. It's the night, he thought. Insane thoughts, irrational fears bubbled up from the underside of the mind and simmered after sundown—that is why man was first attracted to fire—not for the heat, because it could hurt, and not because you could cook with it—since for millennia man had eaten his meat raw and liked it—but simply because fire banished the darkness and some of the thoughts that went with it.

Scott thanked Dave for the movies and got out of the car. He hesitated as if he wanted to say something else, but then turned and made for the house.

"I keep thinking it could be him lost down there instead of Bobby," she said. "Two years ago last winter two duck hunters got into those bottoms. They haven't been heard from since." She shivered. "God, I hope Bobby is safe."

At the door she turned to him, her eyes reflecting moonlight.

"Thanks again." She touched his arm. The muffled sound of voices drifted from inside. When she went inside, he felt regret and relief at the same time. She was a nice, attractive girl, and he realized he was afraid of her.

LUCY had been reading a novel in the living room and had seen Scott to bed. Now as Sharon began to undress, she appeared in the doorway.

"Will called while you were gone. I told him you had taken Scott to a movie."

Sharon looked at her step-mother. "You told him I was with Dave?"

"No. I thought you would want to do that yourself. Or maybe not." Lucy fingered the collar of her nightrobe. "Would you like a glass of milk, dear?"

"No thanks. I'm going right to bed."

40

"Then I'll say goodnight." She started away, then turned. "Do you think it's wise to be dating another man when you and Will . . ."

"We're not married. We're not even engaged." She hung the pantsuit on a hanger and put it in the closet.

"All I'm suggesting is that you wouldn't want to jeopardize your relationship with him. Somebody like Will doesn't come along every day."

"You mean wealthy."

"That, and the fact that he's nice looking and will be successful in his own right. And you two seem to be very close."

Sharon eyed her in the dressing mirror. What you really mean is you think we're sleeping together, she thought. "What do you have against Dave?"

"Nothing, dear. I'm grateful for what he did for Scotty. But we hardly know him."

"You mean as far as the town goes, he's an outsider and besides he doesn't make much money. Isn't that it?" She felt her cheeks flush with anger. Lucy's eyes met hers steadily in the mirror as she brushed her hair with quick, rough strokes.

"I want what is best for you. You know that. You're as much my concern as Scott."

At thirty-seven, Lucy was only fifteen years older than she was. She was still attractive, although there was a brittle quality to her features—if her lips were fuller, her nose not quite so sharp, her eyes softer, she might have been beautiful, Sharon thought. She had grown up poor, her father a house painter when he was sober, which was not very often. Her mother had run out on them when Lucy was very young. She had worked her way through a business college, worked as a secretary to a real estate agent, had become one herself, and met and married Sam Gates ten years ago.

Sharon turned to her. She wondered if Lucy had ever really loved her father, or had married him for security and the respectable Gates name. Whatever her reasons she had been a good wife and a good step-mother, and there was a genuine affection between them.

41

"I know you're concerned about my best interests. But I have to decide some things for myself, including who I go out with."

"Of course." Lucy left.

Sharon looked at the photograph of Will Lawton on her dresser—the broad shoulders and craggy face, the familiar, slightly crooked smile—and thought of Dave Stewart who was thin with a shock of unruly black hair, and whose hazel eyes were serious, even somber. Lucy had said they did not know him, and maybe that was his allure. Will held no unpredictability or mystery for her. She was fond of him, but she was not ready to marry him—not now. She wondered if she ever would be.

She sighed, took off her bra and panties, and put on a blue nightgown. Then she walked down the hallway and looked in on Scott. He was sleeping with his knees curled near his chest in the fetal position. She stared at him for almost a minute, then bent and touched his cheek with her hand. When Scott had been born, she was twelve and she had been afraid her father would love him more than her. But she and her father had remained close and, as she had told Dave earlier, she had grown to feel like Scott's second mother. She pulled the sheet over his shoulders and again thought of Bobby Bowen, lost out there in the darkness, perhaps dead. Had someone really chased Scott into the swamp and made Bobby flee into the swamp too, or worse? Scott had always had such an active imagination. . . . There had been that business with the scarecrow and Mama Celia, the old black woman they had held partly responsible for what had happened. For a long time they had been very worried about Scott. . . . With him it was hard to tell where reality left off and fantasy began.

RUFUS Johnson had fed the two mules and put them in the shed for the night. Now, after eating a late supper of sidemeat and cornbread, he sat on the porch with his pipe and watched the horned moon rise over the bottoms. He had heard in town that afternoon that a white boy had

42

got lost out there, and a bunch of people from town were out looking for him. It was none of his affair. He sucked at his pipe and gazed across the dirt road at the pale headstones behind the old frame church. He could see Annie Mae's stone like a white tooth shining in the moonlight. It had been a fine funeral, and he, Rufus, would miss her. When they were seeing each other, the two of them had drunk a lot of wine and had some sweet times together. Then he had married Sarah. Funny thing, he had been all set to marry Annie Mae and then one day he woke up and it was like he suddenly saw Sarah for the first time, even though he had known her most of her life. They had seen Annie Mae at church last Sunday, strong and stout. Sarah had said too stout. Now, she was in the earth. He never thought her heart would give out. He remembered her able to work in the fields all day like a man, but after dark she had been soft and womanly. A wave of loneliness struck him, and he sighed. His pipe had gone out. He tapped the ashes onto the bare earth beside the porch.

"You sorry scoun'rel," he said to the hound lying beside him. The dog raised his ears and thumped his tail half-heartedly against the porch planks. "You pay 'tenshun tonight." A fox had already grabbed two chickens.

Rufus heaved himself out of his chair, scratched his chest, and gazed again at the gravestone. It had hurt his heart when they threw the dirt in on Annie Mae. He went inside where Sarah was already in bed asleep. He undressed quietly in the light of the kerosene lamp, lifted the glass chimney and blew out the flame, then padded barefoot across the plank floor and got into bed. The moonlight shone dully on the iron, potbellied stove in the middle of the room, and he remembered he would have to get up early and chop some more wood for it.

Sometime in the middle of the night he awoke. Sarah was shaking him.

"Rufus," she hissed. "Rufus!" Through the fog of vanishing sleep, her eyes gleamed directly above his face.

"What is it?" he said thickly.

"Somethin' be out there."

"Be a fox out there," he said, swinging his legs out of

43

bed. The hair rose on his neck. A sub-human sound like crazy laughter broke from the darkness. It was the high braying of one of the mules. Rufus sprang up and, moving with swift agility for a big, fifty-year-old man, snatched the shotgun from the wall, fumbled two shells into the breech, and burst out onto the porch. In the darkness he could see nothing. He raced for the shed where the mules were.

Half the shed had disappeared. Both mules were gone. He stared where the vanished wall had been. The mules had kicked it down; a few of the planks lay splintered at his feet, and all around him was silence and darkness. The moon hid behind heavy clouds.

He ran back into the house and lit the kerosene lantern.

"What is it?" Sarah cried. She sat in bed, the covers up around her shoulders.

"The mules. Gawn!"

He went back outside to the shed. He held the lantern close to the earth and found the mules' tracks leading toward the swamp. He and the dog had run many a coon on darker nights than this, but whatever had panicked the mules was no fox or coon. He called the hound.

The dog crept out from under the shack. He slunk toward Rufus, tail between his legs, and whined. In the pool of light from the lantern, the dog's eyes glittered with fear. He looked toward the graveyard, his ears stiffened, and a half-growl, half-whine came from his throat. Rufus followed the dog's eyes, but in the gloom could see nothing, not even Annie Mae's stone.

"What you see?"

The dog bristling still stared at the graveyard. Something bad was happening, something the dog sensed, something that had made his mules go beserk and run off into the bottoms. He looked again at the tracks. He needed those mules, needed them for planting, but he would not follow them, not now. Daylight would be time enough, and he would get help.

Clutching the shotgun, he hurried back inside the shack and bolted the door. Outside he could hear the hound whining and scratching at the door.

44

CHAPTER 4

NEAR dawn Scott awoke. He could hear rain falling, and a dull grayness seeped through the window. He had been having a nightmare. He and Bobby were in the ditch trying to cut the car door off with a hacksaw and, as they worked, they noticed a slight space appearing around the car trunk. The crack became gradually wider, and slowly a long slug crept through the crack, then another. They resolved themselves into fingers and the fingers lifted the trunk lid. He and Bobby ran through the Negro graveyard, stumbling over the mounds. All around them the fruit jars exploded silently and tiny daggers of glass flew at their faces. Suddenly, the ground opened up beneath him. He screamed for Bobby, but no noise came from his throat and Bobby was gone. Scott had fallen into an open grave. He could hear shuffling footsteps approaching the grave, and he could not climb out. He was trapped in the open grave!

He bolted upright in bed. The thing that had pricked at his mind yesterday evening when he and Sheriff Loomis were down at the graveyard rose to the surface. When he and Bobby had first gone down to the ditch, there was an open grave near the edge of the woods. But when he had gone back alone to find Bobby, the grave was filled! In his flight to the swamp he had fallen over the fresh mound.

A terrible thought struck him. They were searching the

swamp, but maybe Bobby was buried in that grave. And, with the thought, an icy chill passed through him. It seemed almost a minute before he could breathe.

He thought of John Wayne. Last night in the movie John Wayne had handled everything. He wished he was John Wayne. But he was nine, and Bobby was gone, and he did not know what to do. His father did not even believe he had been chased into the swamp. He got out of bed and stared through the window at the rain falling on the gray earth. The burden of his knowledge was too great, and he knew he would have to tell someone.

LOOMIS ate his breakfast of shredded wheat with skimmed milk and listened to the rain. He had called the searchers in when it got dark yesterday and now the rain would make today's search an even bleaker and tougher affair than yesterday's. He looked out the window at his garden. At least the rain would help there. Each year he planted tomatoes, butter beans, squash, okra, and greens. Betsy would freeze or can them, and they would eat from the garden all winter long. Although the garden needed the rain, Loomis knew the backroads would turn into a quagmire.

As if reading his thoughts, Betsy said, "You should stay home and rest today. There's no need for you to go out there. Holly can handle it."

She was constantly fussing over him, worried that he was working too hard in the office or the garden, afraid that he would suffer another heart attack like the one he had had two years ago. It had been a mild one, but it had slowed him down to the extent that he was thinking of retiring when his term expired this time. He spooned up his shredded wheat with distaste. It was Betsy who made him stick to the low cholesterol diet. He used to eat two fried eggs every morning; now he was reduced to this tasteless stuff, he thought ruefully.

Betsy was right. There was no burning need for his going out today. He could let Holly search that southwest

46

section of the county, the one area of the bottoms that was the most remote. It was unlikely that the Bowen boy had reached that area. Hardly anyone lived there—a few swamp rats and moonshiners. Yes, he could let Holly do it, except for the fact that he had been elected Sheriff—not Holly. He rose from the table and kissed Betsy's cheek.

"All right, you stubborn jackass," she said. "At least get your raincoat."

He walked back to the hall closet and got the yellow slicker and put it on. He left it in the car when he got to the courthouse. Floyd Rogers who was on night duty had left the night report on his desk. He sat down in his wooden swivel chair and, tilting it back, read the report. Two drunks had gotten into a fight at the pool hall and were sobering up in the tank and Hubie Beibers had been peeping again—this time at Mrs. Tuttle who was obese and seventy. She should have been flattered instead of pressing charges, Loomis thought. Personally, he would not peep at her for salary. He laid the report down and left the office. In the patrol car he raised Holly on the radio. He was forming the search party near the old Sanders place where they had left off last night.

"How many you got?"

Holly's voice was remote and static-ridden. "Eighteen."

Loomis nodded to himself. He had expected that. Less than half of those who had searched yesterday had showed up today. The rain accounted for part of it, but also the novelty had worn off. And, with this weather, the Civil Air Patrol would not be able to help either.

"Keep workin' toward the southwest. I'm gonna be out in that area myself."

He slung the microphone back in its clamp beneath the dash. If they did not find the Bowen boy today, the chances were he would not be found. Either he was a victim of the swamp or, if you believed Scott Gates, a victim of someone or something even more sinister. Yet, there was not a shred of evidence to support Scott's tale. Loomis suddenly felt old and tired.

He thought of his garden. Maybe he would plant some

47

corn—at least two rows. Betsy would shake her head and say too much starch. But he decided he would plant it anyway.

RUFUS Johnson stared at the patch of muddy water the boy was already circling. Then the boy let out a yell. "There's one 'um."

The two men plunged ankle-deep through the stagnant pool, mud sucking at their shoes, rain running down their necks. The mule stood motionless under a cypress, rabbit ears drooping dispiritedly, and its eyes rolling like cue balls. It waited until the boy almost reached the tree then lunged away and staggered deeper into the swamp.

"Head 'um!" Rufus panted.

The boy wallowed after the mule swinging a loop of rope around his head. He cast the rope, and the loop missed the mule, but the effort sent the boy head-first into the mire. He scrambled up, covered with mud and spluttering. The two men stared at him and grinned. They all paused to get their breath, then started after the mule again. As they slogged along, Rufus began cursing it in a steady monotone.

"You say you found a candle?" Gann said.

Rufus quit cursing. The two men eyed each other soberly.

"Right by her grave."

"What's your ol' woman say?"

"She say no mule act that way if somebody just gatherin' goopher dust. And doan need no candle."

Gann's facial muscles bunched, turning his face into a rigid black mask. "I doan like that," he said, his voice very low.

The boy yelled again. "There, we got 'um now."

Fifty yards away the mule had come to a halt, its side heaving and its eyes rolling in panic.

It was mired to the knees in a sinkhole.

48

AFTER he awoke, it was several minutes before he remembered it was Saturday. He sat on the edge of the bed and watched miniature torrents rush down the gutters in the street below. Finally, he rose and pulled on a pair of levis, shuffled over to the lavatory, and splashed cold water on his face. In addition to the bed and lavatory, the room held a small bookcase crammed with books, an old dresser, two wooden chairs, and a desk on top of which were a lamp and fifty nine pages of his thesis on the Memphis Cotton Exchange written in longhand.

He looked wearily at his sleep-swollen face in the mirror. He splashed more water on his face and squeezed out some shaving lather. He was rinsing out the razor when a knock sounded on the door.

"Somebody downstairs to see you," Mrs. Anson called from the hallway.

He put on a clean shirt and went down. Dwarfed by the high hallway, his back to the front door with its stained glass transom, Scott stood with a pale face and his blond hair plastered against his skull. He wore a tan windbreaker, dark with rain, and he stood in a small pool.

Mrs. Anson, a portly woman of about fifty-five with dyed red hair, brought him a towel.

"Mercy, boy, you could have telephoned just as well, couldn't you?"

Scott wiped his face with the towel and handed it back. "Thank you."

"I was about to fix me some coffee," Dave said. "Do your folks let you drink coffee?"

"Sometimes."

The boy took off his jacket and followed Dave into the kitchen. Then Dave boiled some water on the stove in a tin pot, ladled a couple of spoons of instant coffee into two cups, poured the steaming water and handed one of the cups to Scott. They went out onto the big covered front porch and sat on some lawn chairs Mrs. Anson had brought in from the rain. They sipped the coffee and both of them grimaced.

"You ought to get married," Scott said matter-of-factly.

49

"It's not very good, is it," Dave admitted.

Some drops of rain blew against his face. It had been a day just like this one except it had been evening. Kay had been driving home from her secretarial job. When he had heard the car pull up in the driveway, he had looked out expecting it to be her, but it was a police car.

The coffee splashed on his hand, scalding him and he almost dropped the cup.

The boy gazed at him, but said nothing.

"Do your parents know you're here?"

"They think I'm over at Jimmy Farese's."

They sat silently and drank the coffee and listened to the rain. Whatever was on Scott's mind, he was not yet ready to discuss it.

"I guess I'd better be going," the boy said at last. He put on his windbreaker. The rain had not let up.

"Wait a second," Dave said. He went into the house and came back with his own jacket. "I'm driving you."

Scott stared out the windshield and fidgeted as they drove through town.

"I enjoyed the movies last night."

"Is that what you came in the rain to tell me?"

"No."

They drove another block in silence.

"I don't know how they could have a funeral that quick," Scott said. "It wasn't filled up and then it was, but they didn't have enough time for a regular funeral."

Dave looked over at him.

The boy looked back at him, his eyes grave and profound.

He pulled the car over to the curb and cut the engine.

"Slow down, Scott. And start from the beginning."

When Scott had finished, there was only the noise of the rain drumming on the car for a minute.

Finally Scott broke the silence. "I guess you don't believe me," he said tonelessly.

"Have you told anyone else?"

"No."

"Not even your father."

"He'd think I was making it up." An edge of bitterness

50

crept into the boy's voice. "But I'm not. I promise I'm not."

Dave was certain he was not making it up. But possibly the boy could have seen a shadow on the grave that made it appear open when it was not.

"You know we're going to have to tell this to somebody. But first I'll try to check out a few things."

The lines of strain around the boy's mouth relaxed and his shoulders straightened as if a heavy weight had been lifted from them. "If we tell the Sheriff, he'll dig up the grave."

"He might. Isn't that what you want?"

"I guess so."

Dave started the engine. "I'll let you out at your friend's house, but first tell me how to get down to the graveyard."

CHAPTER 5

THE dripping trees, the leaden sky, the mounds with their dirt-spattered fruit jars made a desolate scene. He got out of the car, turned his jacket collar up against the rain, and slogged over to the raw mound of dirt. He squinted through the streaming jar, but was unable to make out the name within. Lifting the jar, he read the card, then went back to the car and sat awhile, looking out at the swamp. Finally, he started the car and drove back to town.

The square was jammed with Saturday traffic. The newspaper office was across the street from the courthouse, but he could not find a parking place near the square. He settled for one three blocks away. Walking back, he passed a plate glass window with gilt lettering that caught his eye. His pulse skipped. He looked inside and she was sitting at a desk, beckoning him. He went in.

"You'll drown," she said, "or catch pneumonia." She looked fresh and pretty, her shiny hair flowing over her shoulders. She was wearing a white blouse and black slacks. There was a piece of paper in the typewriter roller.

"Slaving on Saturdays is immoral," he said.

"Don't I know it. But sometimes it's our busiest day."

"I can see."

She grinned. "How about a cup of coffee?" She poured him some from an electric pot into a styrofoam cup.

52

"Dad's out seeing about a car wreck that happened a little while ago in the rain."

"Bad?"

"I don't think anybody was hurt. But the cars were banged up pretty bad." The telephone rang, she answered it and told the caller to hold on. She got up and went to a file cabinet. He drank his coffee and admired her curves. She came back to the phone and told the caller when his coverage expired for his fire insurance. She hung up, and he dropped his empty cup into the waste basket.

"Let's see," she said, "maybe I can sell you some insurance. How about a cropduster's accident policy?"

"Why don't we talk about it over lunch? I'm thinking about going into cropdusting."

"It's the best offer I've had all morning, but I can't leave until noon."

He checked his watch. "That's fine. I've got something to attend to. I'll see you at twelve."

"I'll be ready."

At the *Progress* office, a young woman with a bad complexion pointed to a door when he asked for George Burke. He walked into a big room with a long table, and George was bending over it pasting proofs on a dummy page. He peered over his horn-rimmed glasses at Dave and nodded a greeting. He was nearing forty, balding, and had a slight paunch. He had written several feature stories on the baseball team and attended most of the home games.

"I was wondering if I could pick up this week's paper," Dave said.

"Sure. Judy would have given you a copy."

"Do you remember writing an obit on a Negro named Biggs?"

"Judy does most of those. It wouldn't be in this issue if he died after Monday night. That's when we go to press."

"I don't know what day he died. But he was supposed to have been buried in the past couple of days."

George gave him a curious look. "Judy," he called.

When the girl appeared, he said: "Check next week's

obits and see if you've got a Biggs."

"Why the interest?" George said after the girl left.

"I was wondering if it's a Biggs I know."

The girl reappeared with a typed sheet of yellow paper. "Here it is. I remember writing it Thursday." She handed it to Dave.

> Louis Biggs, 48, of Leeville community died May 3 at his home after an apparent heart attack. Services were held at 2 p.m. May 4 at Bethel Grove Cemetery, the Rev. Elijah Young officiating.

May fourth. He glanced at the wall calendar. That had been Thursday. Burial at two; yet Scott had been down there near dark.

George looked at him shrewdly. "Your Biggs?"

"No. I appreciate it."

"Sure. My predecessor didn't run Negro deaths. I run 'em in agate. That's progress. Maybe in a few years I can run 'em with the same size type as white obits and not lose advertising or have white supremacists calling me."

"I guess that will be true equality."

George Burke grinned. "Nobody needs that kind of equality."

Outside the rain had nearly stopped. He went to the nearest pay telephone and looked in the directory under the Leeville listing and found the Reverend Young.

He got lucky. The Reverend Young was at home. When he hung up the receiver a couple of minutes later, it was with a deep uneasiness in his belly.

BY noon some of the small band of searchers were ready to give it up and go home. Holly did not blame them; if he had the choice he would go home, change into dry clothes, drink a couple beers, and get some sleep. Except for freeing a mule from a sinkhole with the help of its nigger owners, the morning had been a wasted effort, leaving them all wet, muddy, and exhausted.

Holly had asked the three blacks if they had seen any

54

sign of the boy. All had shaken their heads, but the old one had looked a little funny, like he might know something he did not want to tell.

You can't tell about them, Holly thought. The white man who says he understands them is either a liar or just fooling himself.

The rain had almost stopped, not that it made much difference. They were already as wet and muddy as they could ever be. Most of the men were resting on a narrow strip of land surrounded by muddy water and dead trees. Bowen stood by himself ankle-deep in ooze, leaning against a willow. He looked out across the swamp with blank eyes. Probably resigning himself to the fact they would never find the boy in this hell-hole, Holly guessed. It was tough, especially for the mother. He had heard she had broken down at work yesterday and was under heavy sedation.

Something bit him on the side of the neck. The rain had at least kept the mosquitoes away. Some of the men had brought sandwiches and candy bars and were eating, but Holly was not hungry. He was too weary to be hungry, too weary even for sleep. He wondered where Loomis was—probably snug and dry in the car. He thought of Janine, the little waitress at Logan's. One of these days soon he was going to score with her. He almost had the other night, but she had left him in a sweat and lather, like that damn mule in the sinkhole. Another mosquito bit the back of his hand, then one hit his cheek.

"Aw right, men. Let's move out!" he bawled.

The men stirred. One muttered something, but another shook his head and everyone looked over at Bowen, who seemed oblivious to them and his surroundings. Only after they had fanned out and were slogging through the muck again, did he rouse himself and start after them, stumbling and almost falling into the brown, turgid water.

ON some weekdays few came down to the cavernous basement, but on Saturdays Sheed usually was assured

55

customers—a tenant farmer needing a used refrigerator, a factory worker looking for a bed because the kids had broken the old one for good, women pretending to look for "antiques" but actually buying something cheap—a lamp, a chair, a chest of drawers.

Some just came to wander through the labyrinth of junk he had acquired at auctions, garage sales, and from people who brought down a family "heirloom" when they desperately needed cash. Sometimes Sheed viewed himself as a curator in a museum of family histories. As he shuffled past a sofa at night, he sometimes imagined that the squeal of the mice was the laughter of lovers who had lain on it, and sometimes when he would catch his own reflection in the glass of a china cabinet, for an instant it was like seeing the ghost of the cabinet's original owner come back to view a once-prized possession.

Then there were those people who came down simply to see the old man in a greasy coat who lived like a hermit and who was rumored to have a fortune squirreled away, maybe in the old grandfather clock over there— one hundred dollar bills clogging the gears and stuffed under the pendulum. Sheed guessed the girl belonged to this last category.

She had come in while he was selling a Negro woman a kitchen table, and had wandered around looking at items, inspecting a wardrobe, examining the grandfather clock, but covertly looking his way from time to time. She had watched him take the money from the Negro and thrust it into his coat pocket. In the other pocket he kept the thirty-two caliber revolver.

"Are you looking for something particular?" he asked when they were alone.

She was a beautiful girl with black hair and dark, compelling eyes. He had never seen her before.

"I'm just looking," she murmured. "You have a lot of interesting things down here." She turned her eyes on him. "Where do you find them all?"

"People bring them to me. Sometimes I go to them." Her eyes were like black wells.

"I've never seen you around here." He licked his lips.

56

His eyes strayed to her firm breasts. He could see her nipples poking against the fabric of her sweater. But her eyes drew him away from even these delights.

"Don't you get lonely down here?" the girl said softly. Her eyes were luminous and seemed to expand while her face was blurring.

"Yes," he said. "I'm lonely." He wet his lips again.

Only her eyes seemed to exist for him—everything else was vague and fuzzy.

"You can tell me," she murmured. "You know you can tell me."

He began to feel outside himself. The walls receded and her eyes were enormous and he was falling into them, being sucked into their dark depths. From far away he heard her voice again; then he was answering her, but he could not make out his own words.

He did not know how long it was before he realized he was alone. When he did, he went to the door and opened it. There was no sign of her. He locked the door, pulled the shade and rushed to a pile of newspapers against one wall. He yanked down a bundle of newspapers from the middle. He reached into the hole and removed a concrete block, weighing almost forty pounds. A board supported the papers and magazines above the hole, and he eased the concrete block onto the floor and with trembling hands reached inside the cavity and groped for the tackle box. His fingers found it and dug into the metal. He pulled the box down and in an instant his sweating hands found the key and he fumbled at the latch. It clicked and he opened the lid. The thick stacks of bills divided neatly into twenties, tens, fives, and ones lay undisturbed.

He wiped his forehead and wondered if he had suffered some sort of attack, or if he was going mad. Had the girl fled in fright? Had he told her anything? Had there been a girl at all?

He closed the lid and carefully placed the tackle box back in its niche. Then he heaved the concrete block back into place with the other blocks. Finally he replaced the bundle of newspapers. His eighty-three thousand and seventy-five dollars was safely hidden once more.

57

WHEN Sharon came back from lunch, the office was unlocked. Her father was searching the file cabinet. "I can't find Meacham under the M's," he said irritably.

"I put the file on your desk. You asked me to, remember?"

"That's right. I forgot."

She put her purse on the desk and pulled off the scarf from around her hair. She tossed her head and her brown hair swirled.

"I saw Dave out there with you."

"We had lunch."

"Getting serious."

"I don't know. I invited him over for supper tonight. Do you mind?"

"No. But you better check with Lucy."

"I will."

She watched him go into his office, sit down, and pick up the Meacham file. She wondered if he felt about Dave the same way Lucy did. She wanted him to like Dave.

At lunch Dave had been very quiet as though something heavy were on his mind. He had kept looking at her and once or twice she thought he was on the verge of telling her what it was, but in the end he had kept silent.

She also had something on her mind. Will had called just before Dave came by at lunch, and they had gotten into an argument when she told him she already had a luncheon date. He had found out from somebody that she had been at the drive-in with Dave last night.

"What's with you and this guy?" Will had said. His tone and attitude irritated her. "First last night, now lunch today. You're my girl."

"Listen to me, Will Lawton. I'm nobody's private property."

There had been a long silence on the other end of the line. Then he had hung up, leaving her confused and angry. Knowing Will, she was sure he would not leave it at that. She liked him, maybe she even loved him, but she was not his handmaiden. She had not intended to ask Dave for supper, but during lunch she decided to. She wondered now if she had done it because she wanted to

58

be with him or partly to punish Will. Probably both, she decided.

She picked up the telephone and dialed Lucy.

A HEAVY iron gate with a shiny new padlock blocked the driveway leading to the old mansion. Huge oaks and dark cedars hid the house from the road. Loomis got out of the patrol car and climbed over the barbed wire fence that stretched away to either side. In front of him a sign nailed to the trunk of an oak warned against trespassers.

The rain had stopped, but the sky was still overcast. The leaves dripped around him. It was getting late in the afternoon, and he had already decided this would be his last stop today. There was only a slight chance the Bowen kid could have wandered out this far, Loomis thought. But if he had run away, somebody around here might have seen him. It was a remote chance, but at this point he was grasping at straws.

His feet grated on the gravel drive. The Graves' place possessed an evil reputation left over from slave days. Local legends told that Talbott Graves had once or twice set a slave loose for sport—then hunted him down and slaughtered him. All who had known him claimed he was strange. Some maintained he was insane. Yet he had wrested a great plantation out of wilderness and swamp. After the Civil War much of it had been sold for taxes, but enough had remained so that the Graves were prominent people still, when Loomis was growing up. Eventually they had all died or moved away, except Letitia, an eccentric woman who had died in the house only last year, well into her eighties. She had been old Talbott's niece. Strange stories had always been whispered about her. When Loomis was a boy, she had disappeared for a year—gone to the West Indies, it had been rumored, where her family came from. Some said she left because she had become pregnant by the mulatto who virtually ran the plantation for her. The other blacks were in constant awe of him because he reportedly sacrificed goats

59

and chickens in magic ceremonies. Later, he had been committed to an insane asylum while Loomis was still in high school. At the time these stories had made an impression on Loomis, but as he grew older, he had discounted most of them as idle gossip. When Letitia had returned to the plantation, she had not been accompanied by any child—only a West Indian Negress called Mama Celia who was a wart healer and fortune teller for the more gullible. Some claimed she was a conjure woman and that Letitia herself had turned her hand to conjuring. For all he cared they could have been hippies as long as they did not violate the law. Whatever Letitia believed, she had let the place go to ruin, not planting crops, allowing the undergrowth to turn into a jungle, letting the mansion itself fall into disrepair.

Several times Loomis had raided stills some enterprising moonshiners had set up in the old lady's bottomland. He had always been scrupulous about getting her permission first, even though he had a warrant—partly out of courtesy, and partly because he enjoyed seeing the inside of the old mansion. But he had not been out here in nearly two years. First the old Negress Mama Celia had died; then a few weeks later Letitia. He had heard that the property had passed to distant relatives. They had taken possession only a few months ago.

Suddenly, he rounded a curve in the driveway and glimpsed the house through the trees—a big, dilapidated structure with square columns and flanked by two immense brick chimneys. The house was gray, its columns peeling and leprous. All the windows on the upstairs floor were shuttered up. To the side of the house were parked a flat-bed truck, the kind used for hauling timber, a pick-up truck, and a blue Volkswagen. To Loomis the house belonged to a different world than that of machines—an aristocratic, feudal world apart from Volkswagens and pick-up trucks. Slaves had hacked out a plantation from the wilderness, made it thrive; and when slavery had died, the plantation had gradually fallen into ruin. He did not envy the new owners the job of making the place prosper again.

60

From the outside, the house looked as if nobody lived in it. He wondered if they had any plans for restoring it. Maybe it was the decay or the dreariness of the day that made him hesitant in approaching the portico. For a moment he thought of turning around and going back.

When he knocked on the heavy oak door, a stocky Negro in soiled khakis opened it and stared at him. He was holding a hammer in his hand. His head was bullet-shaped and rested on a bull-neck; he regarded Loomis unblinkingly with small, red eyes.

"The owner home?"

The man said nothing. Loomis looked at the hammer. From down the dark hallway came quick footsteps.

"It's all right, Mosely," a female voice said. "Can I help you?"

She had dark hair and striking brown eyes. He guessed she was not yet twenty. He took off his hat.

"We're looking for a missin' boy. Maybe you've heard about it."

She nodded.

He gave her a brief description of Bobby and asked her if she had seen anybody matching the description in the last two days.

When she shook her head, he said: "Maybe your folks have seen him. Could I talk to them?"

"My brother's sleeping right now." She gave him an apologetic smile. "I'd hate to disturb him. But if he had seen anybody around here, I'm certain he would have mentioned it to me."

"He might have spotted him out on the road if he was driving into town."

"He seldom gets into town."

"Well, maybe your mother—"

"My mother's dead."

"I'm sorry." He stared past her into the hall. An old gas chandelier hung from the ceiling. He wondered if they planned to install electricity. Letitia had not been impressed with Mr. Thomas Edison or his inventions. The Negro had disappeared back into the bowels of the house,

61

and the girl seemed impatient to be rid of him. She really was quite beautiful.

"Well, Miss—?" He had heard the name in town, but was not quite sure of the pronunciation.

"Villiers."

"Miss Villiers, I appreciate your time."

She must have sensed he was not quite satisfied, because her tone became warmer. "I wish I could help you, Sheriff. That poor little boy. But we're so remote out here that, if any stranger happened by, we would surely notice."

Suddenly from somewhere back in the house came a sound of hammering.

"Your brother must be a sound sleeper," Loomis said dryly.

Her brow creased with annoyance. "Mosely's forgotten. We've been making so many repairs. If you'll excuse me. When my brother wakes, I'll have him call you if he did see the boy. Goodbye!" She gave him a ghost of a smile before closing the door.

He could not pinpoint it, much less define it, but there was something wrong. Something wrong about this place. Maybe the wariness in the girl's eyes had tipped him, or her reluctance to let him talk with her brother, but she was concealing something. Yet he had no idea what.

"I've been a cop too long," he muttered. He started down the drive toward the car. He decided that he would get a couple of the boys out here tomorrow and have a look around. The kid could have mired in those bottoms and not be found by these people if they passed within fifty yards of him. He turned and gazed back at the house in the gloom. Off to one side almost concealed by the cedars was a cabin, built of cedar logs. Letitia had told him it had once been part of the slave quarters. As he looked, he saw for a moment what appeared to be a face in the cabin window. He blinked and the face was gone, leaving him wondering if he had actually seen it or in the fading light had witnessed an illusion.

Maybe Villiers' help lived there now and possibly had

62

seen the boy.

He turned back toward the car. He was tired and wanted badly to get home. But after he had covered a few yards, he knew he would not rest until he went over to the cabin, if for no other reason, than to verify if he had actually seen a face.

He veered off the drive and walked rapidly through the trees toward the cabin. Although he did not sneak, he tried to keep himself from view of the big house. He was not sure why.

The last twenty yards were open ground. He crossed quickly. There was one small window in front and one in back. He stepped to the door and saw the new padlock. He felt his breath beginning to come faster. He could not have seen a face. The padlock meant nobody was inside. Next he would be seeing ghosts sitting in trees. He looked at the house. All the windows on the side facing him were shuttered tight. Going around to the rear of the cabin he was shielded from view from the big house. He was breathing fast as he moved toward the window. Cupping his hands to his face, he peered through the glass and into darkness. Slowly his eyes adjusted to the gloom and his heart jumped. Less than three feet away a face gazed back into his with idiot impassivity. The eyes were unfocused, apparently unseeing. His first thought was that the Negro was blind. A movement behind the Negro caught his eye. A smaller figure drifted into view.

In the dimness the boy's face looked like a transparent jellyfish floating through murky water. Bobby Bowen's eyes held the same vacant idiocy as the man's.

They must be drugged, he thought.

He reached for his revolver an instant after he heard the sound behind him and spun around to glimpse the hammer arcing like a pendulum toward his face. He barely had time to turn his head before the hammer smashed his temple.

63

CHAPTER 6

AFTER supper while the women cleared away the dishes, Dave and Sam Gates retired to the pool table. All during supper Dave had been mulling over Scott's story and wondering if he should tell Sam. If Scott really saw what he thought he saw, his father should be the one to go to the police. Yet Scott did not want to tell his father.

At supper the boy had watched Dave during most of the meal; then he finally excused himself, having barely touched his food. Now as Sam was racking the balls, Scott came into the game room. Dave shook his head and received a reproachful look. The boy turned and left.

"A moody kid," Sam said. "Sometimes I don't know what to make of him. Seems like he's in another world most of the time. You break."

Dave finished chalking his cue, sighted down the stick and sent the mass of colored balls flying, dropping the three ball in a corner pocket.

"What made you decide to go into teaching?" Sam asked.

"I tried some other things and didn't like them." He missed his shot.

Sam lined up a shot on the ten ball and sank it deftly in a side pocket. He sank three more striped balls before missing.

"Don't get me wrong," he said. "I respect teachers. There's just not a lot of money to be made there."

64

Before supper they had drunk expensive Scotch; they were playing on a thousand dollar table; out in the garage were two big cars. Dave smiled wryly.

"You're right about that."

He often asked himself why he stayed in teaching, and he never came up with a completely satisfactory answer. He searched the table for his best shot.

Sharon appeared in the doorway. "I should have warned you my father is a shark."

"That's no way to talk about your poor, old father," Sam said.

Dave sank two more solid-colored balls, then missed. He did not get another chance. Sam ran the rest of the striped balls; his final shot was a beautiful bank into the side pocket.

"I told you," Sharon said. "You should listen to me." She came over to him. "Any chance of your taking a girl for a walk?"

He found Lucy in the living room and thanked her for supper. She gave him a smile that did not quite reach her eyes and walked with them to the front door. As he shook hands with Sam, he decided not to tell him Scott's story. He looked around for the boy, but he had disappeared.

Outside it was cool and misty. The street lamps shone on the wet grass and on the glistening leaves of the silver maples. They walked down the street toward the older section of town.

"That's the best meal I've had in a long time," he said.

"I'm pleased to say I cooked most of it myself." She slipped her arm into his. "Lucy made the pie though. I'm still having trouble with pie crusts."

"She makes a good one." They stepped around a puddle. "I don't think she likes me very much."

"I know. I'm sorry. But Daddy likes you."

"He's found a pigeon."

"True. But still three out of four is not bad. Scotty likes you, you know."

"He visited me this morning."

"Scotty?" She looked at him. "In all that rain? Why?"

65

"He had something he wanted to get off his mind."

"What?"

He felt her breast against his arm. The night smelled of wet leaves.

Under a big sycamore they stopped and he drew her to him, smelling the cleanness of her hair. She pressed against him, turning her face up, her eyes glittering beneath half-closed lids. She reached up and touched his hair in a gesture so much like Kay's that he abruptly released her.

She looked at him questioningly a moment then turned away.

"Is it me?" she said.

He shook his head, at first not trusting himself to speak.

"No," he said finally. "It's not you."

They turned and walked back toward her house in strained silence. With each step he could feel her growing more distant. As she started up the walk toward her house, he touched her arm.

"Would you take a ride with me?"

"Where to?"

"I don't know. Around."

He opened the door of the Pinto. She hesitated, her eyes on his. Finally, without a word, she slid into the seat. He started the car up, and they drove awhile in silence with only the tires whispering on damp asphalt. Ahead of them a street lamp glowed softly in the mist, and they passed over a deep culvert.

"We used to wade down there," she said. "Sometimes after a hard rain, it was almost deep enough to go swimming. The first time I skinny-dipped was down there. I was seven."

"Listen," he said. "About back there. I'm sorry."

"It's all right." She touched his hand.

"Do you want to go swimming tomorrow?"

"Skinny dipping?"

Their eyes met. "I'll settle for a bikini—if I have to," he said.

Suddenly she pointed to a shabby little house they

66

were passing.

"That's the Bowen's."

It was dark except for one light in the back.

They drove wordlessly for two blocks then he pulled the car over to the curb.

"Why are you stopping?"

"You asked why Scott came to see me this morning." He switched off the engine. He told her. Then he told her about his trip to the graveyard and his call to the Reverend Elijah Young.

"He confirmed the *Progress* obit. Louis Biggs was buried Thursday afternoon at two. He conducted the graveside service."

"But you said Scotty told you the grave was open about—it must have been at least four-thirty or five when they were down there." She stared at him. "Oh, no! He saw some other grave. That's it. He saw some other grave that they had just dug."

He shook his head. "When I went down there this morning, there was only one new grave. It was right on the edge of the woods like Scott said."

She stared out the windshield into the darkness.

"He wouldn't tell me," she said. "He went to you."

"He didn't want to upset you."

"No. He thought you might believe him." She gave a short laugh and turned to him. "Do you?"

He remained silent.

"Do you?" she said.

"I don't know. He almost had me convinced this morning."

"Scott is very imaginative."

"Most kids are."

"I suppose so. But when Scott was five, there was this scarecrow in the field behind our house. It used to be a cornfield, but Mr. Sanders quit growing corn in it the year before. The scarecrow just stood in this empty field, its rags flapping in the wind. Then one day Scott began talking about a Mister Bojo. Then for days that was all he talked about—Mister Bojo this, Mister Bojo that. And when we asked who Mister Bojo was, he would just give

67

us that kind of secret smile the way little kids do. Of course, Mister Bojo turned out to be the scarecrow. One evening I saw Scott out in the field standing there talking to it. And the crazy thing is while I watched, the wind must have started up because I could almost see the scarecrow nodding and moving. There was something frightening about it. Then Scott began having dreams—terrifying dreams. He began to talk about Mr. Bojo coming to his window and whispering in the dark about going away with him."

Headlights from an approaching car lit her face for a moment then swept past, leaving them in darkness again.

"If you could have seen him after one of those nightmares—the fear in his eyes, and he kept repeating over and over that Mr. Bojo wanted to take him away from us. Then Scott's dog, a little terrier, died. We found him in the field, not far from the scarecrow. We figured he was poisoned. But Scott carried on terribly, saying Mr. Bojo had done it because he wouldn't go away with him. One day Lucy looked out the kitchen window and the scarecrow was afire. Scott had taken some kitchen matches and was sobbing and dancing around it. We were all pretty upset and for awhile Daddy debated on taking Scott to a psychiatrist."

"Did the bad dreams stop?"

"Yes—after Daddy got rid of Mama Celia."

"Mama Celia?"

"An old black woman who looked after Scott on Lucy's club days. She told him tales and he got very caught up in them."

"What kind of tales?"

"Oh, bizarre things. She was originally from some island in the West Indies. She lived on the old Graves place outside of town and was—a kind of conjure woman. The kind that would sprinkle stump water on your warts and after awhile they would go away—that sort of thing. We all thought she was harmless. But one day Lucy came home early and overheard her telling Scott about a tree that possessed an evil spirit, something out of primitive African religion."

68

"Our own ancestors believed in tree and river spirits too."

"Anyway, when Dad heard about it and some other things she had been telling Scott, he was furious. He said it wasn't hard to see where Scott had gotten his notions about the scarecrow. Mama Celia was banished from our house and Scott was forbidden to talk about the things he had heard. Eventually he seemed to forget all that rubbish. At least we thought he had forgotten it—until now."

He gazed at a misty halo around the street lamp. "You're saying I shouldn't take his story seriously?"

She shook her head. "I don't know." The misty light from the street lamp gave her hair a burnished glow like fine copper. "But why on earth would that grave be opened? He may have seen a shadow that looked like an open grave."

"Maybe. But it's not Scott's imagination that Bobby disappeared. And I'm not sure it was his imagination that somebody chased him that evening into the swamp." He ran his fingers restlessly over the steering wheel.

"It could be some crazy cult that's into grave robbing."

"Good Lord!" Her eyes widened. "You think the boys really stumbled into something like that?"

He shrugged. "Or it could be I've got too much imagination myself."

She gripped his wrist. "Listen. If Scott really saw that grave open, then we should go to the Sheriff."

"Yes."

"But if he didn't—" she began. "How can we know for certain."

"There's no way. That's why I told you. I didn't want to go to Loomis without your family knowing. Maybe I should tell your father."

She released his wrist. "I know what Daddy would say. If Scott made it up, the whole thing would be very embarrassing to him. Can you imagine digging up that poor Negro's grave, violating it for nothing?"

"It could be sticky," Dave agreed.

Neither spoke for awhile. "Let's hold off for one

69

more day," she said finally. "If Bobby's not found tomorrow, then I'll go with you to the Sheriff. I've known Fred Loomis all my life. Another day won't make any difference, will it?"

The mist hung heavily around them like damp cotton. The downtown lights cast a red glow against it.

"Where's Mama Celia now?" Dave asked.

"Dead." The whites of her eyes looked pink in the strange light. "She died a year or so ago, I think. She was very old."

Dave started the car and drove downtown. In the fog the courthouse tower loomed above them like a medieval turret. Sharon pulled her sweater tighter around her chest. "I don't like this," she said suddenly. "I've got this bad feeling."

"It's the fog. It can spook anybody."

"No. I usually love it. It's beautiful. I just can't shake this feeling something bad is going to happen. Bobby won't turn up, will he?" She shivered, and he put his arm around her.

"I shouldn't have given you that body-snatching business. I've seen too many horror movies." He drove her home.

A Dodge pick-up was parked at the curb in front of her house. Dave parked behind it and got out. At the same time a man emerged from the pick-up, a big man, and as he approached them, Dave recognized Will Lawton. As he opened the car door for Sharon, Lawton stopped directly beside him.

"You brought her home," Lawton said. "I'll see her to the door."

"Will," Sharon said.

They could smell the whiskey, but he did not look drunk. He was wearing a windbreaker and old khakis; his tanned, handsome face was stubborn. "Go on home, Stewart," he said. "Just go on home."

"Will," Sharon said sharply. She stepped between them.

Lawton took her arm. "You're my girl. You've had your little fling." He began propelling her up the walk

70

toward the house.

Dave grabbed his shoulder. Lawton let go of her and spun around. Dave slipped most of the punch, but the next one caught him on the cheek and sent him reeling against the car. For a big man, Lawton moved fast and landed another left as Dave bounced off the car. Sharon grabbed Lawton.

"Stop it!"

As Lawton brushed her away, Dave hit him in the mouth with a looping left and threw a right hook, then suddenly lights exploded before his eyes.

He heard Sharon's voice from a long way off and felt the wetness on the nape of his neck that he gradually recognized as grass. He heard Lawton's voice; then a door slam and an engine start. He was struggling to get to his feet and one side of his face felt like it was clamped by a heavy vice. The engine noise faded away in the fog. He was on his feet now with Sharon's arms around his waist. She was virtually holding him up. Her voice sounded like it was coming through a drainpipe.

"What?" he mumbled. A warm salty taste filled his mouth and trickled into his throat.

"I'm going to have to take your jacket back to the dry cleaner's."

He looked down and a fresh spattering of crimson speckled his lapel.

"Hold your head back," she commanded.

"Glad you're not the kind that faints at the sight of blood." It hurt him to talk.

"Give me your keys. I'm driving you home."

"I'll drive myself home."

She withdrew her arms from his waist. "Give me the keys."

"Go into the house," he snarled.

He tottered around to the driver's side and heaved himself into the car. Fumbling the keys into the ignition, he started the car and drove away. In the rearview mirror he saw her dim figure still standing on the sidewalk, staring after him.

71

SHE looked up suspiciously from the TV set as Holly got his jacket. He had just finished talking to Thelma Howe on the telephone.

"Where are you going?"

"Somethin's funny. I've got to go out."

"Yeah, there *is* something funny," she said in a meaningful tone.

He looked at the big pink plastic rollers on top of her head; they gave her thin, sullen face a frightening, alien aspect, he thought. She could have been a woman from Mars.

"Listen, Delores. Don't start that again."

"I want to know where you're going."

"Loomis ain't back yet. Thelma can't raise him on the radio."

"What are you? His keeper?"

"You're a real pain in the ass, Delores. You know that?"

She shot up from the chair and blocked his path. "Don't talk to me like that. Your son is in the other room."

"I've got to look for Loomis, ain't I. Nobody, includin' his wife, has heard from him since before noon."

"Loomis is plenty big enough and old enough to take care of hisself. I want you home tonight."

He brushed past her and went outside. She followed him out onto the porch. The rollers looked like giant caterpillars tunnelling into her head, and her face was a tight mask. "You stay away from that waitress," she hissed. "Or Kevin and I ain't gonna be here long when you get back."

He strode to the car and heard the screen door slam behind him. He started the patrol car, jammed the gear into reverse, and squealed out of the driveway, spewing gravel behind him.

Minutes later he was out of town and driving down the swamp road. It was foggy, and he had to drive slowly. As long as he had known Loomis, the man had never failed to call his wife and tell her if he were going to be late for supper. Tonight he had not called. Betsy Loomis had

72

called Thelma several times since darkness had fallen, wanting to know if Loomis had checked in yet. Each time she had seemed more worried, Thelma had told him. Earlier he had tried to raise Loomis at dusk for permission to call off the search. He had finally done it on his own initiative when he had failed to reach Loomis. Bowen had not wanted to leave the swamp and had begun to cry when Holly and the others forcibly put him into the car and drove him home.

He looked out at the fog blanketing the swamp and felt uneasy. Loomis could have wandered in there himself and fallen into one of those sinkholes like that damn mule they had pulled out this morning.

For a moment he allowed himself to think how it would be if Loomis were lost in the swamp. He would be Sheriff and the whole town would have to look at him differently and treat him with more respect, including Janine. She had gone out with him a couple of times and let him feel her tits, but would not come across. If he were Sheriff, she would spread her legs for him fast enough. Women loved power and except for Judge Summers and old Emmett Lawton, who owned half the town, Holly would be one of the most powerful men in the county.

He dismissed the thought and strained his eyes trying to penetrate the fog that was getting thicker all the time. Now he could barely see more than a few yards ahead. He slowed the car down to fifteen. He could not even drive, let alone find Loomis' car even if it passed him. He would head back to town before he was stranded out here in the car for hours. Loomis would show up soon. His radio could have gone haywire. He might be on his way home right now or already be there.

As soon as he found a convenient spot to turn around, he would head to Logan's and see if everything was under control there. Sometimes a drunk got out of hand, particularly on Saturday nights. Janine would be there.

He tried to raise Loomis once more on the radio. He received no reply. The fog was so thick that he had the sensation he was alone in the world, the last survivor

73

of some kind of great catastrophe. It was a queer feeling and he began to feel scared. He wished he was at Logan's right now instead of out here in this soup. He had been a fool to come out here in the first place. Delores was right about one thing. Loomis was certainly old enough to take care of himself.

CHAPTER 7

THE two boys ambled along the edge of the dirt road still muddy from yesterday's rain. The sun had not yet risen above the pines. Both carried cane poles and the older boy had a rusty can filled with worms he had grubbed out of his mother's vegetable garden.

The younger boy stepped into a fresh tire track in the road. Ahead he could see the bridge across the river. It was an ancient wooden structure with no rails.

He glanced slyly at the older boy. "You goin' to hell if you don't go to Sunday School."

The other said nothing.

"I'm goin' soon as I catch me a few fish. You goin'?"

"Naw," the older boy replied. "And the only reason you're goin' is your folks make you."

"You goin' to hell." Doodlebug shook his head gravely. "But I ain't."

"Shut up, Doodlebug."

Doodlebug ran on ahead in the grooves the tires had cut in the mud. Ignoring the Condemned sign, he ran out onto the middle of the bridge and stared into the murky water.

The other boy sat down on the bridge and threaded a worm on the hook so that the steel ran the entire length of the worm. He swung the line out and the hook dropped into the slow-moving current.

Doodlebug, who had been scanning the water for a

turtle or snake, saw something else and his cat eyes widened. He put his pole down and started for the opposite bank, peering all the while, intently, at one spot in the water.

"Jeff!" he yelled.

The older boy ignored him.

"Jeff!" A shrillness in his companion's voice caused Jeff to look up. He gazed at where Doodlebug was pointing. He could see nothing but muddy water.

"Comere quick! It looks like a car."

"Sure."

"I ain't lyin! One of them po-leece cars. I can see the light on top."

Jeff got to his feet and looked again. This time he thought he detected a faint shadow beneath the surface. Probably just a snag. He sauntered over to where Doodlebug stood. It looked like a sunken skiff, dim and wavery.

Then suddenly protruding above the shadowy mass he made out the small glass dome.

HOLLY woke with his head pounding, his mouth tasting like a septic tank. There was a staccato sound in his ears. Delores was tapping around the house in high heels. Tap, tap, tap, he could hear her tapping from one room to another, and he wished she would stop. He groaned and tried to remember why his head hurt. At Logan's Janine had brought him five or six beers, then Will Lawton had come in and he had drunk a couple more with him. Lawton's lip had been freshly split; he had been morose and sullen.

It came back to him. Janine had left with Lawton. The little slut! He had waited for her until closing time and then she had left with Will Lawton. All the time she had been making up to Lawton and he, in his beery stupor, had thought they were just kidding around. After they had left, he had bought a six-pack from Logan and drunk it out in the parking lot. He barely remembered driving home.

76

Delores tapped into the room. She was dressed up in a tan skirt and jacket. She must be going to church, he thought. She began dragging things out of the chest-of-drawers and throwing them into a suitcase.

"What are you doing?"

She did not answer; she went to the closet and pulled out several dresses. The telephone rang, and she tapped out of the room to answer it. When she returned, she said it was for him, and slammed the lid of the suitcase down and locked it.

He stumbled out of bed to the telephone. When he returned to the bedroom, he had forgotten his headache. His face was pale.

She started past him, lugging the suitcase.

"Where are you going?" he said thickly.

"I'll get the rest of my things later," she said. "Kevin's comin' with me."

He sat down on the edge of the bed.

"Loomis," he muttered. The front door slammed as he spoke. "Wait!"

He heard the car back out of the driveway and roar down the street. He sat listening to the silence.

Two boys had discovered Loomis' car at the bottom of the river. Floyd and Clyde Lee were out there now with the wrecker, preparing to haul it out.

Delores had left him. And he had not laid a hand on Janine last night.

He wondered if he was dreaming. Except for the stabbing pain he was becoming aware of again at the back of his skull, he would have been certain he was dreaming.

HE sat on the side steps of the house and sipped a cup of coffee. His jaw was stiff and swollen. Mrs. Anson's cat rubbed against his ankles, purring. Cars carrying people dressed for church streamed by the front of the house. He finished the coffee, stroked the cat, and debated whether to call for awhile. She might already be at church. Finally he rose, got into his car and drove a

77

block to the pay telephone at the gas station and dialed her number. She answered.

They decided on Greer's Lake, twenty miles outside town, and he picked her up thirty minutes later.

"You look terrible." She eyed his face, wincing visibly.

"You look good," he said. She wore a green tank top and white shorts. She had long, lovely legs.

He took the picnic basket from her and they walked to the car. "How do you feel?" she asked.

"All right except for my pride."

"He was an all-conference linebacker."

"Great." He held the car door open for her.

"I thought I knew him. But after last night, I don't know."

"It's simple enough. He loves you."

She looked at him and did not answer.

They drove most of the way to the lake in silence. The paved road gave way to gravel and then the lake gleamed before them in the sunlight, surrounded by thick pines. There was a narrow strip of sand where a few people were sun bathing. Out in the middle of the lake a speed-boat towed a skier who, even as they watched, toppled head-first into the water. The boat made a fast, tight arc and returned to the spot where the skier's head bobbed cork-like in the wake.

He parked at the edge of the beach. When they got out, she quickly slipped out of the tank top and shorts. She stood before him in a black bikini, her breasts and buttocks almost bursting out of the thin fabric. She smiled. "You said you'd settle for a bikini."

As he gazed at her, a tightness gripped his throat. His tongue felt glued to the roof of his mouth. They spread the blanket she had brought on the sand, and she lay down while he unbuttoned his shirt and pulled off his trousers. When he had stripped down to his faded trunks, she handed him a plastic bottle of sun tan lotion. "Do my back?"

He poured the oil and began working it into her warm flesh. His finger tips caressed her shoulders and neck, then traveled down her spine, close to the swelling buttocks.

78

When he finished, he stretched out beside her, watching the skier on the lake, conscious of the warm sun and the smell of her hair and the lotion on her flesh.

A few yards away a small boy and girl were running into and out of the water, shrieking. Watching them approvingly was an enormous woman in a one piece bathing suit that looked like a tent, sagging around her massive thighs, girdling her great bosom.

Sharon pointed to a float sixty yards from shore. "Sanctuary."

She rose and walked into the water, tossing her head so that her hair swirled around her shoulders. When she was up to her hips, she splashed her upper body with water and turned to him. "Come on! I'll race you."

By the time he reached the water, she already had a good start on him. He swam hard, but she was waiting for him when he reached the float. They clung to the edge with one hand, breathing deeply, their legs touching.

"Slow poke," she said.

"I didn't want to embarrass you with your headstart."

She put her hands on his head and pushed him under. When he came up spluttering, she was heaving herself onto the float. He clambered up, and she looked at him lazily, then stretched out on her back. He eyed the curve of her belly and thighs and again felt the catch in his throat. Lying down beside her, he closed his eyes. He was almost asleep when he heard her murmur something.

He opened his eyes and saw her face close to his. She was looking at him intently. She leaned over him and brushed his lips with hers, then pulled back. As he reached for her, she put her hand to his mouth, and looked toward the beach.

"Let's go back," she whispered.

They swam back to shore, gathered up the blanket and the picnic basket and wandered into the trees. They found a small glade concealed from the beach by almost a wall of pines and spread the blanket. They ate ham sandwiches and drank iced tea from her thermos. After they finished, she lay back on the blanket, one knee raised. "It's so peaceful here. I don't want to leave," she said.

"We'll pitch a tent and live like gypsies."

She smiled and closed her eyes. He gazed at the rim of white flesh between her tan thigh and the bikini bottom.

He bent over her and kissed the hollow of her throat, then the side of her neck. She kept her eyes closed and he kissed her mouth, feeling the firm pressure of her teeth; then the pressure gave way and their tongues met, parted, met again. His hand slid up her belly and cupped a breast.

She broke the kiss and opened her eyes, their gray depths still.

"Dave?" Her cool fingers touched his swollen jaw. When he kissed her again, she sighed and lowered her knee. Their bodies strained against each other.

"No," she said, but it was half-hearted as he pulled down the bikini halter. His mouth and tongue glided over the erect nipples, then she pulled his head back.

She gazed at him steadily while her hands went to her thighs and she wriggled out of the bottom. When he bent to her again, yellow flecks rose in her eyes. Her fingers roved through his hair and for an instant he thought of Kay, but only an instant before the girl beneath him took his thoughts and sensations completely.

Late that afternoon, as they approached town, they heard on the car radio the news of Loomis' death.

HOLLY drove into his driveway at dusk reflecting that it had been a very long day. Some people were speculating that Loomis had died of a heart attack and crashed off the bridge, but they had not seen the gash in his skull. He was still waiting for word from the medical examiner in Memphis as to the exact cause of death, but he was pretty damn sure it was no heart attack.

He had reached the scene just as the wrecker had hauled the car dripping onto the bank like some monstrous turtle. He had opened the door himself as water streamed out of the car, over the crumpled figure lying

80

on the floorboards. Loomis stared up at him with bulging eyes as though they held the image of horrifying sights seen in the muck of the river's bottom. Clyde Lee, seeing Loomis, turned white and walked off into the trees. After they had removed Loomis' body and put him in the ambulance, Holly had knelt and picked up the steel-rimmed glasses still lying on the floorboards. For a moment he had difficulty swallowing. Then as senior deputy he had ordered Floyd and Clyde Lee to retrace Loomis' movements yesterday and reconstruct his exact route in searching for Bobby Bowen. The doctor at the local hospital told him Loomis had been in the water at least twelve hours or since early last night.

The hardest part had been telling Betsy Loomis. He had dreaded going over there. She had stared right through him as he spoke, then went to the window and stared out at the garden. He had left her still staring at it. She had a kid who lived in Atlanta. It would be up to him to try and comfort her, and maybe after the funeral he would take her back there with him. Much of the afternoon he had spent in paper work and filling out forms on Loomis' death. The Mayor had called him and made him Acting-Sheriff until a special election could be held, which might not be for some time. He had gone over to Gray's garage to check on Loomis' car which turned out to have very little damage. Gray already had the engine going when he got there, but Holly knew he never wanted to drive it. He could never forget the car had been Loomis' tomb or shut out the eyes staring up at him from the floorboards.

He got out of his own car, realizing with a sudden twinge the house would be empty. By now Delores must have heard that he was Sheriff. Across the street car doors slammed and a man and woman approached him. The girl was Sam Gates' daughter and the man was that new baseball coach at the high school.

"Could we talk to you a minute," the man said and introduced himself.

Holly tipped his hat to Sharon as the man began: ". . . found out something yesterday . . . maybe should

81

have notified you right away . . . ."

Holly eyed him closely. His jaw was swollen and his left cheek had an ugly purple bruise. He must have been in a fight. Suddenly, remembering Lawton's split lip last night, he guessed he knew who with and why. Sharon Gates was supposed to be Lawton's girl. Now he understood Lawton going off with Janine last night. Ordinarily he would have thought she was beneath him. As Stewart went on talking, Holly found himself eyeing him even more closely. After Stewart finished, Holly looked away. Across the street it was completely dark under the big oak in Widow Foley's yard.

"Kids think they see a lot of things," he muttered at last. "My own boy Kevin once saw the tooth fairy sitting on the roof wearing a tooth necklace and a halo."

"We don't think Scott imagined this," the man said.

"Why?"

Stewart looked away. "Would it hurt to check?"

"You need a court order to dig up a grave, Mister. Even a nigger's grave." He shook his head. In his seven years with the Department he could not remember Loomis ever having run into something like this. Now his first day as Acting-Sheriff, this pair comes along and wants to dig up a body.

"Can't you get a court order?" Sharon Gates said.

"I don't think I can get one on the basis of what you've told me. Your brother imagines his friend might be in that grave. Do you believe the Bowen kid really is?"

It was the girl's turn to look away. He did not want to offend her, particularly since her father was an alderman but, on the other hand, he certainly did not want to go himself to Judge Summers with such a flimsy story and ask for any court order.

"Maybe if your father thinks we should look into this further, I might be able to do something. What does he say?"

Even in the deep twilight, he could see her face reddening.

"I see. He don't take this story seriously—" Holly started to add 'either,' but checked himself.

82

"You'll act if my father says so, but not if we ask you," the girl flared. "That's it, isn't it?"

Holly said nothing.

"That's what law amounts to in this town—who has the influence and who doesn't, right?"

Stewart took her arm. "Come on," he said.

"All right," she said. "We're not going to do any good here."

Holly watched them cross the street, get into the Pinto, and drive away in the darkness. He stood watching until the car was out of sight. Then he thought of the cold beer in the ice box and suddenly felt a great thirst for one. He let himself into the darkened house, shaking his head. What a day, he thought to himself, what a damn day!

"FIRST Bobby, now Loomis," she said. They sat in the Pinto in front of her house gazing out into the darkness. "Even with a heart attack, to be on a bridge at the time, well, I just don't believe it. And he certainly wouldn't be on a condemned bridge—not in his car anyway."

They sat in silence; finally she reached in the back seat and got the blanket and picnic basket.

"Maybe I should have talked to your father in the first place," Dave said.

She shook her head. "He wouldn't buy it any more than McAfee did. Even while we were talking to him, I have to admit, I began to have doubts all over again about Scotty's story." She looked at him. "Do you really think telling Daddy would make any difference?"

"I don't know. Maybe not. I don't believe Bobby is in that grave, but I think something weird happened down there. And now Loomis is dead looking for Bobby." He opened the car door and took the blanket and basket from her. "Anyway we've been to the police. Frankly, I don't see what else we can do."

They walked beneath the silver maples to her door. They lingered for a while on the steps. After she went inside, Scott met her in the hallway. She noticed purple

83

shadows under his eyes and his face seemed even paler than usual. "You know about the Sheriff?" he said.

"Yes. Where are they?"

"Mom's at church. Dad's watching 'Columbo.'"

She went into the kitchen, drew a glass of water from the tap and drained it. He had followed her and was watching her with troubled eyes. She set the glass down and walked over to him. She did not like those deep shadows under his eyes.

"You haven't been getting any sleep, have you?"

He shrugged.

"I know you're thinking about Bobby and I know how you feel. But you've got to try and put it out of your mind. I'm getting worried about you."

"But now the Sheriff," he said. "Dave was going—" he trailed off and studied his shoes.

"Dave was going to tell him what you saw. The open grave."

His head jerked up. "He told you."

"Yes. And we went to the police and told them."

He looked at her gravely. "What are they going to do?"

She turned back to the sink and rinsed the glass.

"They didn't believe it," he said. "But it's the truth. What did they say? Tell me."

She wondered if she should. She decided not to lie. "If Dad believed and went to them, maybe they would open the grave. That's what the man we talked to said."

He looked at her with bitter eyes. Without a word, he turned and walked out the kitchen door. Sharon started to go after him, then checked herself. What could she say that would make any difference? She went back to the sink, washed out the thermos, and put the picnic basket away. She knew she felt guilty because she still doubted Scotty herself. "Damn," she said. "Damn!"

She snatched up the blanket she had laid on a chair and walking into the hallway thrust it up onto a closet shelf. Then she went into the game room. Her father glanced up from the TV set, and she thought his eyes held the old unspoken question. In the past when she had seen it, she had always been able to meet his eyes

84

boldly. This time her eyes slid away from his.

"Did you have a good time?"

"Yes." She made her voice nonchalant. "The swimming was fine."

"You know about Loomis?"

"Yes."

His eyes were still on her. He knows, she thought. Maybe the scent of sex is still on me.

"It's hard to believe," she said. "He was just here the other night."

He was still gazing at her intently. Just when the silence was becoming unendurable, she heard the front door open and close. In a moment Lucy came into the room. Her eyes immediately went to Sharon. They were a bit too bright.

"Why didn't you tell us?" she said.

"Tell you what?"

"About the brawl."

"What are you talking about?" Sam said.

"There was a brawl in front of our house last night. I only found out about it a little while ago."

At church, Sharon thought. Mabel Dunham. She was the nastiest gossip in town.

Lucy turned to Sam. "Between Will and Dave Stewart. Right in front of our house like two mooses in mating season. It's disgraceful!"

"Will had been drinking. Did Mabel tell you that?"

"Who won?" Sam asked.

"Is that all you can say?" Lucy snapped.

"Excuse me," Sharon said. She left them staring after her and went to her bedroom. She flopped down on the bed and kicked off her sandals. Her skin felt gritty and smelled of sweat and suntan oil, and her breasts felt swollen and sensitive against the mattress. She lay there awhile listening to the murmur of their voices in the game room, then sat up and peered at herself in the dresser mirror. It's time for me to move out, she thought. It's way past time.

A knock sounded on the door. She got up and opened it. Scott stood there. She went back and sat on the bed

85

and Scott came into the room. He did not usually come in here.

"You and Dave were gone a long time," he said finally.

"Hey. You're not going to start, are you?"

He shook his head.

She smiled. "You know you're my favorite."

His blue eyes flicked to her face, then around the room. "You should teach him how to make coffee. His is awful."

"I'll keep that in mind. And since when did you start drinking coffee?"

He grinned, but it vanished as quickly as it had appeared.

"Anyway," he said, "I wanted to tell you I've decided to tell Dad about the grave." He stuffed his hands in his jean pockets. "Who knows, maybe he'll even believe me." He gave her another quick look. "Do you?"

She had asked herself that a dozen times since last night, and still she did not know whether she believed he had actually seen the open grave or imagined it. He saw her hesitation. His eyes became stony. He turned away.

She made up her mind. She rose and put her hand on his shoulder. "I believe you. I'll go with you."

A light came back into his eyes. "No. I want him to believe *me*."

She nodded. "All right."

After he left, she lay on the bed staring at the ceiling. A few minutes later, she heard him come back and go into his room. She got up from the bed and went to him.

His face was tight; his lower lip trembled. "He says I've got to quit imagining things." He turned his back on her and began fiddling with a model airplane on top of his bookcase.

She went to the game room. "Why don't you believe him?"

"Because it's nonsense," her father switched off the TV. "Bobby is not buried in some Negro grave."

"Maybe not. But there could be other explanations for what Scott saw."

"Thought he saw. Name one."

86

"What if somebody were digging up the corpse and Bobby happened to see it?"

Her father shook his head.

"Listen, somebody chased Scotty into that swamp."

"Somebody he admits he never even saw."

"Are you saying grave robbers are responsible for Bobby's disappearance?" Lucy said. "And then chased Scotty?"

Sam's eyebrows shot up. "When did you decide somebody actually chased him?"

"It's possible. There are certainly enough perverts in this town. But I don't think even they would consider grave robbing or body snatching or whatever."

"Hell, he was alone in a graveyard at night and panicked. I can understand that. But why he has to make up this other stuff. . . ."

"He thought you wouldn't believe him." Sharon felt the blood rising to her cheeks. "Do you know he went to Dave Stewart instead of you, his own father, or to me, because he didn't think we would trust him or believe in him—because you forbade him to ever come to you with any of his so-called 'nonsense' again."

"Calm down. Don't you think I want to believe him?" Sam said. "Don't you? But he lives in some fantasy world half the time. He's to the point where I wonder if he knows the difference between what's real and what isn't. Remember the scarecrow business. Was I to believe that because some crazy old woman fed him some mumbo-jumbo about spirits being everywhere? And now I'm supposed to take this latest story seriously. Well, what would you have me do? Get the poor nigger dug up, then apologize to his widow and kids and look like an idiot because Scott had another Alice-in-Wonderland vision?"

"Is that why you won't believe him? Because there's a chance you might look foolish?"

Her father's face reddened. "I don't want anymore discussion about this. I mean it!"

She spun on her heel and strode out of the room. She flung open the front door and went out, slamming it shut again. She breathed deeply, big gulps of fresh air.

87

In the moonlight the silver maples looked frosted and, despite the warm night air, she felt cold and alone.

Yes, it was long past time for her to leave this house.

AS he was going up to his room, Mrs. Anson came out in the hallway and called to him. Her henna tinted hair seemed to glow like neon. "Isn't it terrible about Sheriff Loomis?"

He nodded.

"He wasn't that old, you know. We went to school together. Of course, he was several years ahead of me." She squinted up the stairs at his bruised face. "What on earth did you do to yourself?"

"A little accident. Nothing serious." He turned to go on up the stairs.

"By the way," she said. "Somebody called you several times on the phone while you were out. She wouldn't leave her name."

"Thanks. I guess if it's important, she'll call back."

In his room he switched on the light, undressed, and threw his damp swim trunks in the lavatory. He rinsed them out, wrapped a towel around his middle and journeyed down the hall to the shower. When he got back to the room, he put on an old bathrobe and sat down at the desk. He stared at the untidy heap of notes for his partially written thesis. He needed to write, but he was too keyed up. Any excuse not to work, he thought. He stared out the window into the darkness, listening to the crickets. Somewhere close, a car engine started up. He listened to the car go by and its engine noise fade down the street into silence. It had sounded like a small, foreign car, almost a motor-scooter grumble. For some reason he thought of Marie Villiers. She had a Volkswagen. Maybe she had been the one who had called him, and not being able to reach him, had decided to come here and wait, and . . . he grinned. Vanity, vanity. Marie, like many teen-aged girls, might have a highly developed romantic imagination, but he did not seem to be exempt from it either.

88

He wondered if Sharon was still up. He looked at his watch and saw it was only nine o'clock. He realized he had not had any supper, and immediately felt hunger pangs.

He got up from the desk, dressed, and went down to the car. When he got to the small diner, it was getting ready to close. The waitress, a gaunt woman, with tired eyes, took his order impatiently. As he waited for her to bring the food, he wondered again who the caller had been.

He wished he had asked Mrs. Anson about the time of the calls. He had come straight home after leaving Sharon and besides, if it had been her, she certainly would have left a message. Again, the only other person he could think of was Marie. The waitress brought his order, but after the first few bites, he found he was not hungry after all. Why did he feel so jumpy? His mind alternated from thoughts of Sharon to Loomis' death to his neglected thesis and back to Sharon again. It was like a long-playing record with a familiar melody repeated over and over, except that occasionally a new note would break in and that new note was Marie Villiers.

He pushed his half-eaten food away, paid his check, and left the diner. He drove aimlessly around town for a while and finally drove back to Mrs. Anson's, and still unaccountably restless, forced himself to go up to his room.

When he finally got to sleep around two in the morning, it was a restless, fitful slumber filled with menacing dreams.

CHAPTER 8

"HAVE you seen his face?" Millie Thornton said.

Tina Burtram giggled. They were standing by the window waiting for class to begin. Millie was a big-breasted blonde while Tina was thin with a hoyden face.

"Sharon Gates would be worth a punch in the face," Wade Haskill said.

"Watch yourself!" Millie punched his arm. He barely noticed. Out of the corner of his eye he was watching Marie who had entered the classroom a minute before and was apparently listening to them. He turned and winked at her. She gave him an aloof smile. He had been trying to date her for weeks and his lack of success galled him. Most girls wanted to date him. Hadn't he been voted "Outstanding Athlete" in the yearbook? He was quarter-back of the football team and the best hitter on the base-ball team. He listened as Millie and Tina made a few cutting remarks about Sharon Gates. Both girls had ceased to be of much interest to him. He had taken Tina in the back seat of his car one night and thought she was having hysterics when they finished. The closest he had come with Millie was one night against the refrigerator in her kitchen while her parents watched "Hee-Haw" in the next room. At the critical moment he had been interrupted when her kid sister had wandered into the kitchen for a Coke.

Oblivious of Millie's dirty look, he sauntered over to

90

Marie's desk and bent near her.

"What do you think?"

"About what?" The indifference with which she seemed to regard him caused his cool facade to crumble.

"Stewart getting beat up." His tone became low and wheedling. "I know you like him. I've seen the way you look at him. But he's hung up on Sharon Gates. So why not you and me tonight? I guarantee you we can have a good time."

Her dark eyes seemed to become softer, more luminous.

"You know what?" she said.

"What?" He stared at her eagerly.

"You bore the shit out of me."

His cheeks flushing, he glared at her. The bell rang. He whirled away and stalked over to his desk. When Stewart entered the room, Wade gazed with malicious satisfaction at the purple bruise on the teacher's cheekbone.

Despite himself he could not help but glance over at Marie. Her eyes were fastened on Stewart with an intensity he had never seen before, an intensity that somehow chilled him.

WHEN the bell rang ending class, the students milled out the door, some smirking a little as they passed him. He turned away and walked over to the window, reflecting on the fact of a twenty-eight-year-old school teacher ardently wishing he had inflicted more damage on his opponent during a fist fight. Undoubtedly word of the fight had by now spread all over town; some parents might have already called Simmons to protest the poor example he was setting for his students.

"Well?" A voice said behind him.

He turned. She had waited until the rest of the students had left. Wearing a green dress that left most of her shoulders bare, she stood close to him. Her full lips curled faintly. "You're not going to say you bumped into a door, are you?" For a moment a hard glint appeared in her eyes.

91

"No. I'm not going to say that."

"Maybe you should watch the company you keep." She moved closer to him. "I called you yesterday," she said. "More than once."

"What about?"

He felt the sudden warm pressure of her breast against his arm.

"I thought we might get together," she said.

"I don't think it would be a good idea." He shifted his weight so her breast no longer touched him.

"Why?" Her eyes held his and again he felt the insistent pressure of her breast against his arm.

Dammit! Since Kay's death he had been unable to make love to a woman until yesterday with Sharon. But this girl had aroused him first and now she was doing it again.

"If you're worried about your job, we wouldn't have to be seen together," she said smoothly. "In fact, I would prefer it that way. My brother is—strict." Her fingers brushed the back of his hand. "I know a secret place. We could meet there tonight if you like." Her eyes glistened. They seemed enormous.

His throat was dry and for an instant he was tempted to take her up on it.

A fat girl poked her head in the door, looked around, and withdrew. They heard her heavy footsteps shuffle away down the hall. He moved free of the nudging breast. "You know this can't work."

"It can if you want it to."

"But I don't." He wondered if he was not half lying.

She flashed him a quick, piercing look then her lips curled derisively. "I'm sure Sharon Gates will appreciate your—fidelity."

Without another word, she turned and walked rapidly out of the room, brushing past two students who had drifted in for the next class. After she was gone, he thought of the small leather bag he had seen hanging from the thong around her neck on Friday. Today her neck was bare.

92

OVERHEAD a buzzard circled lazily. Rufus stared at it, then batted away some gnats buzzing around the mule's eyes. Since early dawn he had been riding through the bottoms searching for his other mule. Now ahead of him loomed a white, leprous trunk of a dead sycamore that marked the boundary of the old Graves plantation. Rufus felt a slight uneasiness stir in the pit of his stomach. Strange tales had attached themselves to this place, and nearly everyone avoided it after dark.

Lonnie Ledbetter had sworn he had seen the ghost of old Talbott Graves gliding silently one October night through the dark pines. Lonnie said he knew it was Talbott from the old-timey clothes he was wearing and the hell-fire glow in his eyes. "He be lookin' like the devil himself," Lonnie said. "My Granpappy tol' me once in the slavin' days he set aloose one of his slaves, then tracked him down and killed him like he was huntin' a rabbit." Lonnie had run the eight miles back to town without once stopping or looking back, he said, after seeing Talbott's ghost. "He was crazy in life. Got so even the other whites didn't want no truck with him. Reckon I don' need no truck with him neither, even in the spirit."

But Lonnie had probably been drunk that night or he would have never gone possum hunting on the Graves place to begin with.

The mule's ears pricked up. Rufus reined in, cautious, and listened. Far away came the faint whine of a power saw.

He remembered Hurley Gann saying the new owner of the place was cutting timber and dynamiting stumps. They were supposed to be clearing more fields for planting. Hurley, when he first heard about it, had come out asking for a job, but a strange Negro said they already had enough hands, although Hurley had not heard of anybody around here who had been hired. Hurley believed the cutting and dynamiting were just a show to fool the whites—to make them think the new owners were going to farm.

"They into somethin' else out there," Hurley had said. "Somethin' bad. Somethin' real bad."

93

When Rufus had tried to pin him down, Hurley had refused to say anymore, except that the Graves place had always belonged to the Devil and still did. Sarah believed the same thing, even though Rufus had argued with her about it. She had begged him not to come out here.

"Hurley be right," she said. "They's dynamitin' just for show. Wickedness is what they's up to, the same things Miss Letitia, that crazy yeller nigger Bastian she had a baby by, and Mama Celia was up to."

He had told her she shouldn't listen to Hurley who was acting near as crazy as Lonnie Ledbetter.

Still it was strange. If they were planning to plant after all that chopping and dynamiting, why hadn't they hired some folks?

Rufus wondered if they were using wetbacks. He and the mule skirted the edge of the bottoms and rode up a gradual incline into the pines. The shriek of the saw grew louder. Suddenly the mule shied. Through the pines ahead of him was a clearing. In the center of it stood a portable sawmill surrounded by tree stumps. He could see two figures moving about in the clearing. As he watched, he saw them heave a log up onto the conveyor belt of the rig. It was a huge log and he marvelled at their strength.

A hundred yards off to his right, another figure was attacking a pine with a chainsaw. It shrieked, then was drowned by the louder shriek from the headsaw in the clearing. His gaze fell on the figure who was guiding the big log into the headsaw. It was a woman. Something about the thick body and heavy shoulders seemed strangely familiar to him, but there was also something unnatural about her movements. Then he noticed her partner moved the same way: slow and dreamy like both were working underwater. Their heads were bent, so he could not see their faces.

The mule suddenly snorted and sidled against a pine, almost knocking him off. Rufus fought to control the animal, and slowly the woman lifted her head toward him, like a diver struggling to the surface. As she gazed at him vacantly, Rufus felt like the mule had kicked him in the belly.

"Dear Jesus, no," he gasped.

94

The mule reared. At the same instant, someone reached up behind and yanked Rufus down. He struck the ground heavily and lay on his back stunned, trying to regain his breath. Above him stood a stocky Negro with a bullet-shaped head. Nearby the mule plunged and kicked, its bridle in the grasp of a white man who struck the animal's nose with the butt end of a riding crop. The mule screamed and reared again. The Negro sprang over and grabbed the bridle and the two men managed to finally tether the mule to a pine sapling.

"Vicious brute," the white man panted. He turned to Rufus, staring at him with cold eyes that were almost colorless in his narrow face. Something about the thin, curved nose and slightly stooped shoulders reminded Rufus of a turkey buzzard, but the eyes made him think of Lonnie Ledbetter's description of Talbott Graves. He was dressed all in white except for the black leather riding boots. He flicked the riding crop against the top of one boot. "You've been spying on us," he said in an unexpectedly soft voice.

"Nossir," Rufus said. He could not keep the tremor out of his own voice, and he knew they must see the fear and horror in his eyes. He struggled up to his knees.

"You think he knows?" the Negro asked.

"Oh, yes." The white man tapped Rufus lightly under the chin with the riding crop. "You can see it in his face."

"I don' know what you all talkin' about," Rufus said. He was beginning to pant. "I jus' come here lookin' for my mule that run off the other night."

But even as he spoke he could not keep his eyes from the woman in the clearing. Any minute now, he told himself, I'm going to wake up. This is a dream—a nightmare. Because the woman at the conveyor belt could not be who he thought she was except in a dream. Three days ago he had seen her, Annie Mae Willis, lowered into the grave. Right now she was in the cemetery across the road from his house, not here in these dark woods.

Any minute I'm going to wake up now, he thought as the stocky Negro advanced toward him across the sun-dappled pine needles.

95

CHAPTER 9

THE mingled smells of stale cigar smoke and lysol assailed George Burke as he entered the courthouse. His steps echoed down the high-ceilinged corridor and stopped at the door with Sheriff on the frosted glass. He went inside.

Thelma Howe, wearing a large blonde wig that lent her puffy face a baby-doll innocence, glanced up from her typing. "I'll see if he's busy." She disappeared behind another frosted door. He had noticed she was wearing cowboy boots.

Burke lit a cigaret and gazed at the faces of felons-at-large on the bulletin board. He had once been a police reporter for a large daily, and the wanted posters, the impersonal metal furniture, the heavy atmosphere of bureaucracy stirred a slight nostalgia within him. But the three deadlines a day over a long period had given him king-size ulcers and a bad heart as well as a permanent distaste for pressure. Three years ago he had bought *The Progress*. A steady diet of stories about school bond issues, lawn-of-the-month winners, and weddings with only a weekly deadline had rid him of the ulcers, but sometimes he still found himself yearning for more exciting stuff.

Once in awhile a fire, a brawl at Logan's, or a knifing during a Saturday night crap game would spice *The Progress'* otherwise bland front page, but not very often. Now suddenly he had two stories that would not embarrass

96

any front page man in the country. The A.P. man in Memphis had called him this morning asking for details on Loomis' death and Bobby Bowen's disappearance.

"What's happening down there?" the A.P. man said. "Give us anything you've got."

"That's the problem. I don't have anything—yet. When I do, I'll get back to you."

But, although he hankered after a big story, the Bobby Bowen thing touched a raw nerve. Once, as a young reporter for the New Orleans *Times-Picayune*, he had been sent on assignment to a small town a hundred miles above New Orleans. It had been a nice town—neatly painted frame houses, well-kept lawns, big live oaks dripping Spanish moss—a quiet town, the kind of place where generally the most excitement was the annual Christmas Parade. He had grown up in that kind of town, peopled for the most part by quiet, decent men and women.

The town was running a new storm sewer to a recently built subdivision. It had rained for several days and work had been suspended. Two kids were playing in the twelve-foot deep trench when a wall of mud caved in on them. One of the boys was buried completely—the other trapped up to his chest. His screams were heard by a passing motorist and soon the fire department and police arrived to attempt the rescue. But the muddy walls kept caving in and soon the boy who had been chest-deep was buried up to his neck in thick, heavy mire. Outside help was called in, and the newsmen arrived. By nightfall the story had made all three TV network newscasts. The second evening it was the lead story on two of the networks and strangers—sightseers—had begun to swarm into the town. The local restaurants and motel did a booming business.

The TV cameramen, newspaper and free-lance photographers crowded close to the ditch trying to get close-ups of the boy's face, but cops managed to keep them at bay. The newsmen had to content themselves with interviewing the parents and wheedling old snapshots of the boys from them. They were in shock, of course, but TV cameras and microphones recorded their dazed faces and

97

stumbling replies to questions for millions of avid viewers.

Burke had observed himself, with a kind of cynical detachment, asking the parents the same questions as the others, then trying to inject a little more drama and pathos into his telephoned accounts to the paper than the others. He had camped on the doorstep of the surviving boy's parents to register each moment of hope as a new method was tried to free their son—once authorities brought in a crane and tried to lower a man into the ditch without touching either bank—followed by increasing despair as each method in turn failed. The third day the rain began again, the whole bank gave way and smothered the boy.

He phoned in the grim finale, went back to New Orleans and was surprised to find himself a week later suddenly filled with self-revulsion. It seemed to him he was a vulture picking over the bones of others' misery. He thought about quitting the newspaper and finding another line of work. Instead, he went on a bender on Bourbon Street and wound up in the drunk tank of the city jail, his mouth tasting like the town dump and his skull feeling like it was being bored into by an electric drill.

The parents of the dead boys had sued the city and the local construction company building the sewer for criminal negligence. One of the mothers sold her story to the *National Enquirer* and blamed local officials by name in its pages. Bitter feelings were aroused and battle lines drawn between people who worked for the construction company, their relatives, and city hall on the one hand, and the friends of the dead boys' families on the other. Shortly afterward one of the mothers had a nervous breakdown and was sent to the state sanitarium. The woman was the one on whose doorstep Burke had camped, and he had grilled her several times when she had been in no shape to talk to anybody. Others had done the same, but even after all these years he sometimes saw her thin strained face and bleary, red-rimmed eyes in his dreams. And while he knew better than to blame himself for what had happened to her, he had been

98

caught up in a ruthless competition for a story and in the carnival atmosphere that had swirled around the town for those three days. He had a nagging feeling that something of value had slipped away from him during his coverage of the story, something he could not retrieve.

Thelma returned and motioned him to go into the other room. Holly sat at Loomis' old desk, looking haggard. He turned his bloodshot eyes on Burke and waved him to a chair. Burke knew his wife had left him; the whole town knew by that mysterious small town grapevine that spread gossip at the rate of jungle drums.

"How did Fred die?"

Holly slumped back in his chair and stared at a point above Burke's head. His high Indian cheekbones seemed even more prominent and his lean jaw was badly shaved with several razor nicks. Looking at Holly's eyes, it occurred to Burke the man was suffering from acute hangover.

"What does the medical examiner's report say?"

Holly appeared not to have heard; he continued staring at the spot above Burke's head. Burke was tempted to follow his gaze. He might find something entertaining like two cockroaches mating on the wall.

"May I see the medical examiner's report?"

"No."

"Why not?"

"Official police business."

"All right. If he didn't die of a heart attack—"

"I didn't say he didn't."

"Well," Burke said, trying to control his exasperation, "did he?"

"No."

"Listen, Holly. This may come as a surprise to you, but people want to know how their Sheriff wound up in the river. I have a paper to get out—tonight. All I'm asking for is the facts of Loomis' death."

Holly eyed him bleakly, then suddenly straightened up in his chair. He grabbed a manila folder off the top of his desk and opened it. "Facts! Probable cause of death," he snarled, "'a blow from a blunt instrument.' Somebody

99

bashed his brains in." He shut the folder and slid it into a drawer in the desk. "How are those facts? That should give your readers somethin' to sink their teeth into, hey."

Burke stared out the window and felt his stomach tighten into a hard knot. He had genuinely liked Loomis. Most people had. He had been an honest cop and everybody knew it. But obviously somebody had not shared the town's good opinion of him.

"When did it happen?"

"Sometime Saturday evenin'."

"Any leads?"

"We're workin' on it."

Which meant not a clue, Burke thought. He had been down at the river yesterday and gotten a picture of the patrol car a few minutes after it had been hauled out of the water. He would run it in the middle of the front page. He would give the story a banner head. He sighed.

"Anything new on the Bowen boy?"

Holly slumped back in his chair again. "No. Officially the search is off." There was another long silence. Outside traffic hummed around the square.

"You think he's still alive, maybe?"

"There was no ransom note. So he wasn't kidnapped. It's possible a sex pervert got hold of him, but I doubt it. Most probably he fell into quicksand. Only don't print none of this about the boy. I'll deny it. His folks been through enough already. His momma's on the verge of a nervous breakdown."

"Did Loomis think Bobby might have run into a child molester?"

"He didn't tell me. He hunted that nigger graveyard for footprints and took the Gates' kid with him to show exactly where they had been."

"Did he find anything?"

"No. Only the kids' footprints by the ditch. The Gates' boy said he heard some noises."

"What kind of noises?"

"Like somebody was in the brush chasin' after him. Most likely his imagination."

100

"Couldn't somebody have snatched the Bowen kid and covered his tracks?"

"Maybe. But why? The Bowens don't have money."

"You said yourself maybe a pervert."

"Child molesters don't make a habit of hangin' around graveyards. School playgrounds is more their style."

Burke left Holly gazing at the same spot on the wall. Outside the courthouse he sat down on a wooden bench and watched the traffic circling the square. Loomis might have run across a whiskey still in his search for Bobby Bowen. Some tough characters lived in those bottoms and a few would kill to keep out of the Federal Pen. But most of the moonshining had died out and Loomis was an old hand at dealing with that kind of people.

Another thought struck Burke. Loomis had been searching for Bobby. What if he had found him?

Maybe he ought to talk to Scott Gates about what he had heard down in that Negro graveyard. He rose and started across the street to his office. He had to write a murder story and telephone the A.P. man. He suddenly remembered Dave Stewart had come in Saturday and wanted to get some information about somebody who had been buried in that same Negro cemetery.

"Funny," he muttered aloud. "Maybe I should talk to Stewart too."

At the time he had not believed Stewart was simply checking on somebody he thought he might have known. But what in the devil had he been up to?

AT mid-afternoon the girl entered the insurance office.

"Can I help you?" Sharon asked.

"I'd like to talk to Mr. Gates, please."

"You just missed him. He left a minute ago." Sharon eyed the girl, a striking brunette. "May I help you?"

"May I sit down," the girl said suddenly. She put her hand to her temple. "I feel a little faint."

"Of course." Sharon rose and motioned her to a chair near the desk. "Can I get you something?"

101

The girl smiled apologetically. "If I could have a glass of water—"

"Certainly." Sharon picked up her coffee cup on the desk next to her purse. She went over to the water cooler, rinsed the cup, and filled it. "I hope you don't mind drinking from my cup," she said, her back to the girl. She turned and brought it back.

"No. Of course not." She took the cup gratefully and took several swallows. "Thanks."

"Do you want me to call a doctor?"

"Oh no. I just have the cramps, that's all. I walked a few blocks over here and I guess I got a little overheated. It's nothing. I feel much better now." She handed the cup back to Sharon and started to rise.

"My father won't be back for at least an hour. If you tell me what you need, I might be able to help." She really has lovely eyes, Sharon thought.

"No, really. It's something I'd rather discuss with him personally." The girl smiled, revealing perfect teeth. "I appreciate it. I'll drop by again later."

"If you give me your name and phone number, I'll have him call—"

But the girl was already going out the front door.

Sharon returned to the water cooler and rinsed the cup.

Through the window she saw the girl cross the street and disappear around the corner. She shrugged. Sam had taken some papers over to Betsy Loomis for her to sign. Sharon was glad he was gone. They had barely spoken to one another today. More than ever she was determined to break away. The only questions were when would she leave and where would she go.

Walking back to the desk, she saw that her purse was lying open. She started to close it, glanced outside quickly, then pulled out the billfold. After she made sure the ten dollar bill was still there, she inventoried the rest of the purse's contents. Car keys, compact, lipstick, kleenex —everything seemed to be there. Except the comb.

She looked again.

She had used it right before going to lunch and again when she had come back.

102

It was only a cheap, green plastic comb with a few missing teeth, not to mention some loose hair.

Why then did she feel a sudden constriction in her throat as though an invisible hand clamped her windpipe.

Nobody would want an old comb unless . . . . She bit her lower lip. She must be mistaken. She had probably lost it sometime during lunch. But she thought she distinctly remembered combing her hair at the desk when she had gotten back.

Certainly the girl would not have stolen it while leaving the money. And she had been perfectly groomed with every hair in place. Even if she were a kleptomaniac, she could have done better than stealing that comb—unless she *needed* it for a special purpose.

Calm down, she told herself. The graveyard business and Loomis' death are making you paranoid. But what if Scott were right? Just what if? What if he had encountered something very evil in the graveyard, something beyond ordinary experience—some black magic cult? What if the girl had actually stolen her comb?

Wasn't that how black magic worked? Seize a personal article of your intended victim and then cast your spell. She tried to laugh, but it came out like a choked sob. Next she would be wanting to consult Mama Celia—if the Negress had still been alive.

Get hold of yourself, she thought. How can you even think such superstitious gibberish? Dave would laugh in your face if you told him. She shook her head and, closing the purse, sat down to finish typing a fire insurance policy for Mabel Dunham, that gossiping old biddy. She made several typos in one line. Angry with herself, she ripped the form out of the roller and crumpled it into the wastebasket. She got up and went to the window and gazed out at the sunlit street. Despite the sun's warmth streaming through the glass, she felt cold.

HE swung into the ball and felt the clean impact as he hit it solidly. The ball shot away. Far out in center Larry Rice

103

began back-peddling and made a one-handed lunge for the ball that brought catcalls from his teammates. Dave motioned Wade Haskill in from third and handed him the bat, then walked behind the batter's cage where George Burke had been standing for the past few minutes.

"Did you come out here for the sunshine or to do another feature?"

Wade hit a drive over the centerfielder's head. Larry Rice watched the ball drop beyond the chain link fence and shook his head. Then he scrambled over the fence after it. Haskill picked up another ball, threw it up, and tapped a grounder to first.

"That boy could be a major leaguer some day," Burke said. "Yeah, I came over here partly to get out of the office. I've just finished a story on Loomis' murder."

"Murder?" Dave stared at him. "It's official then."

"It's official. Somebody cracked his skull before driving him into the river."

The good feeling he had while batting drained away. Shadows were beginning to lengthen across the outfield. He let Haskill hit a few more to the infielders then told them to go to the showers. He noticed Burke was eyeing him intently.

"Did you ever find out what you really wanted to know about that Negro—what was his name?"

When he did not reply, Burke continued: "It's funny. The Bowen boy disappeared down at the graveyard the same day that Negro you inquired about was buried—Biggs, I believe his name was."

Dave pulled his cap off and wiped the sweat on his forehead with the back of his hand. "What are you driving at?"

Burke offered him a cigaret. He shook his head while Burke lit one and inhaled.

"Just that you might know something I don't." He let the smoke out lazily. "That kind of thing drives a newspaperman crazy. So I said to myself why suffer. Just come out and ask him outright. So here I am. If you don't want to talk . . . ."

The players had trooped into the dressing room

104

leaving the field empty; the base bags cast shadows in the slanting sunlight. Dave walked away from Burke toward first. Burke followed.

"Yep. There hasn't been a burial in that old Negro cemetery for months. Then on the evening they finally have one, a boy disappears there and another is so scared he runs into the swamp." He squinted at Dave through the horn-rimmed glasses, stooped, and handed the first base bag to him.

Dave tucked it under his arm and moved toward second.

"I've got a theory if you'd care to hear it. A little wild but the best I can do for right now."

"All right," Dave said. "I'm listening."

"Let's say for a moment somebody did grab the Bowen kid. What was he doing at the graveyard to begin with? He could have followed the boys from town, but it would have been just as easy to go after them in the woods on the way down there, actually better because he would have had more cover."

Dave reached for second, unfastening it from the spike that held it in place.

"You think somebody was after Biggs' body."

"That's the idea. How about you? Isn't that why you came by my office Saturday—to check the time of Biggs' burial? Or was it something else?"

"No. You got it."

The two of them trudged to third in silence.

"A friendly neighborhood ghoulie," Burke said at last. "Every town should have one. Or maybe just some poor sicko, a necrophile wanting his jollies with Biggs."

"But he hears the boys coming, then scares them off and goes back to his work. Only Bobby comes back alone, sees him, and goodbye Bobby? Is that how you read it?"

Burke stared at him. "I only said it was a theory."

"Why tell it to me? You should try the cops."

"I've thought about it. But I doubt whether they'd believe me. But say they did dig up Biggs and found him undisturbed in his box. Thereafter I'd be known as the

105

town nut. As newspaper editor I can't afford that." He watched Dave lift third. "On the other hand, since we both are thinking along the same lines, you might . . . ."

"Let them believe I'm nuts?"

"Something like that." Burke smiled. "Or maybe both of us might try. Share the burden of nuthood."

Dave eyed the newspaperman. "Afraid we can't share," he said at last. "It's all mine."

Slowly Burke pulled the cigaret from his mouth. "You already went to the cops?"

"Yesterday."

Burke whistled. "And?"

"Like you said."

He felt the newspaperman's eyes studying his bruised cheekbone. Burke shook his head. "Well, unless we're prepared to dig up the grave ourselves, and I'm not, it doesn't look like we're ever going to know." He shrugged. "I've got a paper to get out. See you."

Dave watched him walk slowly across the infield toward his car. Even without Scott's story, Burke had come up with conclusions close to his own. Yet both of them could be wrong and the cops right. Anyway their major efforts now would be concentrated on finding Loomis' murderer, not in seeking answers to what had happened down at the graveyard.

The bases were dead albatrosses as he lugged them to the locker room.

CLYDE Lee stood outside the iron gate gazing at the "No Trespassing" sign. In the setting sun the trees looked blood-like. They formed a dark tunnel over the gravel drive that led to, he guessed, the old Graves place. Something about the dark, silent tree-tunnel filled him with foreboding. Most of yesterday and today he had spent visiting shacks and lonely farm houses, questioning tight-lipped whites and sullen blacks. Those that lived out here in the bottoms were a special breed, suspicious and hostile. They did not like outsiders, particularly lawmen. But

106

gradually by a word, a nod, or even an evasive look, he had traced Loomis' progress to this place. Now he felt a deep reluctance to enter that drive, to walk beneath those dim trees.

He took a deep breath, then scrambled over the padlocked gate. The thirty-eight at his hip slapped against him reassuringly as he lit on the other side. His feet crunched on the gravel and immediately he was in deep twilight.

As he rounded a bend in the drive, a man suddenly materialized ahead of him as though stepping out of a mist.

Clyde Lee's hand darted instinctively toward his hip.

"You won't need that," the man said softly.

He was lean with stooped shoulders and was wearing a white dinner jacket. As he drew close, Clyde Lee noticed he had a switch in his right hand. The man's eyes seemed very light in his dark, narrow face. They regarded Clyde Lee Intently. Except for the eyes the man was almost dark enough to be a Negro. But his features were not Negroid with the exception of full, sensual lips.

Overhead an owl screamed. Clyde Lee's shoulder muscles bunched.

The man flicked the switch against his pant leg and smiled. "The cry of the hunter."

Clyde Lee swallowed hard. "Are you the owner here?" He tried hard to suppress a quaver in his voice.

"I am. May I ask what brings you here on my property, officer?"

Clyde Lee did not like the note of condescension in the man's voice. "Was Sheriff Loomis out here Saturday?" he asked curtly.

"Saturday? No. Nor any other day to my knowledge. I heard about what happened to him. Unfortunate."

Clyde Lee met the other's steady gaze.

"I suppose it was an accident?"

He ignored the question. "Were you here all day Saturday?"

"Oh, yes."

107

"And you are certain Sheriff Loomis was not out here?"

"I didn't see him. But this is a big place. He could have been here without my knowledge. Even though it is posted, some people tend to ignore that fact," Villiers said sardonically. "And that could be dangerous. You see, I'm in the middle of dynamiting stumps and then there's the swamp. Would you believe I've seen mocassins in there as big as your leg? And, of course, the quicksand." He shrugged, and his stooped shoulders, for an instant, seemed deformed.

Clyde Lee inwardly recoiled from him. Then he heard a chilling, yet plaintive, cry rise from the nearby brush. He whirled toward the sound which he recognized as the death cry of a rabbit.

"The hunt was short tonight," Villiers said. He seemed to hum a few notes under his breath.

Clyde Lee turned back to him. The man was regarding him steadily with those pale, cold eyes.

"If you have no more questions," he said at last, "I'll walk with you to the gate." From the dinner jacket pocket he produced a key. "This time you won't have to climb over the fence."

The man walked with a slight limp, Clyde Lee noticed. Combined with the subtle hunch of the shoulders, it gave him a sinister quality. Clyde Lee tried to pinpoint what it was about the other that spooked him so much and was at a loss to account for it except that the unnaturally pale eyes and twisted foot gave the man a not quite human, almost goatish, aspect.

After he reached the car and started the engine, a sense of relief flooded him. He drove away from the place quickly, radioing Thelma that he was coming in. He had gone less than half-a-mile when the mule loomed in the headlight beams directly in front of him.

He swerved and hit the brakes. The car skidded into the ditch and his head went into the windshield. For several moments he was peering through a red mist, then he began cursing, a steady string of obscenities. Finally he reached into the glove compartment for the flashlight

108

and got out to inspect the damage. He circled the car and bent to look under the chassis. Except for a crease in the oil pan and a crack in the windshield where his head had struck, there seemed to be no other damage. The mule had disappeared.

He got back into the car and started the motor which had died when he went into the ditch. The ditch was shallow, and he regained the road without any difficulty. He backed the car up to where the mule had stood. A gap appeared in the pines to his right and peering hard he could just make out rutted wagon tracks winding down in the direction of the swamp. The mule must have come up from down there, then plunged back when the car missed him.

He mashed the accelerator and started once more toward town. His head had begun to ache. Probing his forehead gingerly, he discovered a knot nearly the size of a boiled egg. People were getting damn careless with their mules. He remembered the one belonging to the Negros he had helped rescue from the swamp Saturday when they were hunting Bobby Bowen. Vaguely he recalled the Negro saying he had another mule missing. He wondered if this could be the same one. At any rate, it had almost killed him.

Buckling his seat belt which he had been in the habit of ignoring, he drove more cautiously toward town. Before reporting in, he decided he would stop at the funeral home. Loomis had been damn good to him and his death had shaken him more than he cared to admit even to himself.

Maybe that is why he had been so jumpy at the Graves place, so jumpy he had forgotten to get that guy's name, although he was certain it was Claude Villiers.

There was something very fishy about him, also scary.

Clyde Lee felt the darkness pressing in on him and pressed a bit harder on the accelerator. He suddenly longed for the lights of town.

109

PAXTON'S Funeral Home with its turrets and ginger-bread had once been a private residence and the town's showpiece before it catered to the dead.

Paxton, a plump, bald man with a suitably mournful air, met them at the front entrance and led them down a high-ceilinged hall to a room where several people stood. A smell of flowers and floor wax filled the room. Wreaths and floral displays were grouped around the coffin. Inside the coffin Loomis looked like wax. In death his nose had become his dominant feature, a cruelly caricatured beak from which the rest of his face seemed to slide away. The mortician had done his job well, however; Dave saw no evidence of the skull gash.

He and Sharon signed the register. She exchanged a few whispered greetings with some of the others, then they quickly left. As they stepped outside into the cool night breeze, a young deputy passed them going inside. Above them, the leaves whispered stirring in the wind and the fresh air was a cleansing tonic after the cloying smell of flowers and death.

"He was an honest cop," she said. "He only had a small life insurance policy. He told us he couldn't afford any more."

They walked a block in silence, both wondering who had murdered Loomis and why. She, like most of the people in town, had heard over the radio in the last few hours that Loomis had been murdered.

They had walked to the funeral home from her house and on the way he had told her about his conversation with Burke at the baseball field.

In the breeze was the smell of rain now. Dark ragged clouds scudded beneath the moon, hiding it. Yet, despite the storm threat, when they came to the park entrance they turned in instead of continuing toward her house. Neither of them spoke a word as they followed the walk-way winding through the trees down to the pond.

They sat down on the bank. He broke a twig in two and flipped the pieces into the black water. Then she told him about the quarrel with her parents last night over Scott's account of the open grave. He put his arm around

110

her shoulders.

"I'm sorry."

"I'm moving out as soon as I can find a place," she said. "I came to several conclusions last night."

He smelled the fresh scent of her hair. Out in the middle of the pond he made out several dark shapes gliding across the water.

"What conclusions?" he asked.

"I've used Scott as an excuse not to go out on my own. And the idea that Dad needed me in his business."

Three ducks emerged from the pond, shook themselves, and came forward looking for a handout.

"I don't even like the insurance business," she said wryly. "I never have."

"What will you do?"

"Maybe go to Memphis. Find a job there."

He took his arm away. The ducks, receiving no encouragement, started back to the water. Far away thunder growled.

"You could at least say you'd miss me," she said reproachfully.

He turned her face to him and kissed her mouth. Her lips were slack for several moments, then gradually she returned his pressure; their tongues met tentatively. She pulled away and leaned back against the bank, her eyes glistening. He bent to kiss her again, but she put her hand to his mouth.

"I'm not easy. Yesterday—"

"I don't want you to go anywhere." The words came before he thought. But as he kissed her again, he realized they were true. Her arms came around his neck and their bodies strained against each other. His hand cupped her breast through the thin blouse, then something sharp struck his ankle. Before he could disengage himself it struck again. He looked down in time to see the duck strike his ankle angrily a third time.

"Go away!" He kicked at the enraged creature. Its wings were spread and its neck stretched like a snake's. The duck retreated, then darted in for another peck.

Sharon started giggling.

111

The duck, apparently satisfied, waddled toward the pond, turning for one loud victorious quack.

Sharon's peals of laughter accompanied the duck into the pond.

Dave glared from the duck to the girl. Suddenly he began to chuckle.

"Thwarted by a mad duck," he said.

"My cavalier," she murmured. "Protecting my honor."

They held each other a moment. The thunder rumbled again, closer and more ominous. He rose and helped her up. They hurried up the walkway toward the street as the leaves rattled in the trees and the first drops of rain blew into their faces.

On the way home she was silent and preoccupied. Something else was on her mind.

"What is it?" he naid finally.

A serpent tongue of lightning flicked down the sky and for an instant the street, trees, and houses stood out in eerie light, then blackness swallowed them again.

"It will sound stupid," she said.

"Tell me."

"I lost a comb this afternoon—only I'm not sure I lost it. I thought I had it in my purse; in fact, I'm almost certain I did. Then we had a girl come in wanting to talk to Dad about something. After she left, I missed the comb. For a while I imagined it might even have been stolen, but I guess I just misplaced it." She turned to him in the darkness. "Look, I think all this stuff is beginning to get to me. Next I'll be seeing that tooth fairy Holly McAfee said his son saw."

Before he could say anything, the rain began to beat down hard.

She grabbed his hand. "Come on—let's run for it! My hair is going to be ruined!"

LONG after he heard Sharon come in and go to her bedroom, Scott lay awake. In the light the street lamp cast against his wall, he watched the shadow pictures made

112

by the tossing branches of the silver maple; a witch on a broomstick, a sinister jester dancing an insane two-step—then suddenly a new shadow appeared, a lady with hair streaming in the wind. In her hand she clutched something that looked like a crude figurine. The shadow glided across the wall and disappeared, leaving only the witch and the jester. Scott rubbed his eyes, got out of bed, and peered out the window into Mr. Sanders' field. The sky and the field were black, the windowpane was wavery with raindrops. He could see nothing out there. He climbed back into bed, wondering if he had been dreaming.

In a few moments he drifted into sleep.

SHARON awoke from a dream in which she and Dave were standing on top of a cliff over-looking the sea. In her dream she had suddenly slipped and had started a long sickening fall. She sprang up in her bed to a sitting position, her throat dry and her whole body burning, despite the cool wind sweeping through her open window.

Got to get a drink of water, she thought. She rose from the bed with difficulty and started for the bathroom. She felt strangely light-headed as though she were detached from her body.

She knew she must have a fever. The hallway began to spin. Her knees buckled; she staggered against the wall. Her whole body felt as though it were on fire.

"Momma," she moaned. Then, just as in her dream, she fell into a sea of darkness.

113

CHAPTER 10

SCOTT sprang up in bed. Thunder seemed to rock the room. A hard rain drove through the screen onto his bed, and he got up to shut the window. Lightning flashed as he struggled with the sash. For an instant, the woman was seared on his eyeballs. Her long hair dripped down her shoulders as she stared at him; then the darkness blotted her out.

He ran out of his room into the hallway and stumbled, almost falling. He reached down and cried out.

A light came on in his parents' room and shone on Sharon's face. Her eyes were open, but they were cold and bleak without a flicker of recognition.

"What's the matter?" He shook her shoulder. "Sharon!"

Then his father was there.

"My God!"

He knelt and picked her up in his arms.

"Lucy! Call the doctor. Quick!" His father's voice shook.

Scott followed him into the bedroom. Sam Gates laid his daughter gently down on the bed. Lucy stood by the side of the bed, her hand to her throat.

"Call the doctor, for God's sake!" Sam yelled.

Lucy went to the telephone and began dialing.

Scott backed away toward the window.

When the lightning flashed again, it showed the distant trees. Their branches thrashed in the wind and rain, and

114

he could see the individual branches clearly. But the field was deserted. The woman was gone.

THE girl's pulse was only thirty-eight beats per minute. Cornelia Ramsay pulled back her eyelids and shined a pencil light into the pupils. They contracted slowly. Sharon looked as though she were drugged or hypnotized. Cornelia flicked off the light and probed the girl's skull with deft fingers for any kind of bump or abrasion.

"Has she been taking any kind of drugs?"

Lucy and Sam stared at each other. "No, of course not." Sam said. "What's wrong with her?" His face had turned gray and he looked much older.

Cornelia shook her head. "I frankly don't know, Sam."

She looked away from the desperation in his eyes. How many times had she seen that look of desperation mingled with terror in the faces of patients and their families? When she was not much older than Scott, she had begun accompanying her father on his house calls. After he had retired, she had taken his place, although she would have been the first to say that nobody could replace her father who had been the town's doctor for over forty years. She had never married, and now at fifty she still was making house calls as her father had done.

She looked down at the girl and a chill ran through her. She had been Sharon's doctor since the girl was a baby. Over the years she had watched her develop into a lovely young woman, vivacious and bright. Now she lay on the bed staring at the ceiling with the uncomprehending look of an idiot. She seemed in a catatonic trance. She was twenty-two years old, but her gaze was as vacuous as a two-month-old baby's.

AFTER the ambulance left and they had all driven to the hospital, Scott bolted the front door and checked the

115

back door to make sure it was locked. Then he went into his bedroom, opened the closet and got his baseball bat. He put it on his bed and stared out the window into the field. His eyes strained into the darkness.

For a moment he wondered if he had actually seen her, but then he was certain again. Standing erect in the storm she had seemed beautiful yet ugly at the same time. He knew she was responsible for what had happened to Sharon. She was with the ones who had taken Bobby; and now they had come for him. But somehow they had made a mistake. As strong as they were, how could they have made such a mistake? Unless they wanted to make him suffer by hurting Sharon. Maybe that was it. What had happened to Sharon was in a way his fault because he knew about them, because he had told Sheriff Loomis about what had happened at the graveyard. But Sheriff Loomis was dead now. For a moment he visualized the murky bottom of the Coldwater River. The catfish would chew you up as your body stuck fast in the ooze of the river bottom and your hair floated upward in the current.

Outside water gurgled in the drainpipe down into the dark earth. A joint creaked somewhere in the house.

He gripped the baseball bat.

They were out there.

Maybe now that he was alone they would try to come into the house.

First they got Bobby, then Sheriff Loomis, now Sharon. He had told Sharon about them.

He wiped his eyes with his knuckles and clutched the baseball bat tighter. Who would they get next? He stared out the window into the darkness until his eyes burned.

SHEED listened to the mice skittering under the piles of old furniture. The storm had ended, but he could not get back to sleep. Lying in the darkness he had no idea of the time. Often in the early hours he thought about Louise. Sometimes he still dreamed about her, and in his dreams she was always young and pretty.

116

They had lived in another town where he had owned an appliance store. He knew what they said about him here. They called him a skinflint, a miser, a stingy son-of-a-bitch and laughed at him, but he could buy and sell most of them. With Louise he had never been stingy. He had bought her nice clothes, a car, a fine house. Later he had to sell the house to pay her hospital bills. After she was gone, he could not bear staying in the same town where everything reminded him of her and brought back, daily, the pain of her death. So he had sold the store that he had taken out a second mortgage on to meet the medical bills and moved here. With the little money he had left, he had opened up a used appliance store in this basement because it was the cheapest place he could rent. At first, he had worked hard just to keep from going crazy. He had travelled a lot to auctions and sales picking up items at a bargain. He needed no house; he slept in the basement. Because they had had no children, he had no one to spend his money on, except himself—and he desired very little, not even a car. He simply used the old beat-up pickup truck he hauled junk and used furniture in. Eventually, he found out that there was more demand for the junk than there was for used appliances. Over the years this spartan existence helped the money accumulate until accumulation became his consuming interest.

He did not trust banks. During the Depression his parents had lost every dime of their life savings when their bank failed and forced him out of college his freshman year. No banks for him. He kept every penny hidden down here. Now he seldom went out. Even his groceries were delivered. If anybody had something to sell, they came to him. He knew most of them suspected he had a fortune hidden down here, but he was not afraid of thieves. He had a revolver and he would not hesitate to shoot a thief.

Sheed struggled up from the iron cot and turned on the 40-watt bulb that dangled on a cord from the ceiling. It threw his skinny shadow into the next room. He shambled over to the sink and drew water into the coffee pot. As he turned to put the pot on the hot plate, he

117

heard the rap on the door. The mice stopped moving. For several moments there was dead silence. The rap came again. He looked at the cheap alarm clock which read four thirty-five.

"Go away, damn you," he muttered.

But again the persistent rapping. This time louder.

He pulled his grimy bathrobe over his flannel pajamas, took the revolver from under his pillow, and started into the other room. He turned on another forty-watt bulb and threaded his way through the maze of old furniture.

The rapping was louder, more insistent.

"Hold your horses! I'm coming. I'm coming."

Clutching the revolver, he peered through the small pane in the door. He looked into glassy, unfocused eyes.

Sheed recoiled a step. "What do you want?" he said hoarsely.

He was glad for the dead-lock bolt. He had never seen eyes like that, and he never wanted to again. It had to be some drug-crazy addict out there.

"Get out of here, or I'll call the cops!" he warned.

There was a long silence. Sheed stood uncertainly before the door. Maybe whoever had been there was gone. He listened intently. No noise out there at all. Behind him he heard a mouse squeal. He started to pocket the revolver.

The door exploded inward.

Part of it caught Sheed on the shoulder and sent him reeling back. He sprawled into an easy chair. He was stunned by the impact and sat there for a moment, arms and legs akimbo, staring at the small piece of wood attached to the dead-lock still hanging on the door jamb.

He was aware he still held the revolver.

He fired at the figure which was moving toward him in a swift lurch with peeled eyes and clay-gray face.

Cold hands clamped around Sheed's throat.

The second report of the pistol merged into a roar that came from inside Sheed's head. His last thought was how could he have missed both shots at point-blank range? He could not understand.

118

HOLLY stared out the bedroom window into the misty light of dawn. The yard was strewn with leaves and broken branches from the storm. He wondered if there had been any damage out at Delores' mother's place. He hated to admit it but he was beginning to miss Delores— at least in bed. When he had gone out to Logan's again last night, Janine had not even given him a glance. He had waited until the place closed down, but she had left with Logan. He had watched them drive off together with her wrapped around Logan like toilet paper on a roller.

He sighed, got out of bed, and shuffled to the refrigerator. He wished Delores were around to fix breakfast. Pulling out a can of beer, he popped the top and sat down at the kitchen table.

Here he was, Sheriff, he reflected, and nobody gave a damn. Delores had left him, Janine preferred Lawton and Logan, and his deputies did not have the confidence in him that they had in Loomis. He was sure that went for most of the town, too. They expected him to already have Loomis' murderer in custody, while the truth was he did not even have one solid clue.

Last night Clyde Lee had told him there was something fishy about the new owner of the old Graves place.

"Everybody else out there admits to having seen Sheriff Loomis except him. I think he's lyin'." Clyde Lee had said.

"Why?"

"I don't know, Holly. But he's a weirdo. I got this feelin' about him."

Feelings were one thing, hard evidence another. Yet maybe he ought to go out there and check that bird out himself. He finished the beer.

He had one foot in the shower when the telephone rang. If it's Delores, he thought, I won't make it too tough for her to come home.

But it was Jerry Holmes who owned the feed store downtown.

"Holly, you better get over here, quick."

"What's the matter?"

"It's old man Sheed. I was cuttin' behind his place on

119

my way to the store, you know, and I seen his door open. Open, hell! Splintered clean off its hinges! And he's dead, Holly. Old man Sheed is dead!"

Holly slammed down the receiver. He was almost out the front door before he realized he was naked.

"I RECKON the undertaker won't make much," Wade Haskill said. He was slouched against his locker in the hallway. "Sheed probably had it in his will to be buried in one of his second-hand refrigerators."

"That's awful," Millie Thornton tried to suppress a giggle.

"It's not a joke," Tina Burtram said severely. "A murderer is running around loose. A maniac." She gave heavy emphasis to the last word.

"Nah," Wade snorted. "Somebody just wanted all that cash he had socked away down there. The old man put up a big fight and got killed."

"Everybody knew he kept a fortune down there," Millie said. "My father says anyone in town could have done it."

"You wanna go to Mexico," Wade said. "I just come into some money."

Neither girl smiled.

"Hey, I'm just kidding."

The bell rang and they pushed into the classroom. Everyone was talking about the murder when Dave Stewart entered the room.

"What do you think is going on around here, coach?" Wade asked, and everybody grew suddenly quiet. Wade glanced over at Marie Villiers. For a moment he saw something in her face he had never seen before. He thought she was staring at Stewart with a look compounded of hate and gloating triumph. His heart beat faster. But in a flash her face became utterly impassive.

"Yeah. First Shurf Loomis," Joe Don Castleberry drawled. "Now old man Sheed. And ain't nobody found Bobby Bowen yet."

120

"It's the Devil's work," Mary June Norton announced. She was a plain, heavy girl with thick glasses who sat in the front row. "We're all sinners. The town is being punished for its wickedness."

"We ain't any wickeder than Holston," Joe Don said. "Why ain't they punished?"

Laughter rippled through the class. Holston was an arch-football rival.

"That's right," somebody else said. "Half of Holston High is on dope."

"Settle down," Dave said. "We have a test in here tomorrow. We're going to review."

Groans.

All during the class Wade secretly watched Marie. She was staring at Stewart with such cold intensity that once the teacher faltered a moment in mid-sentence and, although he quickly recovered and the rest of the class might not even have realized the reason for the lapse, Wade did. Something had definitely aroused her against him. Yet the joy he ordinarily would have felt at this discovery was missing. Something he had glimpsed in the girl's eyes scared the hell out of him. He noticed Stewart did not allow himself to look in her direction for the rest of the period. Wade guessed he had seen the same thing.

SCOTT stood in the field where he had seen the woman during the storm. The grass was still wet despite the sun and the bottoms of his pant legs were soaked. He had only been hunting a minute when he found it—a globule about the size of a small wad of chewing gum. He picked it up and turned it in his fingers. He could see his own and Sharon's bedroom windows from here. Despite the sun's warmth, he felt cold. He stuck the glob in his pocket and went back to the house.

"What were you doing?" his mother demanded when he came into the kitchen. She had come back from the hospital to fix his breakfast and see that he got to school.

121

At the hospital they still did not know what was wrong with Sharon.

"Look at your pants. You'll have to change them. Hurry now! I've got to get back."

He went to his bedroom and changed jeans, transferring the wax to the new pants. The wax felt clammy. It was the color of a slug under a rotting log. Maybe it was not candle wax. He had seen her shadow on the wall holding something that had not looked like a candle.

His mother called him into the kitchen to eat his breakfast, but he found he could not eat a bite.

She made him go to school despite his protests. He wanted to be at the hospital, but she dropped him off at school on her way back. He kept telling himself night was the time *they* liked best. Maybe they wouldn't do anything in daylight. It had been almost dark when he and Bobby had been at the graveyard.

He shuffled listlessly across the playground oblivious of the other kids. His hand delved into his pocket for the piece of wax. She had been carrying something, and it had not looked like a candle. It had looked like a crude figure. He snatched the wax out and stared at it in his open palm. It dropped out of his hand as though it were crawling.

He stood staring at it in the dirt while the blood thundered in his ears. A wax doll! They had made a wax doll of Sharon and burned it.

"Hey, Scott!"

He looked up. Jimmy Farese was standing beside him.

"Old man Sheed. Did you hear?" Jimmy's voice dropped. "He was murdered!" Scott stared at him stupidly, then back at the ground.

"Did you hear what I said? What are you lookin' at? What's that stuff?"

Scott picked it up as if it were a black widow spider and thrust it back into his pocket. He started toward the street.

"Hey! The bell is fixin' to ring," Jimmy said. "Where you goin'?"

Scott broke into a run. Behind him he heard the school

122

bell and Jimmy's voice above the other kids'. He ran for several blocks until his breath sobbed in his throat and his lungs burned. Then he slumped down under a maple tree. After awhile he got up again and began walking swiftly toward the hospital.

CHAPTER 11

THE sunlight slanting against the courthouse tower was harsh, and the courthouse looked different like he was seeing it for the first time. All the buildings looked slightly changed, as though he were viewing them in a mirror with a tiny distortion.

Scott passed Duncan Rainey standing in the doorway of the barbershop. Usually the bootlegger greeted him, but now he was silent. His eyes were dark and furtive. Scott noticed that the eyes of other people he passed seemed scared or worried. He cut down an alley and a cat fled silently from a garbage can into shadows, disappearing through an opening in a brick wall.

Emerging from the alley, he saw two police cars parked in front of Holmes' Feed Store.

Sheed was dead. Murdered!

The police were down in the basement below the feed store where he had been many times. It had been like a thief's cave full of old clocks and cabinets and chests. He had wondered if one of the chests contained the money Sheed was supposed to have hidden, and whether it was in silver so the mice would not get it.

He and Bobby had gone down to the ditch to sell the car door to Sheed for enough money to buy some comic books. Suddenly, uncontrollably, he began to laugh.

He put his hand to his mouth, but the laughter would not stop. In his pocket the piece of wax seemed to burn

124

against his thigh. He started running again, and the laughter changed to a long sob.

He ran toward the hospital, the sidewalk cracks flying beneath him faster and faster until they were only blurs.

WHAT it amounted to was that Sheed had fired two shots at extremely close range, Holly thought, and missed. There were no blood stains, no trace of the two bullets missing from the revolver's chamber in the basement itself. Sniffing the barrel had told him the pistol had been fired recently, and it had been lying next to the body which they had found slumped in the tattered easy chair only a few feet from the doorway. And how could the murderer have broken down the door like that? The hinges were sheared off, leaving the dead bolt still fastened. Holly's first thought had been the murderer must have backed into the door with a truck, but there were no tire tracks in the rain-soaked earth outside. The murderer must have possessed super-human strength. He looked at Floyd Rogers, the night deputy, who had been cruising downtown during the early hours, but had heard no shots.

"The slugs must have gone through the open door," Floyd said.

Holly nodded.

Their eyes turned to the wall where the newspapers were still stacked in bundles except for a gap in the middle where a bundle had been removed revealing an empty hole in the wall. They had found the block that had concealed the hole lying on the floor.

"Sheed was so cheap he used a hole in the wall instead of a safe," Floyd said. "Looks like the murderer knew right where to go. He must have forced Sheed to tell him before he strangled him."

"You have any idea what or how much was taken?" George Burke asked. He had slipped in while Sheed's body was being carried out to be transported to the medical examiner in Memphis.

125

"What are you doing here?" Holly snapped.

"The Bowen kid, Loomis, and now Sheed," Burke said. "Do you have any leads at all on any of the murders?"

"We don't even know the Bowen kid is dead—let alone that he was murdered. Now get the hell out of here before I have you arrested for hindering an official investigation."

Burke eyed him speculatively, shrugged, then went outside.

Holly shut his eyes and rubbed his forehead. He had been Sheriff only two days and already he had two homicides. He wished Loomis were here now to tell him what to do. But Loomis was going to be buried this afternoon. He opened his eyes again. The place reeked of mice and death, and he felt an overpowering impulse to get outside and breathe fresh air again.

THELMA Howe was not due in until noon today and they had left him as dispatcher. The office door swung open. Clyde Lee put down the paper. She was tall and stoop-shouldered and could have been anywhere between fifty and seventy, he thought.

"I want the Sheriff," she said, her melancholy eyes looking at a point just above his head.

"He's not in right now."

Her eyes swept the room before coming back to rest at the same spot above his head.

"Maybe I can help. I'm his deputy."

The eyes flicked to his face. "My husband."

"What about him?"

"He ain't come back. He left yesterday and he ain't come back."

An old story. Generally after a night or two the husband would turn up again, sometimes even in a penitent mood.

"I wouldn't worry. He's probably staying with a friend."

"No," she said stonily. "I tole him to quit studyin' that

126

mule, but he had to go lookin' again. I'm afraid he's hurt. The mule he's ridin' has a devil in him."

"Wait a minute. Start at the beginning."

"Ever since that mule be missin', he ain't thought about nothing else. So yesterday he took the other mule and rode over to the ol' Graves place to look. I told him—"

Clyde Lee pulled out his notepad. "What's your name?"

"Sarah Johnson."

"I helped haul a mule out of the swamp Saturday."

"That was one of ours. We lost the pair of them mules the night before that." She went suddenly silent and stared out the window.

"How did they get away?"

She did not answer. After awhile she said: "Rufus wouldn't stay away like that less something happened to him. We married thirty-four years and he ain't never stayed away at night without tellin' me first." Her eyes met his. "You find my man. You find out what's happened to him."

She began to weep softly.

AT noon, Dave drove down to the insurance office and found it locked. He peered in the window.

"You won't find anybody there. I reckon they're all at the hospital."

He turned and saw Saul Druitt who owned the jewelry store next door.

"The hospital?"

"It's Sam's daughter. I hear she's had a stroke."

The sidewalk seemed to heave beneath him.

On the way to the hospital, he felt the same tightness in his chest as that evening when the cop had come to the door in the rain. He and Kay had not had a telephone then, and he had already begun to worry because she was late. She had taken the car that morning, and he had caught a ride home from the University with Jenny Warren, a fellow graduate teaching assistant with whom he shared an office and several classes. They had stopped for

127

a couple of drinks at an out-of-the-way place and had suddenly started getting serious. He had come home late, surprised Kay was not there. Shortly afterward, the police car pulled into the driveway. They had driven him to the hospital, but she died before they arrived. A drunk driver had run a red light at high speed. Later he figured out that at the time of the crash, he and Jenny had been nuzzling each other over their third drink.

A bleak, two-story concrete cube loomed ahead of him. A business-like woman at the front desk told him the room number, but added primly that only members of the immediate family were allowed. He took the stairs two at a time. He found the door, knocked once, then turned the knob.

Sam rose out of a chair, his face the color of the white hospital walls. Dave stared past him to the bed. Her face was turned away, the chestnut hair spilled over the sheets. He crossed to the other side of the bed and blanched.

She gazed at his belt buckle, eyes blank and still. There was a faint smile on her lips. He had seen the same expression on the face of a child once, peering out the window of a home for the severely retarded. He looked away. He remembered her at the pond last night laughing, her arms around his neck. The stillness in the room seemed deafening.

"What happened?" His voice sounded in his own ears like it was far away. He turned his eyes to Sam. For the first time he noticed Scott standing by the window.

"They don't know."

Scott half-turned from the window.

"Scotty found her lying in the hallway early this morning." Sam's words were slow and thick.

Sharon did not move a muscle. Did she even see them?

Anger spurted up in him that they had not told him what had happened sooner, but it quickly died as he watched Sam slump back into the chair; he had been transformed into an old man literally overnight.

Scott was staring out the window toward the pines. The hospital was outside of town and, on this side, faced the woods and swamp.

128

"They have to run more tests," Sam muttered. "We're taking her to Memphis. Lucy is downstairs seeing about an ambulance now."

Dave watched the girl's face intently. Her expression did not change a fraction, she did not even blink. Suddenly, he had to get out of the room. He left abruptly, descended the stairs, and went out into the parking lot. He drew air in deep gulps. After awhile he went back inside, found a telephone booth and called Simmons to tell him he would not be back at school that afternoon. When he hung up the receiver, Scott was standing next to him.

The boy beckoned for him to follow and led him outside. He looked at Dave a moment, then away. "They don't know what's wrong with her. Even Doctor Cornelia doesn't know."

"They have specialists in Memphis. They'll find out. And make her well," he added without confidence. He saw the cop standing in the rain saying, *"There's been an accident."* A deep sense of helplessness gripped him, and he clenched his fists. Don't let it happen again, he thought. Not again!

The boy shook his head. He gazed toward the pines a hundred yards away, sloping down toward the bottoms.

"They won't know about *them*," he said.

Dave looked at him sharply. "What do you mean?"

Scott reached into his pocket and pulled something out. He held it extended in his open palm—a piece of dirty wax.

Dave stared at it.

The boy kept his eyes riveted on the trees. He spoke softly and rapidly. "I saw this lady from my window. I saw her in the lightning. She left this. She used a wax doll and changed Sharon."

The sun glared off the asphalt and glinted on the chrome bumpers of the parked cars. He knew the boy was not lying intentionally. Bobby's disappearance had upset him badly and now Sharon's stroke had pushed him over the edge. He remembered Sharon's story about the scarecrow and felt a sinking sensation in the pit of his stomach. He tried to keep the pity out of his voice. "Let's

129

go back inside," he said gently.

"They killed Sheriff Loomis after they got Bobby." His tone was matter-of-fact, and Dave found it chilling. "Now they want Sharon. I saw her in the lightning. I found this where she was standing." He put it back in his pocket.

Dave put a hand on his shoulder.

Scott looked up at him. "How are we going to stop them? What'll we do?"

"We'll talk about it later. I want to go back and see Sharon now."

Scott stood very still. "You don't believe me, do you? I saw her out there." A shrillness came into his voice. "She changed Sharon!" He pulled away from Dave's grasp. "I thought you cared about my sister."

"I do. Very much. Listen to me. You've gone through a lot . . . ."

Scott backed away. "Why don't you just shut up!" He turned and fled into the building.

"Wait!" He started after him.

When he reached the second floor corridor, the boy was not in sight. He had almost reached Sharon's room when Sam Gates burst out of the doorway. "Have you seen her?" He stared up and down the corridor. He looked groggy.

"Lucy. No, I . . . ."

"Sharon! She's gone."

He looked past Sam and saw the empty bed and Scott staring out the window. "They must have taken her for another test. Were you asleep?"

"I guess I dozed a minute. They gave me some kind of tranquillizer." He pushed past Dave and scurried down the hall.

Scott whirled away from the window, bumped into Dave, his eyes unseeing, then darted past. Dave caught him at the top of the stairs.

"Where are you going?"

"She's out there," the boy said dully. "She's going to them!"

Dave watched him run down the stairs. The boy's

130

madness was contagious; he began to feel an unreasoning panic himself. At the other end of the hall Sam appeared with the floor nurse. She peered in Sharon's room and shook her head, then hurried back to her station with Sam at her heels.

Dave saw through the stairwell window the small figure running toward the pines. A stroke victim just didn't get out of bed and walk away, he tried to tell himself as he started down the stairs. He reached the parking lot in time to see Scott disappear into the trees. He stood there staring a moment, telling himself he was a damn fool. Then he began to lope toward the trees. Before he got beyond the parking lot, he was running.

HOLLY had spent most of the morning questioning people who lived in the row of houses behind Sheed. One woman reported hearing what had sounded like a car backfiring in the early morning. Nobody else had seen or heard anything.

He was driving back to the office when Thelma radioed that Sharon Gates had disappeared from County General.

"You'd best get over there, Holly. They say she wasn't even able to walk, but now she's gone."

He cursed and made a U-turn on Main. "All right, I'm on my way. Tell Clyde Lee to come back in and meet me there."

He had sent the young deputy out to try and turn up something on Loomis' murder. He suddenly remembered Clyde Lee had said something about a nigger disappearing right before he had sent him out.

As he turned into the hospital drive, he wondered about the Gates' girl. She had seemed healthy the other evening when she had wanted him to dig up a grave. He braked the car and started to get out. Thelma's voice broke in on the radio.

"I can't raise Clyde Lee, Holly."

"Well, keep tryin'," he snarled. He slammed the car

131

door and stalked into the hospital. Two murders, three disappearances, he thought. What next?

CLYDE Lee stood in the creek bottom gazing at the horseshoe tracks in the wet sand. He had abandoned the car when the wagon ruts led into this creekbed. He had driven down the wagon trail trying to retrace the path the mule had taken after he had nearly struck it last night in the patrol car.

By now he guessed he must be on Villiers' property. He found it strange and frightening that both Loomis and Rufus Johnson had been nosing on or around Villiers' place and now one was dead and the other missing.

He followed the tracks for another hundred yards before they veered out of the creekbed into the pines. He stared into the trees wondering if Johnson had simply been thrown from his mule or maybe had stumbled across something in these woods that had cost him his life.

He stood there uncertainly. He did not want to enter those dark pines alone. Somewhere in there a dove mourned, its cry low and plaintive. The sound galvanized him into movement and in a moment he was walled in by trees. He picked the tracks up for a few yards, then lost them in the gloom. He found them again and they led into heavy brush. It took him several minutes to cover a few yards in the thicket of creepers and he lost the tracks again. He searched a long time without finding them. Finally he gave it up and emerged into the creekbed once more and the sunshine. Looking at his watch, he realized he would have to hurry to get back in time for the funeral. He would return later and bring Floyd with him.

As he trudged toward the car, he heard a dull explosion off to his left. It sounded like dynamite. He remembered Villiers last night saying he was blasting stumps.

The damp sand was hard to walk in, and he had gone farther from the car than he thought. By the time he reached it, he was sweating profusely. When he got inside, he was glad he had left the windows down. Even

132

with that, the car was stifling from sitting so long in the sun. He would have to push it to get back for the service. He started the engine. The ruts were too narrow to turn the car around and pines crowded along both sides of the wagon trail. He would have to back up over a quarter of a mile to the road. He turned to peer out the back windshield and out of the corner of his eye caught a sudden movement from beneath the front seat.

He yelled, jerking his foot off the accelerator. He felt a needle-like jab in his right calf; at the same moment his other foot slid off the clutch, the car lurched, the engine died. He grabbed for the door handle. The snake's head darted up between the seat and door, its fangs lancing into his arm just above the elbow.

"Christ!" he yelled. He flung himself against the opposite door and rolled out head-first. Through the open door he saw the cottonmouth flowing toward him across the seat like dirty dishwater.

A pungent smell like that of old dirty brass came from the seat. He did not remember drawing the pistol. The first shot missed. Then he was emptying the .38. The snake's skull exploded in a spray of blood.

The stench of cordite in his nostrils, he stared stupidly through the haze of smoke at the thick, twitching body still on the seat. He shuddered.

Crimson drops oozed from the angry puncture marks on his elbow.

Almost instantly he began to feel light-headed. He rose to his feet, but had to hold onto the door. His first impulse was to make a dash for the road, but in a moment he had control of himself again. Of course, he would have to get into the car and drive for help, but the one that nailed him in the leg was still under the seat.

Sweat dripped into his eyes as he reloaded the revolver. He had trouble getting the bullets into the cylinder. One dropped to the ground as he tried to jam it into the cylinder chamber. He leaned against the door, his breath ragged and labored, waiting for a movement inside.

The moments crawled by, and his heart pounded speeding the poison through his bloodstream. Maybe he had

133

been mistaken; maybe there was only the one he had killed. His ankle throbbed; his arm ached. Panic roared through him and his heart pumped faster and faster until he insanely fired a bullet through the seat.

The shot had a calming effect. He whipped the belt out of his pants, coiled it and with a flip of the wrist flicked the buckle end beneath the seat. The belt struck something and he heard a hissing.

"Come out," he whimpered. "Come out, you sonuvabitch!"

He flicked the belt beneath the seat again. More hissing, but the snake would not show itself. If he blindly stuck the Smith & Wesson under the seat and fired, he could hit the gas tank. He had to find a stick.

He stumbled away from the car, sweat blinding him, the blood pounding in his skull. His arm felt numb. Unbelievably, he could find no sticks on the ground around him. It occurred to him finally to break off one of the overhanging pine branches. But he had to try three of them before he found one he could snap away without too much difficulty.

He knelt by the seat. He poked the limb savagely under it with his left hand, the revolver ready in his right. Another hiss. The stick moved in his hand, and he yanked it back, bringing the blunt V-shaped head into view, the little yellow eyes glittering wickedly.

Clyde Lee yanked the trigger three times after the skull disintegrated into bloody mist.

He could see the ground through the holes the bullets had made in the floorboard, and his ears still rang from the noise of the shots. With the pine branch he flipped the one off the seat outside. A wave of nausea swept over him, and he dropped the stick. To remove the one under the seat he would have to pull it out with his hands. He left it alone.

When he reached for the radio, the microphone was smashed. He could not radio for help. One of the bullets must have ricocheted off the car's floor or the opposite door and smashed the mike, he thought.

He crawled into the car and pulled himself up behind

134

the steering wheel. He turned the ignition key. The engine ground and sputtered, but did not catch. Frantically, he mashed the accelerator to the floor and pumped it. For a moment the dashboard swam before his eyes. Then the engine roared to life.

It was a narrow track. Even with the steadiest nerves, backing over it to the road would be no easy matter. Now with the sweat flowing into his eyes and his hands shaking on the steering wheel, Clyde Lee wondered if he could make the first fifty feet.

CHAPTER 12

WHEN Will Lawton entered the living room, he found it crowded with people. He looked around the room for Betsy Loomis to express his sympathy, but he did not see her. He had been out of town all morning on a construction job in the next county and had gotten back only a little while ago in time to shower, shave, and change for the funeral.

Verdo Pardee, a real estate agent, came up to him. "She's upstairs with her boy. He got in from Atlanta last night."

The two of them wandered into the dining room and helped themselves to chicken, roast beef, and potato salad set out on the table.

"I don't know," Verdo said, lifting slices of cold beef onto a paper plate, "what's goin' on around here."

Lawton began eating ravenously. He had not realized how hungry he was.

"I mean the whole town is edgy about these killins. A lot of folks are buyin' guns. There was a run on Akin's place today. He says they cleaned him out, shotguns, pistols, even that little bitty foreign automatic that all the boys laughed at him about carryin' in the display case, said it wouldn't slow down a canary, let alone kill it, damn if somebody didn't buy it. He wouldn't say who."

Lawton grunted. The chicken was delicious. He wondered who had brought it.

136

"You know," Verdo said lowering his voice, "a lot of people are wonderin' whether Holly is up to all this. Catchin' speeders and nabbin' drunks is one thing, but if you ask me, we oughta call in outside help for what's happening 'round here."

Lawton nodded. He had gotten word about Sheed at the construction site.

"They got any ideas about who got Sheed?"

"Hell, no."

Lawton reached for another piece of chicken. Holly drank too much, but then, he was part Indian, so you could expect that. Still, he had been a reasonably good deputy, but being deputy was one thing, being Sheriff another. Pardee was probably right. If they ever expected to find the killer or killers, outside help would be needed.

Verdo was silent for a moment, his gaze drifting out the window. "Anyway, I reckon you got your own problems without me bringin' up this other stuff," he said, his eyes returning to Lawton. "How's Sharon doin' now?"

He looked sharply at Verdo. Was the man mocking him? His blue eyes seemed mild and innocent enough.

"Why ask me?" he growled.

"Well," Verdo faltered. "I just know how close ya'll have been. It's shocking, a girl her age."

"What are you talking about?"

Verdo stared at him. "You don't know?"

"I'll know when you tell me. Now tell me!"

"Lord, man. She's in the hospital."

The forkful of potato salad froze half-way to Lawton's mouth.

A minute later he was in his Triumph driving toward the hospital. Half-way there he spotted Sam Gates' yellow Cutlass in the opposite lane. As it passed, he saw Lucy was driving and Sam was slumped in the passenger seat.

He wheeled the Triumph into a tight U-turn, tires squealing, and pursued the Cutlass. He caught up with them and hit the horn. They did not even seem to notice

137

him. An on-coming truck forced him to drop back behind them. He followed them home.

Before the Cutlass pulled into the garage, he was out of the Triumph running toward them. They emerged from the garage with glazed eyes, their faces gray and empty. Lawton's heart jumped nastily.

"I've just heard. How is she?"

They stared dully at him.

"My God!" he said. She's dead, he thought.

"Both of them," Lucy said. Suddenly her face crumpled. She began to cry.

Lawton turned to Sam. "Tell me!" he demanded.

Sam grasped his wife's hand. "I told you he's with Stewart. He must be."

Lawton eyed the sobbing woman with rising panic. He clutched Sam's shoulder. "Tell me what's happened?" he pleaded. "For God's Sake, tell me!"

THE rank odor of the swamp filled his nostrils. Scott stopped to catch his breath.

From the hospital window he had only caught a flash of white disappearing into the trees. He had plunged into the woods at the spot he had seen it and had headed straight and unerringly toward the swamp. The pines had given way to cypress and willows. He began moving again.

The sneakers made squishy, sucking noises in the soft mud. A steady hum of insects rose ahead of him. Then the smell of sour water struck him like a fist, bringing back memories of his nightmare struggle in the swamp the night Bobby disappeared.

His breath began whistling in his throat.

I'm not going any further, he thought. I won't.

But he was still moving forward, his sneakers heavy with mud.

To his left he saw a moving patch of white through the willows. She was less than fifty yards away gliding ghost-like through the willows. She looked neither right nor left even after he shouted, then she stumbled once, and he

138

realized she was already in water and marching straight into the swamp.

He began running toward her, floundering through the ooze. It seemed to him that he was outside himself watching himself flounder, hearing somebody else's breath, hoarse and panting, not his own. He barely felt the water creeping above his ankles.

She moved ahead of him slowly in the stagnant green water. The hem of the soiled hospital gown floated out around her thighs.

He made a lunge for the gown, missed, and went under. The water pressed against his eyeballs like warm sewage.

When he surfaced, she was ten feet away, the water above her breasts. He struck out after her, crying her name and was choked off as his feet slipped and he went under again. He came up spluttering, his feet scrabbling for bottom. She was gone.

He began swimming, realizing dimly they were in the river. There had been no bank to warn him, the swamp had simply merged into the river channel.

She surfaced two arm-lengths away and went under again before he could grab her hair. He dove for her. His hand wound around her hair, and he pulled her to the surface. She turned her streaming face to him, her eyes glittering through the strings of hair. Her arms snaked around his neck and dragged him under.

He struggled against her, but she clutched him tightly. He jammed his knees against her belly, and tried to push away. But her arms were heavy weights around his neck forcing him down. She was too strong.

His chest grew tight. It felt like it was going to explode. His arms pushed against her feebly. The water seemed to turn red, and yellow pinwheels of light danced before his eyes.

His knee jerked up into her pelvic bone and the weight on his shoulders was suddenly gone. Desperately he fought to the surface with a great roaring in his ears.

He gulped air in huge gasps and blinked in the sunlight. A few yards away were clumps of sawgrass and some willows marking the river's edge.

139

As he started for the willows, she was on him again. He hit her in the face as hard as he could. She bared her teeth soundlessly, her face contorted in animal rage.

They both went under locked in a grotesque dance beneath the surface, but this time he slithered out of her embrace and reached the air and began swimming toward a projecting cypress root. With a great lunge, that nigh broke his heart, he grasped it. She was right behind him. She grabbed one of his legs and pulled herself up his body, her breasts slapping against him. Her teeth sank through his shirt into his shoulder.

He cried out, strangling on a mouthful of water. He writhed free of her, but he did not have the strength left to pull himself up the cypress root. Slowly he slid back, his fingers clawing at the slick bark.

The water closed over his head. He felt a heavy weight pushing him, driving him down into the muddy bottom, and he marvelled vaguely at her strength. Tightness crept back into his chest, his lungs burned.

The pinwheels whirled in front of his eyes.

The pressure inside his chest was unbearable; his eyeballs felt like they were bursting in their sockets.

He began to black out.

Darkness pushed out everything except a tiny pinpoint of consciousness that told him something was gone. The weight. The weight that had held him down was gone and slowly, slowly he was drifting upward toward the light.

SHARON thrashed and twisted in Dave's grasp. He held her from behind, one arm around her waist, the other around her neck. He was up to his chest in stagnant water. Suddenly she quit struggling and went limp against him. Her chin rested in the crook of his elbow, the glare in her eyes died like a guttering flame and was replaced by that idiot blankness he had seen at the hospital.

Scott's head emerged from the water, and he began coughing. His hands scrabbled for and caught a projecting cypress root. His face was dead white, his eyes enormous.

140

Dave had seen her push him under, her face twisted in fury.

"Can you make it out on your own?"

Scott nodded.

"How did you know where we were?" he gasped.

"I heard you calling her name."

Scott dragged himself into shallow water while Dave pulled Sharon toward solid ground. She sagged against him, all dead weight now.

When at last he got her to dry ground, he was exhausted. He let his burden slide to the ground. She lay on her back, her eyes staring vacantly at the bright blue sky. A streak of mud ran down her cheek; her hair was matted with filth; her hospital gown was torn in front exposing one breast. Dave gazed at the brown nipple before he became conscious of the boy standing beside him.

Wordlessly, the boy took off his wet shirt and covered the breast with it. His eyes met Dave's for a moment, then slid away toward the river channel.

They waited until they both got their wind. Then with Dave carrying Sharon in his arms, they started back. After a few minutes, Dave had to rest again. He laid her down in the shade of a willow and sat down himself with his back resting against it. Scott stood silently a few feet away.

"You O.K.?" Dave asked.

He did not reply.

Except for the gnats humming around them there was no sound. Not a leaf stirred. There was not even the faintest of breezes. It was as if they were in a vacuum. The girl did not move; she did not even blink. If he had not seen her struggling with Scott, then felt that ferocious energy directed against himself, he would not believe her capable of wiggling her toes, much less walking out of the hospital. How could she be a vegetable one moment and then suddenly be transformed into what he had seen down at the river—a wild animal, the next? What had Scott said in the hospital parking lot—somebody *changed* her. He stood up and looked around him.

141

What he was thinking was impossible. Somebody must have brought her down here. But why? He walked over to the boy.

"What happened?" he said.

Scott remained silent.

"Did you see anybody with her?"

The boy shook his head.

Dave grabbed his shoulders and spun him around. "Listen, Scott," he said sharply. "I want to know how she got into the river—how both of you got there."

Scott twisted out of his grasp. "Let me alone."

"Listen, I'm on your side. But I can't help if you don't tell me anything."

Scott's blue eyes were hostile. "Why should I tell you anything? You don't believe me anyhow."

"Sharon and I believed you about the open grave you saw when Bobby disappeared. We believed enough to go to the police."

"Yeah. And what good did it do? They didn't do anything. They thought I made it up."

"The point is *we* believed you."

Some of the defiance seeped out of the boy's gaze. There were dark shadows under his eyes and his face seemed thinner than the other morning when Dave had given him a cup of coffee.

"You didn't believe me awhile ago—what I told you in the parking lot."

"No. I won't lie to you," Dave said. "I didn't believe you."

Scott gazed at him a moment longer, then turned away wearily. He walked over to a willow and began picking idly at the bark.

"Look, Scott. There's a lot I don't understand." He followed the boy. "But we have to help her, and I've got to know what happened."

"You can't help her," the boy said tonelessly.

"Maybe not. But maybe both of us working together can. Isn't it worth a try?"

Scott did not look up, but kept scratching at the bark where he had peeled away a thin strip.

142

Dave shook his head and started back toward the girl.

"She walked in," Scott said dully. "She just waded into the swamp."

Dave turned.

The boy was staring down at his mud-coated sneakers. "I went in after her. Then all of a sudden we were in the river. It was like she was walkin' in her sleep when she went into the river. I tried to stop her. I hollered. Then I went in after her." His voice caught. "She tried to drown me." He looked up at Dave. "Even after I got away, she came after me and tried to drown me." He shivered. He looked at Sharon, then away toward the river.

"It wasn't her though," Scott said at last and something in the tone of his voice or the look on his face, a queer, haunted look, sent a chill down Dave's spine. "It wasn't Sharon. It was somebody else makin' her do it."

Only the murmuring gnats disturbed the stillness. Dave had a sudden urge to run, to escape this place, to leave both of them down here and flee.

He fought down his panic. He tried for a moment to convince himself that the kid was crazy or that he himself was asleep and having some kind of nightmare.

A shaft of sunlight shone through the willow leaves on Sharon's pale face. He went over to her, knelt, pulled out a wet handkerchief from his hip pocket, and wiped the muddy smear off her cheek. She did not blink. Her teeth showed a little behind the faint idiot smile.

He turned away. His hand closed into a fist over the tightly wadded handkerchief.

His eyes met the boy's. When he finally spoke, his voice was almost a croak: "Tell me again what you saw last night. The woman in the lightning. What did she look like?"

HOLLY and Floyd were first out of the church. Holly stood in the street and watched his deputy drive away in search of the Gates' girl. Then he walked over to his own

143

car and tried again to raise Clyde Lee, without success. People began trooping out of the church and heading for their cars for the drive out to the cemetery.

Holly felt a deep uneasiness. Clyde Lee would not have missed the funeral service unless one: he was onto something important, or two: something had happened to him. If it was number one, why hadn't he radioed in, Holly wondered.

While he was engaged in these reflections, he suddenly noticed Will Lawton peering in the car at him.

"Any word on Sharon?"

Holly shook his head.

Lawton glanced at the church, then turned back to Holly. His voice was low, but there was an angry edge to it.

"Then why the hell aren't you out looking for her!"

"I've got a deputy out lookin' right now."

"One? That's not enough."

"That's all I got for right now."

Lawton's eyes narrowed to angry slits. "It appears to me you're just sitting here. You've got to form a search party. I've already driven the back roads myself, but it's going to take a lot of people if we're going to find her."

"As soon as I get back from the cemetery—"

"What?" Lawton exploded. "A girl's missing and you're going to waste another hour at the graveyard with a corpse before you do anything, damn you?"

"That corpse you're talking about was my friend." Holly felt the blood stinging his cheeks. "And just because your old man owns half this town don't give you the right to tell me my business. Now get off my back."

Lawton's eyes became murderous. For a moment Holly thought he was going to open the door and come after him. He thought of the way Lawton had snookered him with Janine and he almost wished he would. But apparently the young contractor thought better of it.

"Don't expect to hang onto that badge," he hissed, "if you don't turn her up—and soon."

Lawton turned on his heel and stalked away. Holly slammed the heel of his palm against the steering wheel.

144

At the same instant, the voice of Floyd's wife, Terri, broke in on the radio. She was substituting as dispatcher for Thelma who had come to the service.

"What is it?" Holly snarled into the microphone.

"Holly, Clyde Lee's at the hospital. He's been snake bit."

A moment later Holly was nosing the cruiser through the crowd. When they did not move fast enough, he hit the siren. Heads snapped around and a path opened up for him, then he was through the staring faces and an empty street stretched ahead of him. It was ironic, he thought. Loomis had provided escorts for many of his fellow townsmen to their final resting place, but he, himself, would have no police escort. Not that it mattered to him, anymore, but Betsy Loomis might be grieved.

Holly cut the siren as he turned onto Main Street. Many of the stores and shops were closed, their proprietors at the church. Easy pickings for a crook. The way things were going he wouldn't be surprised if somebody knocked off the bank while everybody was out at the cemetery.

Snake bit! Clyde Lee wasn't the only one, Holly thought.

Two unsolved murders, three disappearances, Clyde Lee hospitalized, leaving only Floyd and himself to handle the situation. And Delores at her mother's with the kid. For the second time in less than three hours he pulled into the hospital parking lot.

Doc Adkins was in the corridor outside the emergency room. He motioned Holly to follow him into a small office. He peered at Holly through rimless glasses, his bald head gleaming in the florescent light. "I pumped a lot of antivenin in him. Mocassin bites aren't usually fatal, but he got nailed twice. I can tell you he's one very sick boy."

"Twice?"

"In the arm and the ankle. Must have stumbled into a nest of 'em."

"Is he going to be all right?"

"I hope so."

"Can I see him?"

145

"Won't do you any good. He's delirious and under sedation. You might want to talk to the fellow who brought him in. He's down in the waiting room."

In the waiting room a leather-faced man in his late fifties rose to meet Holly. He was lean and wiry, dressed in faded khakis and held a maroon baseball cap in his hand. He introduced himself as Lon McIntyre.

"I appreciate your bringin' in my deputy," Holly told him. "Where did you find him?"

"Out near the old Graves place. I was drivin' along the gravel road out there and I seen his dust. He was backin' too fast out of a wagon track, his wheels caught the ditch and he stuck. He jumped out wavin' at me. I figured he was drunk at first. If he hadn't been in uniform and it a po-leece car, I wouldn't have stopped."

"What did he say to you?"

"First I couldn't make it out. He was all pale and wild-eyed, you know. Then I seen he was bit. He said a pair of cottonmouths done it in his car. 'Bout then he started gettin' real sick. I sucked some of the pizen out and brought him in fast as I could. How is he?"

"We don't know yet."

Holly walked with McIntyre out to the parking lot and a battered pick-up.

"Did he say why he didn't use his radio to get help."

"No. And I didn't ast him."

The man donned his baseball cap, climbed into the pick-up, repeated directions on how to get to Clyde Lee's car, and drove away.

Holly went back into the hospital and looked in on Clyde Lee. The young deputy was asleep, his face star-tlingly pale. A nurse asked him to leave. As he wandered out to the squad car, he wondered what he should do next. Should he go out and look at Clyde Lee's car, or deputize some people and hunt for Sharon Gates?

DAVE had thought about sending the boy ahead for help, but he decided not to take a chance on Scott

146

getting lost. He would probably not leave Sharon anyway. He kept glancing at his half-sister, but physically and emotionally he was, Dave thought, about played out.

He, himself, had to stop every few minutes to rest. He was panting now and not entirely from the physical exertion of carrying her up the gradual slope from the swamp. He looked at her face which could have been a plaster cast, and the cold, empty stare was more frightening than the glare of hatred he had seen while he was struggling with her in the river.

He told the boy to stop.

Cradling her head in the crook of his arm like a baby's, he set her down gently on the pine needles. Scott slumped listlessly under a huge oak. He had described the lady in the lightning. Young with long black hair, he had said. All that was left was to believe him or not to believe. To believe meant to believe in a power beyond rational explanation. He wiped the heavy sweat from his forehead and stared at the girl. His heart hammered. If he believed in Scott's "witch", then some other things, beginning with Bobby Bowen's disappearance, Sharon's sudden malady, her trying to drown herself and her brother, her lapse back into a semi-coma, began to make a kind of crazy sense. Suddenly, uncontrollably, he giggled. He tried to choke it off and it came out instead, a wracking sob.

The boy looked up at him abruptly, then away.

He wondered if he was losing his mind. He struggled to his feet, the girl in his arms, a huge, inanimate doll, a floppy Raggedy Ann. Again, the dry racking sob tore from his chest. It seemed incredible that they had made love together only two days ago, that last night she had been a warm, laughing human being. Had been? Yes, because she was not human now—she was no more than a zombie, worse even, at this moment, only a vegetable. And, if it had not been for Scott, she would not even be that.

What was it Scott had said? She had walked into the swamp like a sleep-walker. "But it wasn't her. It was

147

somebody else making her do it."

He glanced at the rigid face of the boy walking beside him.

How easy it was for him to attribute what he didn't understand to witchcraft—the simplest explanation for the young, the unsophisticated, the ignorant. Suddenly, came a vision of a small leather bag nestled between two firm breasts.

Marie Villiers!

His breath whistled in his throat. He told himself he was insane. Yet the girl Scott claimed he had seen in the lightning was young with long black hair.

Quick, frozen moments snapped through his mind like slides in a projector. The look she had given him in class this morning had momentarily rattled him. What was it he had seen in her eyes? Even at the time he had thought they looked cold and held a kind of triumph, a gloating that he had wondered at—evil was the only word that came to mind to describe what he had seen in her eyes at that moment—pure evil. The other night after he had brought Sharon back from the lake and returned to his room, the noise that sounded like a Volkswagen engine in the street below. Then yesterday she had all but offered herself to him, and he had refused. Hell hath no fury . . . .

He *was* cracking up. But that strange little leather bag. He had not imagined that. Some kind of charm. Magic. Bobby Bowen had disappeared at a graveyard; Scott claimed he had seen an open grave. George Burke believed somebody might have stolen Biggs' body. Some satanic cults used dead bodies in their unholy rites. His mind whirled. He tripped over a dead limb and almost fell with the girl.

Ahead of him through the pines he saw the hospital in the middle of its asphalt desert.

"Do you still have that piece of wax?" he asked the boy in a hoarse voice.

Scott fumbled into his pocket.

Dave took it. It was wet and clammy. He stared at it, filled with repugnance and disgust. It was only a few

148

inches from Sharon's cheek. A tremor seemed to ripple across her cheek. Her eyes began to widen and an animal glare seemed to fill them for a moment. With a cry he dropped the piece of wax as though it were burning.

Scott stared at it a moment, blinked, then stooped and picking it up, put it back in his pocket.

CHAPTER 13

SHADOWS from the pines half hid the patrol car that tilted at a sharp angle, the left side still on the road, little more than a wagon track, the other side in the ditch. Holly parked behind the car, got out, and walked over. He peered inside the window on the driver's side.

On the floorboard, half hidden by the seat, thick as a length of fire hose, was a snake. Its head was gone. Blood was spattered on the seat and dash. Bullet holes were in the floorboard; one was in the microphone still slung under the dash. Clyde Lee had fought a war in there.

Holly did not see another snake.

He went back to his car and radioed for a wrecker. He gazed up and down the lonely road, gnawing his thumbnail. How in the hell had one snake, let alone two, gotten inside the car?

In the distance came a sound like low thunder. It came from the direction of the Graves place. Holly had been there before with Loomis hunting moonshine stills. The sound was the same as when they dynamited stills. He wondered what they were blasting over there—more than likely stumps, he thought, to clear land for planting. He wondered if a moonshiner had put a snake in Clyde Lee's car to scare him off.

When the wrecker arrived, Holly was glad to see it. It was damn lonesome out here by yourself. The driver looked inside Clyde Lee's car and blanched.

150

"You gonna leave that in there?"

Holly nodded. "Take the car to the garage and don't let nobody touch it until it's been dusted for prints."

He watched the wrecker disappear down the road trailing the car in its dusty wake. Then he radioed Thelma, who had returned from the funeral, that he was going over to the old Graves place for a while.

He asked if Floyd had turned up anything on the Gates' girl.

"Negative!" Thelma responded.

He shoved the car into gear and drove fast. He almost overshot the padlocked, iron gate and had to slam on the brakes, spewing gravel. He got out and gazed a moment at the "No Trespassing" sign, then climbed over the gate.

The thick trees closed over his head and, before him, the drive twisted like a dark snake.

FROM the window in the corridor he gazed at the pines they had just emerged from, while a nurse cleaned Sharon up in a nearby room. He felt numb. If Scott had not seen her going into the pines, chances were she would have vanished into the swamp, just as Bobby Bowen had vanished, without a trace.

He turned as the elevator doors slid open. Sam and Lucy got out of the elevator and started toward him. He had called them to tell them Sharon was back. As they drew close, he saw their faces were gray and pinched. He had not told them any details.

Lucy stared at him and he was conscious of his mud-stained clothing.

"She's in there." He pointed toward the closest room. "A nurse is with her. Scott's down in emergency, but there's nothing to be alarmed about. He's okay."

Lucy's eyes had widened. "Emergency room! What happened?"

"He got a little wet, that's all."

She exchanged a quick look with Sam, turned and hurried back down the hall. Sam watched her, a bewildered

151

look on his face. After she disappeared down the stair-well, he turned back to Dave. "What happened?"

"They both fell into the river."

Sam started for Sharon's room. Dave grabbed his arm to slow him.

"Listen, Sam, I've got to go somewhere right now to check on something. Don't leave her alone for a moment while I'm gone. Not even for a second. Do you understand? Not even for a second."

Sam stared at him. "I want to know what happened," he said. "All of it."

"Believe me, I wish I could tell you, but I'm not sure yet." Without another word, he left Sam and went down to the parking lot. He drove directly to the high school. He had already checked the telephone directory while waiting for Sam and Lucy. No Villiers was listed. It was nearly four. The building was locked and deserted. He fished out a key and let himself in the front entrance.

His footsteps echoed hollowly down the hallway lined with green metal lockers. He stopped at Simmons' office and tried the knob perfunctorily, knowing it would be locked and he did not have a key. He rattled the knob, then raised his foot and kicked in the frosted pane that was set in the upper half of the door, reached in and unlocked it. In a moment he was walking through the broken glass to the file cabinets where the student records lay.

Pulling out the drawer marked U–Z, he flipped through the folders until he came to the one he wanted. He pulled it and began reading.

She was eighteen, according to the record sheet: her father, Bastian Villiers, her mother Catherine, both deceased. Her guardian was her brother, Claude Villiers. Born in Martinique, she had attended private schools in Fort-de-France where her grades had been good, A's in French, Art, and Music, B's in Science, Math, and English, a couple of C's in History and Social Studies. Her I.Q. was 132. His eyes lingered on the address, Route 4, Box 63. He replaced the file in the cabinet and left the office, closing the door with its shattered pane behind

152

him. He retraced his steps down the dim corridor and, locking the front entrance behind him, stood a minute blinking into the afternoon sunshine, before deciding to go back to the hospital and check on Sharon first. After that, he would pay Marie Villiers a visit.

SCOTT heard all their words but it seemed like they were talking from far away. Doctor Cornelia was sending Sharon to a big hospital in Memphis. His father was asking Doctor Cornelia how Sharon could possibly have walked out of the hospital under her own power. Doctor Cornelia didn't know. His mother was hovering over him and kept asking him if he was all right. He wished she would leave him alone. He felt very tired. Sharon lay in bed, motionless.

"Don't you want to get some sleep?" his mother asked.

"No."

"You really ought to try, Scotty."

He looked away from her.

"Your mother's right, Scotty," Dr. Cornelia said. "You've got to rest."

He looked at his father in appeal, but Sam was gazing at Sharon, his face grim yet pathetic. The boy felt sorry for him. Doctor Cornelia left the room.

"We're proud of what you did—following your sister and bringing her back," his mother whispered to him. "But you do have to get some sleep."

"I can't," he said. "I can't sleep." His own voice sounded distant. His legs ached and his skin felt like it was being pricked by hundreds of little needles from the inside.

Doctor Cornelia returned with a glass of water and handed it to him with a big white pill. "I want you to take this, Scotty. It'll help you sleep. You really need it, you know."

He shook his head.

"Cut out this nonsense," his father said sharply. "And do what the doctor tells you."

153

Scott said nothing. He looked dully at the pill in his outstretched palm.

"It's all right," Doctor Cornelia said. "You don't have to take it." She turned to his mother and said in almost a whisper that he should go home and lie down awhile anyway.

"No!" Water sloshed out of the glass he was holding onto the tile floor. "I'm not going home." He walked over to Sharon's bed. "I'm going with her."

They stared at him. He realized he had been shouting.

"I've got to watch her," he said desperately. "They can get her anytime. Probably even in Memphis too, if they want."

His father grabbed his shoulder. "What do you mean? Who are *they*?"

"Leave him alone, Sam," his mother said. "Can't you see he's out of his head?"

"I'm not! I'm not!" The words rushed out, tumbling over each other. "The ones who got Bobby—they control her. They make her do what they want. She tried to drown me down at the river when I tried to stop her from drowning. They control her. I've got to watch her every second. Ask Dave. He'll tell you—" his voice broke.

His father turned loose of his shoulder, looking scared and angry at the same time. But he said softly, "Come on, son. We're going home."

Scott stepped back from him and looked at Sharon. Her face had the smooth, vacant expression of a giant Barbie doll. When his father took hold of his arm, the glass of water he was holding slipped and smashed on the tile, spraying their feet. Suddenly he began laughing. His mother and Doctor Cornelia came over to him. They were all closing in on him. He tried to pull away from his father's grasp, but the fingers tightened on his arm until they hurt. He could not stop laughing. He wondered why he was laughing; then he saw Doctor Cornelia nodding to the nurse who left the room a moment later, and his laughter stopped abruptly.

"Let me go," he snarled, trying to wrench away from his father's hold.

154

Then the nurse returned with the needle.

"No," he screamed. "No! I've got to watch her."

His father held him from behind as the nurse swabbed his arm with the cotton.

"It won't hurt," she said sweetly. "Don't be afraid—a big boy like you."

He tried to kick her, but she was standing to the side and he only grazed her ankle while his father held him fast and his mother bit her knuckles. The nurse held the needle up to the light, then brought it down, and the prick merged with the tiny needles already dancing beneath his skin.

"Now you'll sleep," Doctor Cornelia soothed. "And when you wake up, you'll feel much better."

In the bed Sharon smiled at him—a plastic, Barbie doll smile.

THE lovely girl at the door regarded Holly coolly.

"My brother's working," she said, a trace of arrogance in her voice.

"That him blastin'?"

"Yes."

"When does he knock off?"

"Hard to say."

Her curt answers irritated him. He studied her full, sulky mouth, the high breasts, the well-rounded bottom encased in tight jeans and wondered if there was some Negro blood there. With a name like Villiers there certainly must be some kind of foreign blood mixture, he thought.

"Well, I reckon I'll go hunt him then. What with the noise he's makin' he won't be that hard to find."

"I wouldn't," the girl said. "It's dangerous."

Of course, she was right. It would be foolhardy to walk into the middle of some blasting, but her manner had angered him, making him a bit reckless.

"Then suppose you invite me inside to wait until he gets finished," Holly said, smiling at her. One hand rested

155

on a column of the portico and he leaned toward her. She certainly was a looker, whatever her blood.

"I don't think my brother would care for that—and I'm sure I wouldn't."

Her dark eyes were openly hostile now. Holly took his hand from the column and straightened up. "Look, little girl, I aim to see your brother. I've got a few questions for him—and maybe for you too, for that matter."

"What is it, officer?"

Holly whirled. He had not heard the man come up behind him and, looking at him now, he understood why the man had made Clyde Lee jumpy. The first thing you noticed about him were those unnaturally pale eyes that looked like chips of ice in his dark face—that and the slight hunch of the man's shoulders produced a definitely unsettling effect, plus the way he seemed to appear out of nowhere.

Yet, despite his light eyes, his features bore a startling resemblance to the girl's. Except for the eyes and the obvious age difference they might have been twins, he thought.

"Heard you blastin'," Holly managed to say at last.

"Yes. Getting stumps out so I can plant. I'm extremely busy. So if you could tell me what brings you out here—"

The girl turned to go inside.

"Just a minute, Miss," Holly said. "I'd like to talk to both of you."

She shrugged and waited.

"Did either of you see Sheriff Loomis out here Saturday?"

"I've already told another deputy last night that we haven't," Villers said.

Holly turned to the girl. "What about you, Miss?"

"No."

"That's funny." Holly looked back at Villiers. "We traced him out here. Seems like he stopped at every place *but* yours."

"I'm sorry we can't help you," Villiers said, "but there you are. Now as I said, I have a lot of work to do. Perhaps you will excuse us."

156

"How much help you got out here?"

Villiers cold eyes looked beyond him. "A few hands—that's all."

"I'd like to talk with 'em."

"Why?"

"They might have seen Loomis. You object?"

"No. But right now it's out of the question. They're working. You've heard the blasting. I can't stop them right now even if I wanted to."

"I can get a warrant."

Villiers smiled. "There's no need. We'll have finished by tonight and, if you come back in the morning, I assure you no warrant will be necessary. Actually, only my foreman besides my sister and myself was here Saturday. Give me a time in the morning and I'll see that he's here at the house to answer any of your questions. Now you really must excuse me. Marie will see you to your car."

Holly shook his head. "As much as I'd appreciate her company, I can find my own way." He looked at both of them. Next time he came here it would be with a warrant all right, and he and Floyd would search the whole damn place. For what, he was not sure, but the two of them were definitely hiding something. The old house itself seemed to hold something sinister and dark.

He turned and felt their eyes on his back as he walked down the drive. Overhead the trees were as thick as a jungle—and for an instant he had the sensation he was back in the jungles of Vietnam—a distinctly unpleasant feeling. He cast a glance on either side of the drive. Snakes could be swarming in that dense undergrowth and he thought of the cottonmouth he had seen in Clyde Lee's car.

"Get hold of yourself," he muttered. This place was getting to him.

Tramping the bottoms out here tonight would not be smart. Even if he knew what he was looking for, he did not relish the idea of falling into quicksand or a nest of moccasins in the dark. But tomorrow morning he would be back with the warrant—he and Floyd. Even after he turned the curve in the drive and was out of sight of the

157

house, he could not shake the feeling that he was being watched. He quickened his pace toward the car. As he scrambled over the locked gate, he heard Thelma's voice on the radio.

Thelma told him the Gates' girl had been brought back to the hospital by Dave Stewart and her brother after she had wandered off on her own.

One less pressure on me, Holly thought. He wondered how Will Lawton would react to his lost love being rescued by his rival, and smiled. But how had Stewart known where to find her? He told Thelma he was returning to town.

"See if you can get hold of Stewart. I want to talk to him."

Stewart and the girl had come to him the other evening about Bobby Bowen's disappearance, then the girl disappears herself for awhile. Maybe there was some connection. But Stewart better not start that business about digging up graves again, Holly thought, as he headed the car toward town. He was glad to be leaving Villiers' place, but all the way into town his thoughts were on Villiers and his sister, and what he was going to tell Judge Summers so the old man would issue a search warrant.

LUCY Gates stared out the window at the long shadows stretching across the hospital parking lot. She had called Judy Farese and made arrangements for Scott to stay with Jimmy while she and Sam went to Memphis with Sharon. Sam had driven a groggy Scott over there and now she waited for his return and the ambulance to arrive that would take Sharon to the specialists in Memphis. She glanced over at her step-daughter lying there gazing blankly at the ceiling. Then she turned back to the window. Where was the damn ambulance and why was Sam taking so long? She put her hands to her temples and pressed so hard her eyeballs ached. Everything that had happened was so sudden, so inexplicable. Even now she was having trouble grasping it. She and Sam had led neat,

158

well-ordered lives. Sam's business was doing well, she had her women's clubs, and there was tennis and their group of friends at the country club and suddenly, in the middle of the night, their assured world had collapsed. She felt again like the lonely, unsure girl from the wrong side of the tracks whose drunken father beat her and her mother.

A great weariness came over her. She watched the sun dip behind the trees, spreading blood-like streaks across the horizon. Below, a car pulled into the parking lot and Dave Stewart, still dressed in muddy pants and a stained T-shirt, got out. What did—had—Sharon seen in the man, she wondered, and again turned to the girl. She uttered a cry. The bed was empty.

She ran out into the hallway in time to see the girl's back disappearing down the stairwell. By the time she reached the head of the stairs, Sharon was on the landing. Half-way down the bottom flight she caught up with her step-daughter.

"Baby! Honey!" She grabbed the girl's arm.

Sharon turned to her, eyes as bleak as gray sky. Her hands clamped over Lucy's wrists and with surprising strength pulled her around. Lucy felt the girl's leg pressing against her left calf. Then Sharon pushed her hard.

The stairwell turned upside down and sharp pain shot through her body as she rolled down the concrete stairs.

Entering the waiting room, he heard the scream. He exchanged glances with the woman at the desk, who had started up, and broke for the stairwell. He opened the stairwell door and found Lucy moaning at the bottom of the steps. Half-way up the flight of stairs Sharon watched him, her eyes burning with demonic light. Suddenly she turned and fled back up the stairs. He started after her and reached her at the landing; grabbing her, he pulled her around.

"It's all right," he said. "I'm not going to hurt you."

She smiled that faint, sweet, idiot smile and her fingernails went for his eyes. He stumbled back against the railing as she lunged for him. He glimpsed her face twisted in hate, then her head bent and her teeth sank deep into

159

his chest. He roared in pain and yanked her head back by the hair, twisting her around so he could grab her from behind. She squirmed, kicked his instep, and broke free. He danced on one foot and she ran up the second flight into the arms of a husky orderly. When Dave reached them, they were on the floor with her on top. Dave pulled her off, and they both held her pinned to the floor.

"My God, she's strong!" the orderly gasped.

Gradually her struggling grew feebler. The fierce light in her eyes faded. She went limp, her breathing became quieter.

From the bottom of the stairs, Lucy whimpered.

A few minutes later they X-rayed Lucy. Her left hip was broken. Sharon had been put in a strait jacket.

"You better let me put something on that," a young intern said, pointing to Dave's chest where blood had seeped through the T-shirt. "You can get a nasty infection from a human's bite," the intern said as he swabbed Dave's wounds with antiseptic. "You remember the old one about the man who bit the dog and the dog died. Maybe we ought to vaccinate people against each other."

Sam returned in time to sign admission papers for Lucy to the hospital. He was badly shaken when he left the room they had taken her to and found out what had happened during the twenty minutes he had been gone to arrange the ambulance. It finally arrived to take Sharon to Memphis and he went back in to confer with Lucy, who was in considerable pain but conscious.

When he came back into the room where Sharon lay, he had the look of a man who has just witnessed a bad automobile wreck. He motioned Dave to follow him out into the hallway. "I should have listened to you," he said. "I shouldn't have left Lucy alone with her."

Dave tried to think of something comforting to say, but drew a blank.

"I wonder if you'll kind of keep an eye on her while I'm gone—you know, see that she gets everything she needs here." Sam bit his lower lip. "I don't know how long I'll have to be in Memphis with Sharon. But we

160

talked it over just now and she says I should go with Sharon. She's a tough woman." For a moment Dave thought the older man was going to burst into tears, but he got a grip on himself. "Scotty will be all right; he's staying with friends," Sam continued. "It's just I hate to leave Lucy like this—lying there in that hospital bed."

"I'll look in on her," Dave said.

Sam shook his hand gratefully. "I really appreciate it."

Two attendants wheeled Sharon into the elevator a few minutes later, her face pale and still. Dave followed them out to the ambulance and watched them put her inside. He caught a glimpse of her rich chestnut hair as Sam climbed in with her. Then the door was shut.

After the ambulance had disappeared in the twilight, he still stood a moment on the almost empty parking lot staring after it. He had never felt more alone.

CHAPTER 14

GEORGE Burke sat alone in his office hunched over an ancient Remington. The newspaper office was dark except for the cone of light from the desk lamp spreading over the yellow copy paper in the roller. He glanced quickly at the story he had just written:

Walden County Deputy Sheriff Clyde Lee, 22, is in serious condition tonight at County General Hospital after being bitten by poisonous snakes, apparently in his patrol car.

The incident occurred this afternoon while Lee was patrolling the Gravel Springs area.

A passing motorist, Lon McIntyre, said he saw Lee's car back into a ditch about 2 p.m. on the Gravel Springs Road eight miles west of here. McIntyre stopped his pick-up to lend assistance.

Lee emerged from his car dazed and claimed that water mocassins had bitten him in his car, McIntyre said.

McIntyre rushed the stricken deputy to the local hospital where he was treated for snakebites in the arm and leg. Hospital authorities say he is presently unable to give an account of what happened.

Acting Sheriff Holly McAfee this evening said he sent Lee out into the Gravel Springs area to try and turn up some leads on the recent murder of Sheriff Fred Loomis whose funeral services were held today. Loomis was found Sunday morning in his patrol car in the Coldwater River. An autopsy revealed he had been killed by a blow to the head with a blunt instrument.

McAfee refused to confirm that Lee was bitten in his patrol car or to speculate how a snake or snakes got into the car. But Lem Dolan of Gray's Wrecking and Towing Service, who towed Lee's car into town, reported seeing a water mocassin on the floorboards with its head shot off. He also said there were several bullet holes in the floorboards and the front seat.

Authorities will not allow anyone near the car at present. McAfee said it is being dusted for fingerprints.

He pulled the copy out of the roller and laid it on the desk next to the story he had done earlier on Sheed's murder. He had telephoned that story in to the Memphis *Press-Scimitar*, but he figured the A.P. man would be as interested as the Memphis papers in this one.

Leaning back in the chair, he looked out the window into the darkness. The streets were unusually quiet, and the town seemed to be in a state of suspended animation except for a lone bat swooping around the street lamp right outside his office. It was as though the town were shell-shocked, he thought. Only a few days ago Bobby Bowen's disappearance had rocked the town, but now it was all but forgotten in the wake of the two murders. A fear as tangible as the mist from the Coldwater Bottoms had settled over the town—it was in the faces of the mourners he had seen at graveside this afternoon and in his own eyes right now reflected in the brass cone of the desk lamp. He could not shake the vision of Sheed's face like a mummified frog's in that evil-smelling basement this morning. He reached into the desk drawer, pulled out a half-full pint of Jack Daniels black label, uncorked it

163

and poured a generous slug into a paper cup.

He savored the whiskey in the back of his throat for a moment before swallowing it. He had put in a long day and he was ready to go home, but still he lingered, staring out into the darkness. Then it came to him. He was afraid to go out there in the dark alone.

He sat there digesting this new fact for a while. He shook his head, then put the cork back on the bottle, thrust it into the drawer and, reaching for the telephone, prepared to call in his latest story to the A.P. man in Memphis.

THE movie was dull and Wade Haskill in the back row of the theater was restless. His hand slid down to Millie's breast, but she pulled it away. They were almost alone in the place; very few had come to see the picture tonight. His hand crept back toward her breast, and he looked at her out of the corner of his eye, wishing she was Marie. He shut his eyes and imagined that she was, while his fingers caressed her breast. She did not pull his hand away this time and he felt the firm breast beneath the sweater, unfettered by a bra. His fingers circled her nipple, rolling it until it became stiff and hard. Millie began to squirm and turned her face to him. "Don't," she pleaded.

He kissed her, their mouths greasy with popcorn butter. No, she was not Marie. He looked back at the screen and pinched her nipple sharply. She gave a yelp and stared at him in the darkness with big cow eyes. For a moment he felt vaguely ashamed, but only for a moment, then he was thinking of Marie again, not even aware of the images on the screen in front of him. She had missed all of her afternoon classes. And the thought that had nagged at him all afternoon came back, giving him a sick feeling in his belly: *What if she had been with Stewart?*

Stewart had not been at school that afternoon either, had not even shown up for baseball practice, even though they were scheduled to play a double-header tomorrow.

164

A picture rose in his mind of the two of them together—Stewart and Marie—making love, and he gritted his teeth. He tried to tell himself she no longer cared for Stewart. If looks could kill, this morning in class she would have withered him into dust; yet, they said, hate was very close to love, and for weeks Marie had wanted Stewart. Wade gnawed his thumb. He was imagining things. If the two of them were going to get together, they wouldn't be that obvious. Stewart would lose his job in a flash if anybody found out he had left during school hours with a student for a lay. Yet Marie would be well-worth losing a job for. His face burned as he visualized Stewart doing those things with Marie that for many nights he, himself, had dreamed of doing with her. He dropped the popcorn box, crushing it beneath his feet, still half-full of popcorn. He heard a sob and turned. He wondered how long Millie had been crying.

"What's the matter?"

She stared at him through swollen eyes. "Go to hell," she hissed. Then she rose quickly and brushed by him. He grabbed her wrist. "Where do you think you're goin'?"

"You dirty bastard." She kicked him hard in the ankle. He yelled and she tore free of his grasp and scurried out into the lobby. By the time he hobbled into the lobby after her, she had already disappeared into the darkness outside.

HANK Bowen slumped in his armchair in the dingy living room, his glazed eyes on the flickering TV screen. Angie was asleep in the bedroom. She spent most of her time in bed now. She burrowed in like a mole, shutting out everything including him.

The house was a mess, especially the kitchen with splotches of food on the table cloth, crumbs on the floor, dirty dishes stacked in the sink. He hated to go in there anymore. She just slopped a meal together, hardly eating anything herself—just popping those tranquillizers

165

the doc gave her, then retreated back to the bedroom to sleep. Yet she still clung to the idea Bobby would come back. Every morning she expected him to show up, and she hovered around the windows peering out at every kid who passed, and she jumped everytime the damn telephone rang, expecting somebody on the other end to say he had found Bobby and was bringing him home.

Bowen knew better. He knew Bobby was never coming home, but he could not tell her. He stared into the kitchen at the mess. Finally he got up and went in and fetched a beer out of the refrigerator. Returning to his armchair, he slumped into it and gazed with hopeless eyes at the television set. It was several minutes before he realized he was watching "Happy Days"—Bobby's favorite program. For a moment a great lump formed in Bowen's throat. Then he got up and switched channels.

OUT in the garden lightning bugs flickered. Betsy Loomis stared at them through the sliding doors of her dining room. She and Fred had moved into this house fifteen years ago and every spring Fred had planted a garden and in the fall she had put up the tomatoes, beans, peas, and okra for the winter. This fall she would not be putting up anything. As soon as the could, she would sell the house and move to Atlanta to be near her son and grandchild. After the funeral, before Tom had left for the Memphis airport to fly home, they had discussed her moving to Atlanta. He had urged her to come and stay with them. Tom had always been a good boy—a fine son. But now staring out at the garden she realized it was going to be hard to leave the only place they had ever owned.

She stepped out through the doors into the smell of trees and freshly turned earth. She thought of Fred sleeping in the earth, and Betsy Loomis began to weep softly.

After awhile she wiped her eyes. Tomorrow she would talk to the real estate people. Probably they could

166

not sell the house right away. Maybe long before the house was sold, Fred's murderer would be caught.

He was out there somewhere now—perhaps waiting to kill again. Maybe he had even attended the funeral. She hated him, of course, but she had lived so long with the fear of something happening to Fred that her hate seemed detached. Maybe the same man had murdered poor Mr. Sheed. After awhile she slipped back in the house, feeling chilled. She hated the silence of the house. She shut the doors and locked them. In the distance a dog began barking. She stared into the blackness remembering that Fred had always checked the doors at night before they retired to bed. Finally she turned and shuffled like an old woman to the lonely bedroom.

THROUGH bare, cavernous rooms Clyde Lee drifted until he came to the heavy door carved with gargoyle faces. He twisted the knob, but the door was locked and his bare feet were cold on the marble floor. He turned to retrace the way he had come. The moon shone through a high window on the pale expanse of marble before him and in the pool of light it formed he saw movement. A dark writhing shape! It wriggled toward him, its evil eyes glittering. He saw now, there were more of them—hundreds. They swarmed out of the heaving shadows into the moonlight, slithering over each other, their scales glistening green, brown, oily black, sickly yellow, in a twisting, undulating mass. They were flowing over each other, a serpent sea, rolling towards him. He screamed, but no sounds came from his throat. All his muscles seemed paralyzed. When the first one was only inches from him, he flung himself against the door, sobbing. He hammered on the thick wood with his fists and felt a queer coldness gliding over his foot. Then something crept up his ankle, wrapping around it, constricting muscles tightening and relaxing then tightening again. It entwined itself around his trunk. The thick coils contracted, squeezing the breath from him. The needle

167

teeth pierced his throat. He shrieked, a long, high wail.

He had struggled up to a sitting position in the bed. The hospital sheet was coiled and twisted around his sweat-soaked body. The nurse who had heard his scream found him crawling across the floor on his hands and knees still trying to fight his way free of the constricting bed sheet.

SHE would spend the night here at her sister's, Sarah Johnson thought. She did not want to go home tonight. She stared dully at her sister frying ham in the heavy black skillet, then gazed out the kitchen window. The moon was a slice of orange just above the horizon and half-obscured by a thin mist creeping out of the bottoms. The knowledge that Rufus would never be found alive had come to her as the darkness settled over her sister's shack on the edge of town. She knew how to read the signs; she had just tried not to. The candles on Annie Mae's grave that Rufus had found the other morning when the mules had stove the shed in and run off. And she had warned Rufus not to go down near that no good place—the old Graves place.

When she was only a girl, a conjure woman down there in the bottoms close to the Graves place—an ancient woman with a wizened black face and eyes sunk so deep in the sockets you could hardly find them—Mama Celia, they called her—lived in a hut. White and black came to her hut. She made warts vanish and toothache. She made mojos and charms and cast spells. Lots of people were afraid of her. With reason. Sarah knew her charms worked. When she was sixteen, Sarah had used a love charm from Mama Celia to get Rufus. She had lured him away from an older woman he had planned to leave the county with. But it wasn't the love charms Mama Celia made out of hummingbird powder and the blood of the wearer and pollen of flowers ground fine and placed in a he-goats scrotum that people feared. It was the business with Sally Beaufort that scared folk so bad. Only it hadn't scared

168

Sarah—at first.

Everybody had known that Sally had been lying with Sis Tarver's man, Manford. Sis had gone to Mama Celia and within three weeks Sally caught the Typhoid and died. Peoples said Mama Celia had given Sis goopher dust to sprinkle on Sally's stoop every midnight for a week.

The night after Sally was buried two boys passing through the graveyard saw a burnt white candle on her grave. They ran home and told their mother who told Sis Tarver. The next day she and Manford left the state. People whispered that Sally Beaufort's mama had paid Mama Celia to bring Sally back from the grave. Sarah had laughed at that talk.

One night months later she had gone down to Mama Celia's to buy the charm that brought her Rufus. As she emerged from a cane thicket into the clearing where the hut stood, she saw a figure coming out the doorway. Something about the way the woman moved seemed familiar, yet strange too. The woman was thin, dressed in a once white, but now torn and filthy gray dress. She walked stiffly past Sarah looking neither right nor left. She passed without even seeming to see Sarah—and her eyes, dull and staring, were like a blind woman's. The moon had not risen, but in the gleam from the coal oil lamp shining through the open doorway, Sarah had recognized the gaunt typhoid-wasted face.

She turned and fled.

Weeks later she had returned in the daylight with a friend for the charm and only then because she was so desperate. The older woman had said she and Rufus were leaving for Memphis at the end of the month and would not be coming back. The older woman had been Annie Mae Willis.

All the years since, Sarah had wondered if she had really seen Sally Beaufort or only a woman who looked very much like her and had come for some charm or cure to Mama Celia. But in her heart she knew. Even after all the years that had passed, she sometimes dreamed of that stiff, familiar figure and the gaunt face with those blank, staring eyes.

169

Some swore Sally Beaufort became a servant to Letitia Graves for years afterward—but one of her old boyfriends saw Sally and went to the police. When the police finally went out to the Graves place, she had disappeared—into the swamp's quicksand, many whispered, because she was never seen again.

She shivered despite the heat from the wood stove and her eyes focused again on the heavy stolid face of her sister bending over the skillet before they shifted once more to the window involuntarily as though she half-expected to see Rufus there demanding that she come home and start supper immediately.

She had paid Mama Celia twenty shiny silver dollars she had saved working as a maid. And she had won Rufus. Annie Mae Willis had gone off to Memphis. Eventually, she had married another man and only returned here a few months ago after he died. She should not have come back. Here no grave was deep enough. The burnt candle Rufus had found near Annie Mae's grave had told her all she needed to know.

She had warned Rufus. The Graves place—it was bad— it had always been bad. Old Talbott Graves had been a devil, and Letitia and Mama Celia had kept the badness going. She had thought that when Mama Celia died and then Letitia that that would be an end of it. But the ones out there now—Letitia's children, some said, even claiming that the older one was the son of that crazy mulatto, Bastian—had lived on one of the islands and learned the old ways too, just like Mama Celia.

The whites were fools. She had gone to the police, but even with their own Sheriff dead, they could not see what was going on right in front of them. Or they would *not* believe. All that dynamiting and talk of planting was just something to fool ignorant whites. Sarah moaned. "Rufus!"

Her sister turned and looked at her.

Sarah stared out the window into the darkness with sightless eyes, her arms hugging her breasts.

Her sister watched her a long time then turned back to the stove and the frying ham.

170

THE mist swirled in little eddies in the headlight beams and seemed to penetrate inside the Pinto. His hands were clammy on the steering wheel and his whole body was damp, not from the mist, but from sweat that stank sourly in his nostrils. A bitter, metallic taste was in his mouth.

Driving through town, he had seen the light in Burke's office and had longed to stop and talk with the newspaperman. But what could he say: "Yessir, there's some sort of powerful hoodoo out there and if we don't stop it, soon the whole town will be chopping cotton for no wages." But even if Burke could eventually be convinced that he did not belong in a cozy padded cell, it would have taken too much time. He did not know how much time Sharon might have before they tried again. He thought of her lying in the ambulance now and wondered if there were any thoughts at all in her mind, or was her mind only a vacuum, as in unconsciousness, waiting to be filled by another's dark intelligence, an intelligence that had reduced her to the subhuman thing he had fought with in the river and in the hospital stairwell. He remembered the hate in her eyes as they had struggled on the hospital stairs, but more frightening than that had been the utter blankness in them as she lay in the hospital bed. He was terrified of losing her, but he already had. Would death be any worse than the way she was now with her eyes like two holes punched in a sheet of white paper?

A cold, numbing despair settled over him. Sharon was gone, and he did not know how or if she could ever be brought back. Maybe the answer, if there was an answer, lay up ahead.

The car plowed on through the darkness and mist. Only the engine's hum gave him any sense of reality. He slowed the car when he came to the cluster of mailboxes, then stopped, got out and read the numbers on them in the headlight beams. Then he drove on. He came to another lonely box perched atop its leaning post and read the number and the bitter metallic taste grew stronger. The next one, he told himself. In the murk he almost

171

missed the sign and, if had he not seen it at the last moment, he would have missed the drive with its padlocked gate. He backed the car up and in the glare of the headlights read the "No Trespassing" warning. There was no mailbox, but from the numbers on the last one, he guessed this was the place.

He drove another two hundred yards and pulled off the side of the road into some trees. Opening the glove compartment he pulled out the flashlight, cut the car's engine and lights, slid out and closed the door quietly. He began walking back in the direction of the padlocked gate. When he was still fifty yards from the drive, he swerved into the thick underbrush. He climbed under a barbed wire fence, then struck out through dense trees in the direction the drive led.

Ahead of him a light glowed. As he drew closer, it looked as though it were shining from the window of a grounded steamboat with the mist lapping softly around it. He emerged from the trees and saw the lighted window belonged to a columned mansion. Between himself and the house stood the dark, squat shape of an outbuilding. Behind him tree frogs sang; everything else was silence. He slunk across the open ground and came up against the rear of the outbuilding—logs chinked with clay, very old, a relic dating before the Civil War, he guessed. Close to him was a tiny window. He peered inside into blackness. He listened intently for a minute, then switched on the flashlight for an instant that revealed an empty room with a plank floor. Putting the flashlight back in his belt, he crept to the corner of the cabin and peered at the big house, wondering if he might have made a mistake and Marie did not live here after all. The light from the window formed a halo in the fog that made it appear he could almost reach out and touch the lighted glass, although the house was probably two-hundred feet away.

He felt his heart beginning to thud heavily in his chest even before he broke for the house. It was close to a hundred yard sprint and he arrived gasping. He crouched below the window beside the old bricks upon which the foundation rested, catching his breath. A smell of rotting

172

wood and mildew filled his nostrils, mingled with another unpleasant odor which he could not quite identify. Slowly he raised his head to the window, keeping his body out of the light that poured from it.

A glittering chandelier, a dining table with a snowy cloth set with a gleaming array of silver, crystal, and china, two persons facing each other at the table in evening dress. The one at the far end of the table, facing him, in a green gown and with bare shoulders was Marie. Her dark face in the light from the chandelier had an almost Egyptian cast with its high cheekbones, wide lips, and slanted almond eyes. Her hand held a wine glass and she was looking intently at the man whose back was to him. He had the feeling he was gazing at a wax tableau until the man suddenly lifted his own wine glass and drank, breaking the illusion. Then Marie drank.

Dave could not take his eyes off her. In the classroom dressed in jeans or tight skirt she had been pretty, but now with a strange catch in his throat, he saw that she was a woman of rare beauty. The light glowed softly on her naked shoulders. He thought of Sharon and swallowed hard. He must be wrong about Marie; he had to be. Nobody could be that lovely and be what he suspected. A couple of jolts to the nervous system and his mind had shucked off its twentieth-century rationality and reverted right back to the dark ages. A cow dies—the witch did it; your house burns—burn the witch; your sweetheart sickens, does things you can't explain—the witch cast a spell, drive a stake through her heart. Only there were no witches, just the superstitions of ignorant peasants and fanatic priests—and damn fool pedagogues. It was time for this fool to go home.

Her dark eyes stared languidly at the man over the rim of the wine glass; then as she brought the glass down, he saw first the thong around her neck. Dangling from the thong, outside the bodice of the green gown, like an obscene brown eye, was the leather pouch.

He let out a quick intake of breath and heard a noise behind him. He spun around in a half-crouch, jerked his head to one side and something grazed his hair and

173

clanged dully against the side of the house. Through a red haze he saw the man scramble after the lead pipe that had been wrenched from his grasp as it bounced off the wall—the wall instead of his skull. Stupidly, he watched as the Negro bent for the pipe and grasped it, right in front of him. As he straightened, Dave put all his weight into the upper cut that caught the Negro in the solar plexus. The air whooshed out of him and he dropped to his knees again, doubled up, and toppled on his side.

A screen door slammed. Dave broke for the trees, the running footsteps angling toward him from the front of the house.

"Stop or I'll kill you!" Cold, authoritative, the voice left no doubt the man behind it would do exactly what he said.

Dave stopped and turned. Light from the window reflected on the barrel of the revolver aimed at his belly.

"Come over here!" the man ordered. He was lean, slightly hunched over, dressed in a dinner jacket. Although he had only seen his back through the window, Dave recognized him as Marie's dinner partner. Behind him, the Negro groaned.

"Get up!" the other rasped, not taking his gaze from Dave. "Who are you?"

"My name's Stewart." His voice sounded shaky. "Does that guy work for you? He tried to kill me." He made an effort to sound outraged, but it seemed hollow in his own ears.

"What are you doing on my property?" The man's eyes were very pale, very deadly. The pistol remained pointed unwaveringly at his stomach. He had come to the right place after all, he thought bitterly—the place to join Loomis. His eyes fell on the Negro struggling to get up and still clutching the steel pipe, and he remembered that Loomis had been killed by a blow to the head. A vision of Loomis entombed in his car at the bottom of the Coldwater River flashed through his brain and panic roared through him. His legs trembled and he felt as though he were going to vomit. The air burned in his

174

nostrils; he felt light-headed. He fought the panic down and felt his thick tongue forming words that seemed to come out in a croak: "Marie. I came to see Marie. I'm her history teacher."

For an instant the gun barrel dropped a fraction, but only an instant.

"And why do you want to see my sister?" The man's voice vibrated with a new and dangerous undercurrent.

"I wanted to ask her out."

Even as Villiers eyed his soiled clothes, he knew how painfully contrived it sounded.

"I thought because I'm older than she is, I should meet you first. I had a blow-out coming here and had to change the tire. I guess I got dirtier than I thought."

"Let me see if I have this correct. You came out here to ask my permission to take my sister out?" Villiers' irises were the color of dirty ice.

"I would have called first, but you aren't listed in the telephone book."

The Negro, short and powerfully built, had gotten unsteadily to his feet and glared at Dave. "He was spyin' through the window."

"I wasn't sure I'd come to the right place. I knocked on the front door and nobody answered, so I went around to the window."

"He lyin'," the Negro sneered.

Villiers regarded Dave silently, the pistol still covering him. Suddenly he motioned Dave forward with the barrel. They rounded the corner to the front of the house, the barrel pressed into the small of Dave's back.

Marie was standing on the portico. As they came into the light streaming from the hallway out the screen door, Marie's eyes fell on his face and widened a fraction, but her face remained impassive.

"You know him?" Villiers said.

She nodded. Dave was struck by the facial resemblance between the two of them.

"Is this the one you've chosen then?"

She was silent.

"I told you not in front of me—," his voice was a hiss.

175

"And not on my land. That was understood."

"He's not the one," she said.

"Indeed?"

"No!" She returned his cold stare but seemed suddenly pale.

"He says he's come to see you. To ask you out." Villiers tone was ironic. "You do know him, don't you, my dear, but the question is how well? Well enough that you care to go out with him?"

She stared down at Dave aloofly. "Hardly."

"I wonder why you went to all this trouble to come out here then, Mr. Stewart. Has my sister ever said anything to you or indicated in any way she might welcome your attentions?"

For an instant Dave saw a shadow pass behind the girl's eyes, although her features remained coldly indifferent. Was she afraid of her brother or herself? He remembered she had told him her brother was strict. It was obvious he could expect no help from her, and he had to admit the justice in that, considering the reason he had come out here; yet if he could tell Villiers she had made a play for him, just possibly he would believe it and put the gun away. But it was not likely.

"Not really," he said. "But I didn't think it would hurt to try."

"And you, my dear?" Villiers voice had turned silky, but the throbbing undercurrent of menace was still there. "Has he ever said anything to you to show his interest?"

Again the shadow behind her eyes for a fraction of a second before she said tonelessly: "He asked me for a date a few days ago. I laughed because I thought he was joking."

"That's all?" Villiers said.

"That's all," she murmured.

The sweat trickled down Dave's ribs. "Look! I come out here with honest intentions and damn near get brained. Now you threaten me with a gun. Do you intend to shoot me for wanting to date her?"

He felt the muzzle of the pistol a moment longer, then it was gone.

176

"No, Mr. Stewart. I don't intend to shoot you." Villiers stepped away from him. He handed the pistol to the Negro, "Put it away, Mosely."

Mosely thrust the pearl-handled .32 into his belt, his red-rimmed eyes never leaving Dave.

"Mosely may have been over-zealous," Villiers said. "We're alone out here and with the murders," he shrugged, and the action made his hunched shoulders look deformed. "Perhaps you'll understand. At any rate you're free to go. Mosely will escort you to your car."

"That's not necessary."

"But it is. We can't have you wandering alone out here. After dark the place is alive with snakes. Just last night Mosely killed a mocassin not twenty feet from where we're standing, didn't you?"

The Negro nodded.

Dave glanced at the girl. She gave him a queer, penetrating look. The mist curled in tendrils around the rotting pillar next to her, and she seemed to shiver as it touched her.

Villiers mounted the steps. "Shall we go in, my dear. There's a chill in the air. Au revoir, Mr. Stewart."

The girl stood rooted to the portico, staring at Dave.

"Marie," Villiers said. He grasped the girl's elbow. Dave watched the front door close behind them. Villiers was right; the night air had turned suddenly chill.

They started down the gravel drive. When they reached the first turn, Mosely pulled the pistol out and gestured toward the woods on the right. "This way, turkey."

"What are you going to do?"

"Move!"

After a hundred yards they came to a little clearing. In the middle of it was a narrow, unpainted structure. As they drew closer it looked like an outhouse.

Behind him the Negro chuckled mirthlessly. "I bet you feelin' the call right now. 'Bout to have an accident in you britches." He shoved Dave forward with the gun barrel. "Go in and relieve yourself."

Dave's hand trembled on the door latch, and Mosely backed away.

177

"Open it!"

The door swung open easily. There was no wooden seat, just a black pit; he could not see the bottom.

"Go on," Mosely ordered. "Get in!"

A vision flashed through Dave's brain with startling clarity. He saw himself at the bottom of the pit with Mosely firing down on him, then filling the hole up with lime and dirt. He would not be dumped in the river like Loomis; he would be buried in a privy. He felt hysterical laughter begin welling up in his throat and choked it off with a gasping noise.

"Get in," Mosely repeated. In the darkness all Dave could make out was his outline some seven or eight feet away and the pale rims of his eyes. He could not see the .32.

He took a small step inside and the door swung against his body. His fingers curled around the metal rim of the flashlight in his belt. He twisted his body so that the door would partially conceal the movement as he pulled it free from the belt. Another half step and he would lose his balance and be in the pit. Below he heard something like the thin rustling of paper, and suddenly he realized that Mosely's intention was not to shoot him. Of course! They wanted it to seem an accident.

I don't intend to shoot you, Villiers had said. Not with two murders already. A third murder and the county would be swarming with state as well as local cops. That is, if he had bullet holes in him. But snake bites. The place is crawling with snakes, Villiers had said. Somebody would stumble across him in the bottoms, miles from here and think he had blundered into a nest of mocassins.

"I'm not alone," Dave said. "I came out here with a friend and if I'm not back soon—"

"Climb down," Mosely whispered. "Or I'll forget I ain't 'spose to use this." Dave heard the hammer click back on the pistol. He inched toward the pit, his body sideways, and his right foot settled on empty air. Mosely was no more than nine feet away. His hand was so slick with sweat, the flashlight almost dropped out of his grasp into the pit. He held it against his right leg away

178

from the Negro.

"What's down there?" His voice sounded high and thin in his own ears.

The low rasping chuckle sounded in the darkness. "You really want to know?" Mosely said softly. "Well, you fixin' to find out." He took a step forward and Dave pivoted on his left foot hurling the flashlight, harder than he had ever thrown a baseball in his life, his muscles tensed for the jolt of the bullet.

There was a sound like an axe thudding into a tree and Mosely toppled backward into a heap. In the darkness and at that short a distance, he must not have seen it coming, Dave thought as he sprang toward him.

CHAPTER 15

MOSELY was unconscious but breathing. Nearby lay the flashlight. The glass was broken, but the bulb was intact and the light worked. He could do one of those dramatic endorsements, he thought—the time a flashlight saved my life. With the aid of its beam he found the .32 at Mosely's feet. Then he walked over to the outhouse and looked down into the pit.

Eight feet below lidless eyes glittered red in the beam of light. Thick, splotched bodies writhed together in an intricate knot. He could not tell how many there were. His knees went weak and he leaned against the privy door. An odor like old brass rose from the pit. He walked unsteadily back to Mosely. A stream of blood trickled down the dark forehead from a deep gash in the scalp at the hairline. He wanted to stomp Mosely, to dance an insane jig on his chest, to drag him over and roll him into the pit with the squirming serpents. He kicked the Negro in the ribs. The man made no sound. Gradually the rage subsided into a cold, hard anger. Up until now what they had done to Loomis, to Bobby Bowen, to Sharon—they had gotten away with. They believed they could do anything. Now it was his turn. The law would not help—it would only be his word against Villiers. Even if he showed McAfee the snake pit, Villiers would claim he did not know anything about it. But he had a gun now, and they would bring Sharon back from that other pit they had

180

plunged her into, or he would throw them to the snakes—yes, including Marie.

Kneeling, he stripped Mosely of his belt and tied the Negro's hands behind his back. He stuffed a handkerchief into Mosely's mouth, securing it with a strip of cloth ripped from the man's shirt. Then, grabbing him beneath the armpits, he dragged him deep into the heavy underbrush, propped him in a sitting position against a young gum tree and bound him to it with the rest of the shirt.

When he emerged from the trees, he was on the opposite side of the house from where he first had approached it. An L-shaped porch ran along this side of the mansion and at the rear of the L, attached to the house, was a small structure he took to be a smokehouse. Close by it, leading off the porch, was a door into what was probably the kitchen. He clutched the pistol and started running in a half-crouch toward this door. Half-way to the porch he ducked behind a black walnut, waiting and listening for any sound from the house. The only light visible was the one from the dining room. Yet from where he crouched it appeared to be empty. He noticed for the first time the moon had risen and, looking behind him, he saw an old barn rising above the mist. Beyond the barn was a solid black wall of pines and beyond that, he knew, lay the swamp. He turned his gaze back to the house and listened to the thudding of his heart. There was no other sound; even the tree frogs were silent now, and the stillness made the house seem that much more menacing, the stillness of a mausoleum inhabited by death. He drew a deep breath and moved out from the tree, then darted back. From the gravel drive in front of the house he had heard footsteps and suddenly he saw a figure leaving the drive and drifting across the yard toward the trees and the little clearing. Villiers was paying a visit to his outhouse. He was carrying what looked like a shotgun.

Again Dave felt the hysterical laughter bubbling up in his throat. It wasn't polite to make your guest go to the bathroom at gun point. A shotgun enema! What had happened to good old Southern hospitality? He choked the

181

insane mirth down. He had to get a grip on himself. In his mouth was the taste of bile and his legs felt suddenly weak again. He watched Villiers' dark figure merge into the blackness of the trees. A moment later he was creeping up the rotting wooden steps onto the porch.

The old planks creaked beneath his feet. He moved swiftly toward the door but stumbled. Looking down, he saw two iron staples protruding from the porch fastened with a heavy padlock. The trap door led probably to a storm cellar. Only a few feet away the smokehouse door was also fastened by a shiny padlock. But the door in front of him had no lock he found as he turned the knob: it swung open with barely a sound. An aroma of woodsmoke surrounded him as he entered. The room was dark, but to his right a thin line of light shone from under a closed door. Soon he made out the outline of a potbellied stove in front of him and a length of tin pipe running up through the ceiling. Cocking the .32 he moved to the door where the light shone, opened it and proceeded into the next room.

The crystal and china still lay on the table with the remains of a roast and an almost empty bottle of claret. Catching movement out of the corner of his eye he whirled to face in the glass of the china cabinet his own face, eyes wide, mouth tight. He entered into the hallway with its fourteen-foot ceiling. Shadows swarmed up the walls and dark doorways opened on either side. They appeared to be empty, so he risked the flashlight. One room was the living room complete with purple drapes shut tight at the windows, a great brick fireplace with massive andirons set with heavy logs, and overstuffed Victorian furniture that reminded him of the furnishings in Paxton's Funeral Home. He was about to switch off the light and leave the room when his attention was arrested by an oil portrait on the far wall of a beautiful woman in a yellow evening gown—a woman who bore a remarkable resemblance to Marie. But she was slightly darker and a good twenty years older at least. Inscribed on a brass plate at the bottom of the frame was a name: Marie Villiers.

182

Was it Marie's mother?

But in the school file they had given her mother's name as Catherine. Puzzled, he looked at the portrait again.

She might have been a Mexican or possibly a quadroon; she was certainly a beauty, except her eyes stared at him with a disdainful haughtiness and her thin nose and full, sullen mouth hinted at an underlying cruelty the artist must have seen. The room to his left was a study: a desk, heavy and solid of maple, shelves of books; a gun rack with several rifles locked in place so that without a key to the lock you would need an axe to liberate them—and one space empty where the shotgun must have rested.

He stood with one hand on the mahogany newel post undecided whether to enter the study and go through Villiers' desk or to go upstairs. Any moment Villiers might come back, might already suspect, when he could not find Mosely, what had happened and that Dave had doubled back to the house and Marie.

Above him on the landing shone the reflection of a light. If she was in the house, she had to be up there.

The gun still in front of him, he started up the stairs. He paused on the landing, straining his ears for any sound. But there was no noise above or below. Slowly he mounted the remaining stairs as though toiling up a steep hill. At the top was another hallway, and a door on either side of him just as below, only both these doors were shut. The light came from beneath the door to his left. He crossed over to it and, twisting the knob, pushed it open.

The light came from a kerosene lamp standing on a chest-of-drawers. Beyond was a huge brass bed. In one corner of the room stood a dressing table with bottles, jars, and vials of perfume and cosmetics arrayed in front of an oval mirror. In the mirror he saw Marie behind the half-open door.

Her reflection stared back at him in the glass. She was standing half in a closet, frozen in the act of hanging up the green gown she had been wearing. For a long moment

183

they stared at each other in the mirror in silence; then he stepped into the room.

"He'll kill you," she said. Her eyes flicked to the pistol, then back to his face.

"He'll try."

"You'd better get out of here. You may still have time." She stood in the closet doorway pressing the gown to her body. Behind her dresses and skirts on hangers were a row of men's slacks, shirts, and coats. Brother and sister were close, all right. Suddenly he understood just how close. He understood now the tension between the two of them when Villiers had been questioning her on the portico, and the fear he had seen in her eyes. *My brother is very strict,* she had said. He glanced toward the brass bed.

"Is he really your brother?" He lowered the gun.

She had seen the direction of his eyes.

"Yes," she said defiantly. Her eyes were flat, her bare shoulders rigid. He could see the cords standing out in her neck. He had the feeling that if he touched her, her whole body would begin to vibrate like a tuning fork.

"He'll kill you," she repeated in a low, strained voice.

"Like the others? Like the Sheriff?"

"I don't know what you're talking about."

"Yes, you do. But I'm not here about them. How did you do it?"

"Do what? What are you talking about?"

He grabbed her wrist. "Sharon! I want her back, you hear me."

The gown fell to the floor. "Who's Sharon?" Her lips curled mockingly. She wore a strapless white bra and half-slip. She did not glance at the fallen gown, but kept her eyes steadily on his. "For the last time—you'd better get out of here."

He raised the pistol and pressed the barrel into the hollow of her throat.

She did not even blink. "What did you do to Mosely? Claude won't like it if you've killed him."

He turned loose of her wrist, slapping her hard, and her head snapped back.

184

Slowly, deliberately her tongue licked the corner of her mouth leaving a tiny spot of blood. The blow had cut the inside of her mouth or tongue. She was smiling at him, her eyes, black and hypnotic, drawing him. He dropped the gun to his side. She took a step forward.

Her arms encircled his neck. Her tongue pushed against the roof of his mouth and he tasted the salt blood. The musky scent of her flesh filled his nostrils, her body strained against his, and he felt a traitorous stirring in his loins. He had wanted her from the first day she had come into his class. She had tempted him, taunted him, and he had tried to deny the lust he had for her. He should take her and be damned. Every fiber of him wanted her, but even while their tongues met, he was filled with a loathing too.

He pulled his mouth away from the greedy suction of hers, but her hand was fumbling between his legs insistently. She murmured his name; her eyes were glazed, the pupils dilated and he saw twin images of his own face in them, taut and flushed.

"Now!" she murmured. "Now!"

"What about him?"

"I don't care. I want you now—I want your child. He was right—I picked you all along." Her mouth fastened on his again and she moaned deep in her throat.

The pistol slid out of his hand to the floor. The sound it made was muffled by the blood drumming in his ears. He wanted her standing up without benefit of the brass bed she shared with Villiers. Her fingers were busy at his belt.

With a groan he pulled his mouth from hers and pushed her back. They stood staring at each other, his breath rasping in his throat, her breasts, almost out of the thin bra, heaving. The glazed look in her eyes began to fade and her breathing became regular.

She saw his eyes on the pouch dangling from her neck and she put her hand to it. He pulled her hand away.

"What did you do to Sharon?" His fingers pressed into her wrist. "It was because of me, wasn't it?"

He tightened his grip, clamping on bone.

185

"You're pathetic," she sneered. "What do the two of you do together? You can't even get it up. Oh, yes! I know all about that. You know why I picked you when I could have had any of those high school studs—especially Wade Haskill? Do you?"

He was silent, but suddenly he knew what she was going to say.

Her eyes glittered.

"Because next to you, they were all innocents. Lambs! But you—you have the same *hunger* Claude and I do. I sensed it right away—and I knew for certain that afternoon after classes. Even with your—problem, you almost took me right there." Her voice seemed to throb. "You can give me the kind of son I need."

He felt like he was burning up.

"Why can't Claude give you the *kind* of son you need?" he snarled.

"Because—," a shadow seemed to flicker behind her eyes for just an instant. "The child must be perfect. Claude, you see, is not just my brother." Her eyes stared right through him. "He and I are twins."

He loosened his grip on her wrist and almost let her go. She was lying. She had to be.

"You're surprised. I told you once there were things I could teach you."

The woman in the portrait downstairs with the name plate: Marie Villiers. His brain felt numb and the room took on a new, alien quality as though he had never been in any room before, as though he were seeing each object—bed, vanity, mirror for the first time in his life. He glimpsed his own face in the mirror—flushed, a mask of lust—and he knew she was right.

He contained the same evil she and her brother shared. He thought of Kay in the automobile wreck at the very moment he was fondling the pretty graduate student, wanting her as Kay was dying.

The face in the mirror smiled at him mockingly.

With a reeling sensation he tore his gaze away.

"The portrait," he said weakly.

"Yes. The portrait is of me. I only have a short time

186

left for childbearing." Her eyes drew him again.

"But you and I—we can share things right now. I care more about you than I do about Claude. That's why he is so jealous." Her face seemed to swim before him. "He knows how I feel about you."

Her free hand reached for him and stirred again an aching need. Her warm flesh pressed into him, her scent, sharp and sweet, was overpowering. He shut his eyes, yet in his mind he saw that mocking face in the glass again— his face. Kay was dead—and now Sharon might as well be. He groaned.

Her lips sought his, but opening his eyes, he turned his face away and took a long, ragged breath.

"You're going to bring her back—or I'm going to feed you to your snakes."

He squeezed her wrist so tightly his hand felt numb.

Her face had turned white and she twisted in his grasp. "Go—to—hell, you—bastard!"

Suddenly she dropped to one knee and was grabbing for the pistol. She moved so quickly he was caught by surprise. He barely had time to get his hand on the barrel as she brought the .32 up toward him. Trying to wrench it away from her, he lost his balance and fell over, freeing one of her hands. She was on him, her fingers clawing. She drove her knee into him, grazing his crotch. He hung grimly to the revolver in her hand. Nails raked the side of his neck. He twisted out from under her, finally wrenching the gun away, but her teeth sank into his hand. He yanked it away staring at the blood beginning to flow and froze.

Beside him the girl was still. She had heard it too—the faint creaking on the hallway steps. She gave him a swift look. He scrambled to his feet and, the pistol raised, stared out the bedroom door.

In the shadows of the landing he glimpsed a hunched shadow and the gleam of the shotgun's twin barrels pointed at him. He ducked back behind the doorjamb; at the same instant the shadow retreated and was cut off from his line of sight.

The girl had gotten to her feet and, seeing Dave's

187

movement, began pulling on a pair of levis. For thirty seconds there was complete silence from the stairwell, broken at last by Villiers' voice.

"Are you all right, Marie?"

She was rapidly buttoning on a blouse.

"Yes. I'm all right!"

"I suppose he has a gun?"

She stared at Dave, her eyes deadly as she tucked the shirt into the levis and smoothed down her hair. "Yes, he does. Be careful!" A touching example of sibling love, Dave thought.

"Ah, I thought so." The voice below took on a slightly pained tone. "That was very careless of Mosely. What did you do with him, by the way, Mr. Stewart?"

He wondered if Villiers was trying to trick him. Maybe he had found Mosely, untied him, and the Negro was out in the yard with a rifle waiting for him to show himself at the window. Yet when he tied Mosely, he had taken pains to conceal him well, and he was certain the man had at least a concussion if not a fractured skull. He glanced around the room to make sure he was not in line from the window and remained silent. His neck smarted from the girl's nails. He heard a faint tick in the wall as his ears strained for any trace of movement on the stairs.

"Mister Stewart," the voice echoed up the stairwell. "It appears we're at a stalemate. What do you propose?"

"Come up and we'll talk about it. Leave the shotgun down there."

"Very droll, Mr. Stewart. Now you listen to me. You have one minute to come down with your hands up and you can leave here unharmed."

"You forget who's holding trumps, Villiers. I've got your sister."

This time a long silence. When Villiers spoke again, his voice was very quiet, very cold. "You have thirty seconds to come down or you'll never come down alive."

"I'm comfortable up here." He looked at Marie. "With your charming sister."

All the color drained out of her face.

"You scum!" Villiers' voice was almost a scream.

188

"You're going to wish the snakes had gotten you."

Dave heard his footsteps going rapidly down the stairs.

He turned back to the girl. She had retreated to the far wall, her hands against it, her body leaning slightly forward. In the flickering light of the kerosene lamp her face seemed to have suddenly aged. Except for the absence of wrinkles, it had become almost hag-like. The nose and chin seemed sharper, her mouth hung slackly open, a trace of spittle showed in one corner. Her eyes glittered, and he thought of the lidless eyes gleaming up at him from the pit. As he started toward her, she broke for the door. He caught her and spun her around, facing him.

"He'll kill us both," she hissed. "God, why didn't you stay away from here?"

He grabbed her chin, his face close to hers. Her face seemed older now than the one in the portrait downstairs. "Listen to me! You're going to bring Sharon out of it! You'd better be able to. Or I'm going to tell brother dear things about us that he'll kill you for and save me the trouble." He released her.

She stared through him at something far beyond, something he could not see. Her eyes were almost all whites. He doubted whether she had heard anything he had said. Her fear and the silence filled the room like mist from outside. Her head was cocked in a listening attitude. The conviction that they must escape this room grew within him suddenly, and grasping her hand he dragged her toward the window. It was nearly twenty feet to the ground. Again he wondered if Mosely might be out there—or another servant, waiting.

He raised the window. There were some shrubs, wild and overgrown, directly below. Marie stood rigid, still in that listening attitude. He fumbled with the hook on the screen. Below and only a few yards from the house something moved in the shadows of an oak. Dave sprang away from the window.

"It's too late," Marie whimpered.

She stood frozen beside the window. Then he heard her quick intake of breath, and she turned toward the door. As she shrank into the corner, he heard the faint,

189

scuffing sounds coming up the steps. He ran to the doorway. He could see nothing in the hall or on the stairway, but heavy, shuffling footsteps were approaching the landing. He riveted his eyes on it.

It seemed an interminable time before the figure materialized amidst the shadows on the landing, a burly figure that was not Villiers and was taller than Mosely. Without pause or an upward glance, he shuffled forward on the landing. He turned up the remaining flight of stairs, head bowed, arms dangling loosely from the heavy shoulders. There was something in that shambling gait that was sub-human and the hairs rose on the back of Dave's neck.

Like a trained bear the figure kept coming, mounting the stairs, his face still in shadow.

"Stop right there!" Dave shouted. He gripped the cocked pistol in both hands forcing it steady.

The man ignored him.

"Get back!"

The face, a gray moon, rose above the top of the stairs. Below the matted hair the bulging eyes were desolate. Devoid of expression, emotion, the man's face was like a mask of gray clay, an imperfect mask, Dave suddenly saw. Where a nose should have been was only collapsed gristle.

"Get back!" He could not pull the trigger. "Damn," he panted. "Damn!"

Arms swaying, fingernails longer than talons, it lurched toward him filling the hallway with the sickly-sweet odor of carrion. For a moment he thought he would vomit. The hallway and the advancing horror swayed in front of him. Behind him, he heard Marie moan. Just as the creature reached out for him, he slammed the door and bolted it.

Marie moaned again, an animal sound from deep in the throat. He stepped back from the door and turned to her. She still cowered in the corner, a froth on her lower lip, her eyes fixed on the bolted door. The knob turned violently. It was a heavy oak door. Dave retreated to the window and looked out. In the thin moonlight,

190

their eyes glimmering up at him bleakly, three more of them stood by the shrubs. A sob tore from his chest.

The door knob quit turning. With a sound like tearing fabric the door seemed to fly apart. Marie screamed as it swarmed through where the door had been. Dave fired three times. Faint puffs of dust rose from the middle of the filthy denim shirt. Then it was on him.

He tried to dodge beneath one of its outstretched arms, but his feet left the floor and he was hurled into the chest-of-drawers with stunning impact. The pistol flew out of his hand and the kerosene lamp crashed to the floor.

He tried to roll under the bed. Flames were spreading near his feet. He was half-way under when the hands clamped around his throat and dragged him back out.

The smell of rotting flesh clogged his nostrils. Dimly he was aware of the orange glow spreading around him. But the hands clamped around his throat were cutting off his wind.

The gray, relentless face whirled above him, the mouth and place where the nose should have been, dark craters. He struggled to free himself from the cold, iron hands, but each moment his struggles grew feebler. The entire room began to spin in a darkening void. Yet, in the center of the darkness, remained a circle of light.

Suddenly the pressure on his throat relaxed. The circle of light became a nimbus around the gray face.

The hands left his throat and the face rose.

The thing was on fire.

Twin columns of flame were its legs; a smell of scorching flesh blotted out the other odor. Its arms flapped like grostesque wings at the flames. Dave realized one of his own pant legs was ablaze. He beat it out with his hands and staggered to his feet.

Some of the kerosene had spread under the bed and the mattress was on fire. Already the flames were licking up the dry walls. He looked around for Marie but she was gone. Another minute and the whole room would be engulfed in flames. In the center of the room the creature staggered. On the ceiling its shadow blended with the

191

reflection of the fire in a grotesque dance.

Already flames had cut Dave off from the window. The only way out was the door.

He ran out into the hall, saw the gleam on the landing, flung himself backward and the noise of the blast roared up the stairwell, raining fragments of plaster down on him from the ceiling in a cloud of white dust. Only then he remembered the .32.

Dave plunged back into the bedroom in time to see what was left of his attacker, the charred face encircled in a fiery halo, rebound off the wall into the window and disappear through splintering wood and glass into the darkness.

CHAPTER 16

ON the floor the pistol glowed red-hot in the flames. A blacksmith could not have gotten near enough to retrieve it with tongs.

Dave stumbled back into the hallway, flopped down on his belly, and began crawling. Cautiously he peeped through the banister slats at the landing, but no Villiers. He sensed his presence though; probably he was waiting just below the landing with the shotgun, still believing Dave might have the pistol. Otherwise what would have prevented him from coming up? He must certainly be aware of the fire by now. Smoke was pouring down the stairwell and the crackling of the flames could be heard even if Marie had not already told him. There was a slight chance Villiers had gone outside, if he had heard his creature crash through the window, yet Dave had no intention of gambling on going down the stairs.

With the fire Villiers would be growing desperate. He would have to try to put it out soon and that meant he would be sending those others up—the ones Dave had seen out the window. He had fired three times and not even slowed down the thing which had splintered the door. His throat felt like a tight noose was around it, and he could barely swallow. In another minute the fire might spread out here into the hallway. He had to get out fast.

He crawled to the other door across from the bedroom

193

and tried it. The door swung open. From the light of the flames across the hall, he could see chairs, boxes, crates stacked in a jumble. The room was evidently used only for storage. He rose and went quickly to the window on the opposite side of the room. Through the mist he made out the shape of the barn no more than a hundred yards away.

None of *them* were visible below.

He wondered how many there were.

Quietly he slid the sash open and thrust one leg out. He had the sensation that what was happening was a horrendous nightmare from which he rightfully should have awakened some time ago. Ducking under the sash he pulled his other leg out and, for a moment, perched precariously on the sill, his pulse hammering, then pushed himself into space.

The impact toppled him over, and pain spurted up his left leg from the ankle. He staggered to his feet and began hobbling across the yard. The pain was agonizing.

Behind him he heard the kitchen door open.

He lunged for the black walnut, diving behind the trunk as bark and twigs exploded around him, their fragments stinging his face and arms. The thunder of the shotgun echoed from the porch.

Keeping the walnut between himself and Villiers, he scrambled up and began hopping toward the pines like an absurd giant rabbit, coming down on his left foot every third hop, his teeth clenched against the pain. Looking back he saw Villiers leap off the porch.

Villiers would cut him down before he reached the pines. He swerved to his right and fell.

He began scuttling nearly sideways on his hands and knees until he came to a barbed wire fence. Dropping under it, he glimpsed Villiers under the walnut, shotgun broken, and fumbling shells into the breech. Around the corner of the house three figures shambled toward him. Dave rose and limped across the barnyard to the refuge of the barn. Inside were the sharp odors of fresh manure and old hay. Somewhere close an unseen animal snorted. He looked around. There was only the one entrance.

194

Ahead of him was a ladder. Grasping the rungs he hauled himself up into the loft and pitched face-forward into the musty hay, panting.

From below came a high-pitched bray that raised the hackles on his neck, followed by a sound like the crack of a pistol shot. He turned and peered over the edge of the loft.

One moment there was only mist and then they were there—three figures in the barn entrance. Two halted; one came on in that eerie shamble. It stopped at the ladder, its dark upturned face like a mole's, sniffing a scent. It started up the ladder.

He scrambled away, wading through the hay. Through the loft window he saw Villiers waiting in the barnyard below with the shotgun. The moonlight shone pale across the loft floor and he searched for any other way out. By now Villiers knew he did not have the pistol and had sent *them* in to flush him out.

As the hulking shadow reached the top of the ladder, Dave's eyes fell on a square opening in one corner where the roof angled down to meet the wall. He hopped, tripped, crawled toward it while the thing behind him followed relentlessly through the hay. Reaching the hole, he peered down into darkness. But something was down there, he could hear it moving. Suddenly came the sharp crack again like an engine backfire. A mule was down there kicking the dry planks of its stall. He looked toward his pursuer, now only a few yards away. As the figure crossed the patch of moonlight from the loft window, he saw it was a woman.

Her thick hair hung long and her body was heavy and muscular. Enormous breasts pushed against the sack-like garment she wore. Her protruding eyes stared through and beyond him, beyond the wall he crouched against, beyond, he felt, this world. Her flesh was the color of dead leaves. She lurched toward him, her arms raised as though to embrace him. He looked down into the stall, then back at her. The panicky animal below seemed infinitely less dreadful.

He dropped through the hole into the stall, the pain

195

shooting from his leg through his entire body.

Hooves scythed past his head an instant after he landed, thundering into the planks at the back of the stall. He rolled against the side of the stall and fought his way to his feet, waiting for the hooves to cleave his skull open or trample him. The mule sidled against him, pushing him into the wall.

Then he saw the short rope around the mule's neck. The animal was tied to a thick post below the feed trough to keep it from rearing. He scrambled in front of the mule to keep from being crushed. Its eyes rolled frantically. Dust and straw filtered down from above. Any second she might come down through the opening used for pitching hay into the stall from above.

Dave looked around for some kind of weapon, but there was nothing he could find in the darkness. He tried the door and it did not budge. Villiers and the other two were out there, even if he should manage to open it. The rabbit was snared.

Sweat dropped into his eyes, stinging and blinding them. His heart felt like it was coming out of his chest. Yet, despite his fear, he felt amazingly clear-headed. He was listening for any sound beyond his heart and the stamping of the mule. If she came into the stall, there was one chance he could stop her if he were quick and clever enough. He stood against the feed trough, his fingers splayed against the rough planks, his eyes on the opening above.

Something gouged into his thigh. The damn beast had bitten him. He struck the mallet head with his elbow. As the mule's head jerked back, a leg, followed by another leg, appeared above, then she was in the stall. The mule screamed; its rear hooves drummed against the planks.

She came at him quickly around one side of the mule. He circled toward the back. In another moment he would be squarely behind those murderous hooves. She lunged for him, catching part of his T-shirt, but he tore away and scuttled under the plunging animal's belly, reaching the other side unscathed. She followed, bent-low

196

and, just as her head emerged on his side, he kicked it as hard as he could with his sound leg. Already off-balance, she toppled into the flailing rear hooves.

She rose, but went down again under the now beserk animal's thrashing hind legs. Twice more she tried to rise, her head misshapen, yet strangely bloodless, then she lay motionless.

A froth covered the animal's mouth and its flanks were wet. It shifted its weight off the body. It had quit screaming, now only panting and groaning, its sides heaving. Dave clutched the planks that made up one of the side walls and gagged. Then he moved around to the front of the stall again. He did not look at the crumpled figure anymore.

Other than the sound of the mule's labored breathing and his own heart, the barn seemed silent But outside Villiers had heard and knew where he was exactly. And gradually Dave thought he heard someone else breathing outside the door of the stall. He held his own breath and moved away from the door.

They were out there, of course, and would be coming in to see if he was dead. With the fire at the house Villiers could not afford to wait any longer. No more cat-and-mouse games, he had to make sure of Dave then get back with his ghastly helpers and try to put out the blaze. The mule stamped nervously, but Dave heard the metallic sound of the key turning in the padlock.

The mule snorted, its eyeballs showing white in the gloom. Dave grasped the rope, his fingers fumbling for the knot under the feed trough that held the animal. The mule butted him with its bony skull and he again jabbed his elbow into the soft nose. His fingers wrenched at the knot in the darkness, his breath rattling harshly in his throat as though he were strangling. The knot was stubborn and the mule tossed its head, drawing the rope taut.

A sob tore from his throat. He yanked the rope down with one hand to give the knot slack. He heard a rasping sound of the padlock being drawn from its hasp.

The knot gave a little bit, but his slick fingers could

not seem to unravel its final intricacy. He wiggled it with clumsy hands and wriggled a forefinger into a tiny loop that began to grow.

The door to the stall sprang open and Villiers stood there, the shotgun levelled, his eyes blazing with a pale light. With two fingers hooked under the loop, Dave gave one last desperate pull and the knot dissolved. The mule, suddenly free, reared up, knocking him into the side of the stall, blocking Villiers' line of fire.

Dave slapped the animal's ribs. The front legs came down, all four legs bunched, and the mule sprang for the freedom beyond the door. Villiers eyes widened. He ducked to one side. The mule's flank brushed him, causing him to jerk the shotgun slightly left as he pulled the trigger. The blast ripped past Dave and tore through planks.

The mule's nudge had caused him to fire off-balance, and the recoil of the .12 guage sent Villiers sprawling on his back. Dave saw his stunned face as he dove on top of him. But even then Villiers managed to get a foot up, catching Dave in the stomach and catapulting him, head over heels, into the dirt. For a moment his breath left him. He tried to scramble up and saw Villiers on his knees reaching for the shotgun and saw, almost at the same instant, the mule wheel with a scream at the barn entrance, and start back toward them. He fell back against the stall while Villiers swung the shotgun toward him. The twin muzzles were almost resting on him when the drumming hooves caused Villiers to swing his head around. He barely had time to raise one arm in front of his face; then the hooves pounded over him.

The mule wheeled once more as it came up against the solid wall at the rear of the barn and started again for the entrance; the pounding hooves gouged up chunks of clay that rose high in the air and spun lazily before falling to earth again. The mule with a scream broke past something in the entrance and galloped out into the barnyard.

Villiers lay still in a swath of moonlight. Dave crawled over to him. Blood bubbled from his mouth. His eyes were already clouding like glass someone had breathed on.

198

A movement in the barn entrance caught Dave's eye. One of *them* was there, shambling toward him.

He grabbed for the shotgun, knowing already it would be ineffectual against the advancing horror. It was the one that must have caused the mule to wheel in panic and trample Villiers. His finger curled over the twin triggers. He would aim for the head waiting until the thing was right on top of him and let loose with both barrels. He remembered then that one barrel was already empty. The figure was moving toward him slowly—so slowly it was as though it were walking under water. It swayed, took a lurching step forward, then another step and toppled face-forward in the dirt. The sickly-sweet odor of decay rose from it. He looked away, back to Villiers. The eyes were completely glazed over now; the blood had stopped bubbling from his mouth. Dave groped for his wrist and found no pulse.

Slowly he got to his feet and stumbled out of the barn, still clutching the shotgun. The ground was bathed in a red light.

Another one lay by the fence gate. He stepped over it carefully like a man avoiding a deep puddle. Behind him, he heard a bray like inhuman laughter and turning, saw the mule at the far corner of the fence, its ivory eyes rolling.

He put the shotgun down, climbed over the gate, reached back through the barbed wire and pulled the gun through the strands and started toward the house. The light on the ground was cast by the flames. Tongues of fire twisted and darted from the second floor windows. The flames had burst through the roof and a line of fire ran along the ridge pole toward the kitchen and smokehouse. Silhouetted against the back porch near the steps was the squat shape of Marie's Volkswagen.

He hobbled up to it and saw nobody was inside, but the keys were in the ignition. He reached inside and pocketed them. Heat pressed against him and inside the house he heard a timber crack. Flaming shingles had begun drifting off the roof. They floated overhead like fiery birds, landing in the trees and grass. It was impossible

199

that she was still in the house—even in the kitchen where the flames had not yet reached, the heat and smoke were intense.

Then he saw the door to the storm cellar flung open against the kitchen wall. He climbed up onto the porch, the heat, an invisible hand, pushing against his face. He peered down the steep wooden steps into the cellar. Fruitjars, reflecting the flames, gleamed redly up at him from spider-webbed shelves. As he started down the stairs on the swollen ankle, a smell of rank earth struck him and he felt a revulsion as though he were descending into a grave. And with the speed the fire was making, it would be his own grave if he were not quick.

At the bottom he was in a small room no more than ten-by-twelve feet; the floor and three walls were of earth, the wall to his right was of ancient brick. Against it stood a rack of shelves high as a man, stocked with Mason jars, some empty, some filled with a dark, gummy substance. There was nothing else.

As he started to retreat back up the stairs, he noticed the rack of shelves was not flush against the bricks. The far end seemed to angle out almost a foot further than the near one. Crossing over, he peered behind it and saw a thin crack of wavering light. He pulled against the edge of the rack and it swung out easily, revealing a small wooden door. Many of these old mansions, he remembered, were reputed to have a secret room where they hid the silver from the marauding Yankees during the Civil War. He shoved the door open, ducked down, and entered a low room, much larger than the other. The moment he stepped in he was greeted by an awful stench and nearly gagged.

Ahead of him a brick arch rose that he realized supported part of the house above. Through the arch he could see a table. It was covered with a black cloth. Breathing through his mouth, he approached it. A black wooden cross stood in the middle, flanked by two black candles in tarnished silver holders. The candles were not lit, the illumination came from a kerosene lantern on the floor that revealed a sneakered foot protruding from

200

behind the make-shift altar.

The reek of corrupted flesh was almost unbearable. Slowly he forced himself to look at the boy's face. It was bloated and looked like a fantastic caricature, but he had no doubt it must be Bobby Bowen. The hot gorge rose in his throat and for a moment he thought he would vomit.

"My God," he muttered. "My God!"

But even then she did not hear him. Her back was to him; she had laid the shovel down next to the lantern and was lifting something from the freshly dug hole in the clay floor. It was a metal tackle box. She opened the lid, stared at the contents, and he glimpsed the green bills neatly arranged, before she snapped the lid shut, and straightening up, turned.

Her eyes widened and for a moment she did not move, did not even appear to breathe. Then she bolted around the altar toward the door. She moved fast; she was almost out the door when he caught up with her. If she had dropped the tackle box, she probably would have made it, slamming the door shut and trapping him.

As it was, she held the box against her stomach, her free hand clawing at his face. Her mouth worked, but no sound came. She tried to knee him in the groin. He slapped her twice, then yanked her, spitting like a cat, toward the steps. Smoke billowed down on them, growing denser by the moment, and they began coughing. He groped for the steps, yanking her by the wrist. He still held the shotgun in the other hand. She stumbled and fell; he hauled her to her feet.

The smoke blinded him and he almost fell over the bottom step, causing him to drop the shotgun. He began groping up the stairs with his free hand, pulling her along behind him. He was choking. The heat rushed down in a fierce wave against his face, but he could see nothing. Panic surged through him. Every nerve in his body signaled him to go back, and he hesitated a moment even while a part of his brain knew that to turn back would mean certain death by asphyxiation. He started forward and the rectangle of doorway appeared through the

201

smoke above him, and he could see the porch ceiling ablaze.

Behind him the girl almost climbed up his back.

"Hurry," she screamed.

Even as she spoke, part of the porch roof collapsed; it seemed to come down on them almost in slow-motion, disintegrating as it hit the porch and showering them with sparks and flaming debris. They ducked, protecting their eyes with their arms, and when they looked up again they saw one of the posts that supported the roof had fallen directly across the entrance, its flames barring their way.

Marie rushed past him, but the flames sent her cringing back. He saw them dancing crazily in the dilated pupils of her eyes. Her face was contorted and her lips writhed out one word to him. It took him a moment to grasp it.

"Dynamite!"

He stared at her stupidly, his heart seeming to contract.

"The smokehouse," she gasped. She broke into a fit of coughing.

He looked at the post, then started for it with his hands, but the heat was too intense. He turned back, looking desperately for something he could roll it away with, and his eyes lighted on the tackle box. Within a few seconds he wrested it from her, and holding it by the handle slammed it against the post, raining sparks down on them.

He lifted the tackle box again, feeling the metal already turning hot, and shoved it with all his strength against the fiery post, felt it roll back. Suddenly he could hold the scorching metal no longer and dropped the box. It clattered down the steps. Marie gave a little cry and started back down.

"Don't be a fool!" he shouted, grabbing her wrist.

The entrance above was clear. He pulled her up on the porch. The kitchen and smokehouse were engulfed in flames, the heat nearly unbearable against their skin.

They were off the porch in a heart-beat, and he was

202

already past the Volkswagen almost to the black walnut when he realized he no longer held her wrist. He turned and she was not there.

Very clearly against the flames he saw her in the Volkswagen, her head bent to where the ignition key should be, saw her look up at him, her eyes like splintered glass as she began scrabbling at the door. She was half-way out when the ground struck him in the face.

SHARON awoke. There seemed to be dozens of fireflies gleaming outside the window. It was strange because they were stationary. She felt immensely thirsty. Despite the room's dimness, she saw that someone had moved the chest-of-drawers to the foot of the bed—then she realized all the furniture in the room was out of place. For several moments she was only puzzled, then fear tightened her throat. She was in a strange room.

She blinked her eyes. She was dreaming and now she had to will herself awake, she thought. She closed her lids and opened them again. The fireflies were still at the window—unblinking. She stared at them for some time. They were lights in far away windows—many windows. She rose abruptly up in the bed.

"Easy," a voice said near the door, a cool female voice, yet with a slight tremor in it. "Lie back down."

A light came on. The woman was pretty, in her mid-twenties, and wearing a starched white uniform.

Hospital, Sharon thought. I'm in a hospital. Why?

The woman had picked up a telephone receiver. "Get Doctor Jardine down here. Hurry."

She put down the receiver and smiled at Sharon. "We were pretty worried about you."

Sharon stared at her. She knew something had happened to her or she would not be here. She wondered what it was. She felt no pain and she had no trouble moving her arms and legs. A dozen questions sprang to mind, but the first words that came out of her mouth were: "Could I please have a glass of water?"

203

CHAPTER 17

THE first thing he noticed, besides the loud ringing in his ears, was the back of his hands—they were bleeding. Then he saw his pants were smouldering. Tiny fires were all around him in the grass. The house had vanished. Part of the staircase stuck up from the foundation like a fractured bone; the tall brick chimneys remained, but nothing else.

He was surrounded by shattered tree limbs, fragments of wood, and particles of glass. He was lying on his belly against the black walnut tree.

Slowly, painfully he crawled over to the Volkswagen. It rested on its side, a mass of twisted metal, the windows blown out. Beneath the wreckage an arm stuck out at a grotesque angle. He reached out and felt for the pulse that he knew was not there. The flesh on her arm began to sag, the muscles became flabby. The veins in the wrist stood out and the skin suddenly felt dry and coarse to his touch. He gazed at her arm dully. A shudder passed through him. Her face was hidden and smashed, and he was grateful he could not witness its transformation.

He held her wrist for some time before it occurred to him to let go. Finally he did, and blinking, got stiffly to his feet. He swayed, steadied himself, then forced his feet to move in the direction of the trees. He remembered that he still had the Volkswagen keys in his pocket. He pulled them out and looked at them as if they were

204

some repulsive alien object. He flung them into the deep brush.

When he reached the place where he had left Mosely, the Negro was gone. He searched the brush and found the strip of shirt he had torn to make a gag. A little further he found the other strip of shirt with which he had bound Mosely to the tree. The man himself would be impossible to find in the darkness. He turned and stumbled back toward the drive.

On his injured leg it was a long walk back to the Pinto. Just before he reached it, he heard the first siren coming from the direction of town. He crossed the road to the car. He waited until he saw the blue flashing lights pull into Villiers' drive before he started the Pinto. He eased the small car out onto the road and with the headlights off drove away fast in the opposite direction. He was a mile away before he switched on the lights.

His first impulse had been to stay and explain what had happened, but then he knew he could not. Without Mosely there was not even the remotest possibility he would be believed. At best he would be committed; at worst, they would probably claim he killed Villiers, dynamited the house, and caused Marie's death. They would be right about the last part. And what would they make over the rest of the bodies? When Villiers died, they had collapsed like balloons when the air is let out. And there was Bobby Bowen's body. He wondered if the boy had been like the others.

Then he suddenly swerved over to the edge of the road and stopped. His hands were trembling on the wheel, and he could no longer fight off the wave of panic that now engulfed him. With Marie dead Sharon could be dead or locked into that other kind of limbo forever. And he would be responsible.

"My God!" he said. "Don't let it be."

He had to know. He had to get to a telephone. If only his hands would stop shaking so he could keep the car out of the ditch. He pressed them hard against the wheel and noticed then for the first time that they were burned. But the pain cleared away some of the panic.

205

After a minute he was able to control the trembling and get the car going again, but he could not stop the fear that squeezed his insides.

IT looked like a battlefield, Holly thought, as he surveyed the scene from the barn entrance. Fanned by a light breeze that had sprung up, the grass fire was sweeping toward the barn. It revealed three bodies in its path; one at the gate to the barnyard and the two others stretched near him. Counting the one he had found in a stall, the one under the Volkswagen, and the charred remains of the one in front of where the house used to be, the total came to six. It was as bad as anything he had seen in 'Nam.

He had dragged the one out of the stall into the open where he could examine it better. Part of the skull was caved in, but it was a Negro woman—a woman he thought he recognized. He had thrown her in the drunk tank one Saturday night recently after she had almost run into his squad car. She had been driving a borrowed Caddy and he had found a nearly empty bottle of T-Bird rolling around on the floorboards. She had been so drunk she could barely get out of the car. He thought her name was Annie Mae something or other.

He eyed the advancing flames.

If the fire department did not get the lead out of their butts, he would have to move the bodies himself to keep them from being Bar-B-Que, a task he did not relish since two of them had evidently been dead for some time. Villiers had apparently died only recently, his body was not yet cold. He had an idea the one under the Volkswagen was Marie Villiers, but he would not know until some help came. As soon as he and Floyd had found the two bodies up by the remains of the house, he had called the Highway Patrol and the firemen in town, but nobody had shown yet. Where the hell were they anyway? He wished he had not left Floyd poking in the house's rubble.

206

He was breathing shallowly through his mouth because of the smell which seemed to be getting worse by the second. The stench rose from the one a few feet away from the entrance. Holly stared at it in outrage then turned away and started out into the barnyard. A sucking noise, obscene and loud, caused him to spin back around in time to see the corpse's belly rising like a yeasty bubble. It burst before his horrified gaze, spewing a ghastly yellowish substance and releasing an unspeakable odor. At the same instant, the staring eyeballs slid back into the skull, the entire face began sliding away like dark wax and Holly caught the gleam of bone beneath.

He did not look anymore. He had never seen anything like that in 'Nam. He staggered to the fence, leaned over, and vomited.

When he finally looked up, he saw the body near the gate. The fire was nearly to the gate now, but he did not have to worry about moving the corpse because there was very little of it left except the bones. In terror yet fascination, he turned to gaze at Annie Mae a few yards behind him, half-expecting the flesh to be oozing from her bones like dark jelly. But she remained intact.

What in God's name had he come upon here? It was so obscene and unreal he would have thought he was hallucinating except for the awful stench of corruption in his nostrils.

Let the fire have them—except for Annie Mae. She was still recognizably human—his one anchor to sanity in the midst of hell. The fire would reach her in another minute. Still breathing shallowly he began to drag her further from the flames. The heat pressed against his eyeballs like fingers and greasy smoke arose from the burning corpses.

"Jesus," he gasped. "Jesus Christ!"

Tears filled his eyes. His mind fumbled for some explanation for those bodies putrefying in a matter of moments.

They had rotted so fast because they had been dead a long time.

He remembered Sharon Gates, and Stewart wanted

207

him to investigate the grave that her kid brother thought had been dug up.

He should have listened. Incredible as it seemed, he should have listened.

He had heard about such things, even read about them, but never believed—until now. To violate the dead and their rest, to pull them from their graves, to do to them what must have been done here filled him with horror, yet rage too.

Let the fire do its work! My God, yes!

He clenched his teeth against a sudden wave of heat as flames ran up the front of the barn. The dry wood popped like firecrackers. He turned loose of Annie Mae and watched as flames shot through the tin roof.

"Let it burn," he muttered. "Let the whole damned place be wasted."

He cried quietly and steadily, the tears leaving trails in his soot-blackened face. He felt like the custodian of Hell.

GEORGE Burke watched dawn seep over the town. He sat on a bench in the court-square, alone in the cold gray light. There was no traffic yet, and the streetlights still burned. He sat silent and motionless, drained by all he had seen in the past few hours.

It was the biggest story of his life, yet even now he suspected he would never know all of it.

He had followed the firemen out to the old Graves place. They had been too late to save the barn, but had managed to stop the fire from spreading into the woods. He had seen three charred skeletons and the bodies of Villiers and his sister, as well as another woman, an Annie Mae Willis who had been dead and supposedly buried for a week. Holly said he had dragged Villiers and the Willis woman from the barn before the fire reached it, but that he had been unable to save the other bodies which he claimed had been dead for some time.

After they had found the opening beneath the rubble of the house, he had followed them down into the secret basement and seen the altar with its black cross and nearby the bloated corpse of little Bobby Bowen. They had found another smaller room with another corpse which had no visible signs of decay but showed deep marks around the neck indicating recent strangulation. The body had been identified by one of the firemen as Rufus Johnson, a local black who had been missing for the past couple days.

Even as he had taken the pictures, he had felt ashamed.

One of the state cops had found the scorched tackle box with over eighty thousand dollars in it. They speculated it might have belonged to old man Sheed, but that was something that could never be proved.

Finally around three a. m. Holly had gotten a court order from old Judge Summers. They had gone out to the Negro graveyard where Bobby Bowen had disappeared and opened the grave of Louis Biggs. When the shovels scraped against the cheap coffin, a kind of sigh seemed to escape all their lungs at once. Their eyes had bored into the lid like termites, but when it was lifted revealing emptiness, each man had looked away quickly, avoiding the others' eyes.

Burke had left them clustered around the open grave and had gone back to write the story. It was one with several big gaps. The official police version was that the house had caught fire, exploding the dynamite Villiers had stored in the smokehouse and was using to blast stumps. The explosion had flipped the Volkswagen over on Marie Villiers.

Right now an autopsy was being performed on Villiers himself to determine cause of death. The doctor's preliminary report said that Villiers' chest and ribs had been crushed, and the state cops theorized that he had been trampled to death by a mule they had found in the barnyard.

But neither Holly nor the state boys would comment on those other bodies. Why were they scattered all over the place if they were already dead, and how and why had the fire started? Maybe Villiers was trying to carry them from the barn to the house hoping the fire and dynamite would obliterate them. Since a woman's remains had been found in the barn and two of the other bodies nearby, that might indicate they were kept in the barn, although one was found in the front of the house and two in the cellar. But why were they kept at all? There was no rational explanation, but then Villiers and his sister could not have been sane. From what Holly had said about the state of advanced decay the bodies were in before they were burned and from what he had seen, himself, of Bobby Bowen, Villiers made Nero seem normal by comparison. He had read of people who robbed graves and used the organs of corpses for some sort of satanic rites. Villiers must have been engaged in a cult de morte. But all this was simply speculation.

He had confined his story to a straight-forward account of what he had seen, factual, accurate, no speculation whatever. It was still in his typewriter in the office. Instead of telephoning it in to *The Commercial Appeal* in Memphis and the wire service when he had finished it, he had come out here. He told himself he needed some fresh air after recreating the horrors of the night, but it was more than that. He did not want to file the story. It was the story of a lifetime, but he did not want to file it, and although he knew he was going to—he wanted to postpone it a while longer. Villiers had perpetrated an outrage on those who were presumed to be beyond outrageous acts, and he most certainly had murdered Bobby Bowen and Rufus Johnson and quite possibly Sheed. Yet it was not reluctance to deal with the sensational and horrible that had kept Burke from telephoning the story in right away. Once the story went out (and it would make all the major papers across the country and all three networks' evening news telecasts), the people would start pouring into town—the sensation seekers, the curious, the ghoulish—like the time he had covered the sewer cave-in as a young reporter for *The Times-Picayune*. Only this time for weeks they would come, maybe months. The town he had grown to think of as his town, small,

210

quiet, yes even dull, would be known hereafter as *that place,* and the town would change. He did not want it to change, at least not in his lifetime, but it would. Some local entrepreneur would start taking tourists out to the Graves place, showing them points of interest. Some idiots would set up souvenir stands selling postcards and plastic models of vampires, ghouls, and zombies. Bobby Bowen's parents were going to be put through a new ordeal of TV cameras and microphones, crank callers, and sob-sisters. The raw wound of the boy's death would be probed again and again, never allowed to heal. The mother of one of the boys who had died in the muddy sewer ditch had been institutionalized and who could say he had not shared at least a small part of the responsibility in the name of news-gathering and his own eagerness to promote himself through somebody else's tragedy? Angie Bowen was already on the verge of a nervous breakdown. This new kind of pressure might send her over the edge, permanently.

Yes, this was his town and he felt a kinship with it. He knew most of its people. He did not want to see what was going to happen to the town. The street lamps were off now. The first rays of sun struck the top of the courthouse tower. Down the street he saw Dayton Phelps in his milk truck. Dayton worked hard. He had four kids and worked at a filling station in addition to his milk route.

Burke stared across the street at his office. As he watched, the sunlight stretched over the faded bricks and onto the sidewalk. With a sigh he rose stiffly from the bench and started across the street. Even if he did not telephone the story into the Memphis papers, it would make no difference. If no one ever wrote a word about what had happened last night, the people in town would still know and would never be able to forget, certainly not Angie Bowen. He wished for her sake, and maybe his, that the boy's body had been consumed in the fire like those others. At least then she would have been spared something. He thought of the photographs he had taken for Holly and himself and felt again a stab of shame. He had

211

the negatives and he could make some money from them.

He would insist on a by-line and copyright the story. In a couple of hours the Memphis media would be here, but he had a big jump on them. He might even work a book out of it, he thought, opening the office door. A book is where the money could be made and with the photographs . . . . He knew the Bowens and would be less pushy and more understanding than outsiders. He slumped in his chair behind the desk and eyed the copy in the typewriter. Smiling sardonically he reached for the telephone, knowing there would be no book—at least not by him. Maybe he lacked the toughness to write it—but he would see to it this year that somebody, some other newspaperman, would record the truth for him. He picked up the phone to call Memphis. When the re-write man for the *Commercial* asked him did he have any art to go with the copy, Burke paused. The voice repeated the question, eager, impatient.

"No," Burke replied. "No art."

"That's a shame." The voice lost some of its enthusiasm.

"Yeah," Burke said. "Isn't it? For some reason my flash attachment isn't working. I've got to get the damn thing fixed."

HOLLY walked down the steps of Paxton's Funeral Home, which had been turned into a temporary morgue, glad to be away from the smell of death. Gratefully he breathed in the scent of fresh dew on the glistening grass. Since the call last night from a farmer living over a mile from Villiers reporting the fire and explosion, he had not had a moment to relax, and he told himself it was not over yet. Soon the out-of-town reporters would begin flocking in and there would be more questions. He had told Floyd to keep his mouth shut, that he would answer all the questions. Floyd had not seen those bodies corrupt in a few heartbeats as he had. He had not told

212

anyone else about it, not even Floyd, nor about what he had begun to suspect. He wanted to keep his badge, and he had no desire to spend time at the funny farm. He had purposely left those putrid bodies to be purified by the fire.

He did not believe the fire was accidental. Somebody else had been out there, somebody who had possibly set the fire to get revenge for what Villiers had done to the body of a relative. He had already questioned Rufus Johnson's widow. Her sister had sworn Sarah Johnson had spent the whole night with her, but with niggers you could never tell whether they were lying. The mule they thought killed Villiers belonged to Johnson. It was weird— Villiers killed Johnson and Johnson's mule finished Villiers. Sarah Johnson had mentioned that Annie Mae Willis' grave had been disturbed. He would have to have that one dug up too, although it was pointless because he knew damn well she was lying in the funeral home with half her skull mashed in. The state cops were trying to collect dental records on Biggs so they could identify which one of those burned bodies was his. Sometime today he would have to talk to Biggs' family to see where they were last night.

His own view was that whoever started the fire had performed a public service. He had little doubt that Villiers had murdered Loomis, who had somehow stumbled onto his secret when he went out there searching for Bobby Bowen. Then, there was the matter of the snakes. One of the state cops had found an outhouse crawling with cottonmouths, Villiers' own private snake pit. Clyde Lee had been nailed by cottonmouths. Knowing these things in advance, he might have set the fire himself, Holly thought, or at least handed whoever did it the match.

He reached his car and radioed Thelma that he was going to the hospital. Earlier she had radioed him that Clyde Lee was improving. His condition was now listed as good.

As he drove, his eyes burned with weariness and his mind drifted back to the events of the night—the flames,

213

the decomposing bodies, the opening of Biggs' grave. A strange thing had happened to him; in the midst of all that grimness he had begun thinking of Delores—of Delores, not with rollers in her hair and that whiney tone of voice she sometimes took on, but as she had been when they were courting—soft, feminine, with a sexy, throaty laugh. And the sight of all that death had made him realize that Kevin needed a Daddy, and he needed the kid. Kids were life. Maybe when he got some time later in the day he would drive out to her folks' farm.

He nosed the car into the hospital lot, parking it beside a dusty Pinto that he recognized. It was the one that Sharon Gates and Stewart had been in when they had wanted him to open Biggs' grave. How had Stewart known? Something about Scott believing Bobby was in that grave. Holly got out of the patrol car and ran his finger over the hood, leaving a trail in the thick dust. He shook his head and walked into the antiseptic smell of the hospital.

SHARON had come out of it about ten-thirty, Sam had told him over the telephone. They were going to keep her in Memphis several days and run more tests. She did not remember anything since going to bed the night before. The doctors would not let Dave see her right away although she had asked for him. He had told Sam he would drive up in the morning. He had left the pay telephone in front of the closed drugstore and driven home, praying that he would not bump into Mrs. Anson going up to his room. He had been lucky, she was not at home, and he remembered that Tuesday nights she played Bridge, sometimes not getting home before midnight.

He had pulled off his burned clothes and poured himself a stiff drink from a fifth of Scotch he kept in a dresser drawer. He had coated his palms with Petroleum Jelly. Although they hurt, the burns were not severe. He heard Mrs. Anson come in. He knew he should take a shower, but he sat on the edge of the bed, his mind awhirl, and poured himself another drink. Ten-thirty,

214

Sam had said. Ten-thirty Marie had died.

He fell asleep for a while and dreamed of Marie reaching out to him and, when she started to embrace him, he saw that her face was gray and rotting and her eyes desolate. Sometime before dawn he awoke shaking and soaked with sweat. He showered, dressed, wadded the scorched clothes into a bundle and drove out into the country and burned them.

Driving back to town he picked up the local news on the car radio. Two county residents had died during the night, the newscaster announced, as the result of a fire and explosion. They were identified as Claude Villiers, a farmer, and his younger sister Marie, a senior at the local high school. The brief report concluded that authorities were still investigating. There was no mention of Bobby Bowen's body or any others at the scene. Dave switched the radio off. He was suddenly hungry. He realized he had not eaten in twenty-four hours.

At sunrise he ate breakfast at a diner out on the highway, then drove to the local hospital. He had promised Sam he would look in on Lucy. She was in good spirits. Sam had called her immediately about Sharon, and drugs had lessened the pain from her hip. She did not seem overly pleased to see him, however, and he doubted that he could ever overcome her antipathy toward him, but he was not going to lose sleep over it. After a few strained minutes, he left her. At the pay telephone in the corridor he called Simmons and told him why he would not be at school.

Hanging up the receiver, he turned around to face Holly McAfee. The man was red-eyed and haggard.

"I need to talk to you, Stewart, as soon as I check on my deputy. Stick around."

Dave felt a hollow feeling in his stomach, but kept his voice steady: "I'm on my way to Memphis and I'm in a hurry. Can it wait?" He jammed his hands into his pockets. What if they had found Mosely?

Holly watched him intently. "I reckon you've heard about what happened last night?"

"On the car radio. Marie Villiers was in one of my

215

classes. I still can hardly believe it."

"Yeah. Since she was a student of yours, maybe you won't mind me askin' you a question."

"Go ahead." If they had found Mosely, he knew he was in for it.

"Where were you last night between eight and eleven?" Holly's inflamed eyes were hard.

"Part of the time I was driving around."

"Anybody with you?"

"No."

"Where'd you drive?"

Dave shrugged. "Around town and out in the country."

Holly nodded. "Your car got a lot of dust on it."

"I hit some back roads."

"Out near the Villiers' place?"

Dave smiled faintly. "If I knew where the Villiers place was, I could tell you if I was near it." He met Holly's gaze steadily. "Are you trying to accuse me of something?"

"Do you expect to be accused?"

"No," Dave said softly. "I don't. Now if you'll excuse me, I really am in a hurry." He started down the corridor toward the parking lot. He had almost reached the waiting room when Holly called after him:

"What happened to your leg?"

He turned. "Fell off the porch. Don't tell my landlady." He grinned sheepishly. "She'd throw me out if she knew I got crocked."

"Bullshit!" Holly said. "You never hurt your leg that way."

Staring into those hard eyes, he was suddenly sure Holly knew what had happened.

"You were playing with fire—or dynamite—out at the Villiers' place."

"You're crazy!" He struggled to keep his voice level, casual.

"I could haul you in just on suspicion." Holly's gaze flicked down to his hands jammed in his pockets. "A feller playing with fire can get his hands burned. Want to show me yours?"

216

Dave remained silent and motionless.

"You know for arson and possible murder somebody could go away a long time."

Dave felt like the other must hear his heart pounding. Damn this cat and mouse game. Did he have Mosely or not?

"I figure right now I have a shot at a possible indictment."

"Is that right?"

"That's right. But the thing is—I ain't so sure it was murder. One man trampled and a girl crushed by a car. I ain't even sure it was arson."

Dave swallowed hard and waited. Their eyes locked. Somewhere down the corridor a telephone rang, a nurse answered it. Neither man spoke for nearly a minute. Finally Dave could stand it no longer.

"How *do* you see it then?"

Holly stroked his lean, stubbled jaw.

"I kind of see it as somebody trying to clean up a bad mess, say an overflowing sewer, that nobody else—even the law—would clean up. I don't approve of how it was done, understand. But I can see the need for doing it." Again Holly's gaze drifted to the hands in his pockets. "I got to check on my deputy."

As he started past, he seized Dave's right wrist, yanked the hand out of the pocket, looked at it and nodded.

"You might oughta see a doctor about that." His retreating footsteps echoed down the corridor.

Dave turned, his jaw slack, and stared after him. Holly ignored the elevator and started up the steps. For several moments after he disappeared, Dave stood rooted to the spot. Then he headed for the door and the parking lot.

In the car he looked to see if Holly had changed his mind and followed him outside. He started the car and resisted the temptation to race out of the parking lot. He drove sedately and soon was on the highway leading to Memphis. They had not found Mosely. Where was he? If he was smart, he would be out of the county by now, but he could be hiding in the bottoms. Someday—maybe tomorrow, next week, next year, Dave reflected, he

217

might open a door and find Mosely on the other side with a knife or gun. On the other hand, the Negro might never come back—either way, he could not spend his time worrying about it; he would just have to be wary for a long time. He thought of Sharon. She had awakened from a nightmare. And for him, the events of last night had a curious, dream-like quality already.

But a few minutes later, when he passed the van with Memphis TV 5 on its side, heading in the opposite direction, he knew the nightmare had been real and more than just his alone and Sharon's.

He wanted to shut it all out. But the image of Marie formed in his mind as she had stood in front of the vanity in her bedroom last night.

"You have the same hunger Claude and I do."

He knew now why he had been so attracted to her from the beginning. He had responded to the darkness within her because it answered the same darkness within himself that he had always tried to hide. And in the bedroom he had wanted her so that even now his hands trembled on the steering wheel, and he felt an aching hollowness in his belly. He had wanted to sacrifice Sharon for her and the only thing that had stopped him was the sudden glimpse of his own mocking face in the vanity mirror that had filled him with self-loathing.

But even now a part of him grieved for Marie.

When he had seen her arm protruding from beneath the Volkswagen, he had clung to it for a long time. He had clung to it as it had changed, grown older, and it was not just shock or concussion that had made him cling to it. He had *not wanted* to let her go.

He met his eyes in the rearview mirror. They were tired and melancholy, but they looked at him without mockery or guilt, only with bleak resignation. He shifted his gaze back to the highway and pressed down harder on the accelerator.

He had to get to Sharon. He suddenly felt a great need to be with her, to talk to her and hold her.

218

AFTER school Scott and Jimmy Farese trotted across the street into the field that adjoined the town's cemetery. They were taking the short cut to Jimmy's house. Around two o'clock the sky had begun to turn gray and now the wind tossed the tree branches and dark clouds scudded overhead. The smell of rain rode on the wind, fresh and clean, making Scott's blood tingle. In the distance thunder rumbled.

They began running through the tall, blowing grass. Before school Scott had seen his mother at the hospital and when they reached Jimmy's, Mrs. Farese was taking him back there again. This morning his mother had told him Sharon was well, that the doctors had fixed her, and that she would be home in a few days.

And they—the ones who had changed her and who had killed Bobby—had burned. They had burned while he was sleeping last night at Jimmy's from the shot he had got at the hospital. All over school the kids had been talking about it. A girl at the high school had been one of them that burned, somebody said, but Billy Patton, whose father was a fireman who had been there, said she had not burned, but she was dead anyway. He was glad. Maybe she had been the one he had seen in the field in the lightning when Sharon changed. Nobody knew how the fire had started, but maybe God had smashed them with lightning. Even now he could hardly believe it was over.

They were running past the graveyard now and suddenly Jimmy stopped.

"Look!" He pointed through the spiked iron fence.

Scott's eyes followed the pointing finger.

There were four figures standing by a plain wooden coffin. The woman's gray hair streamed in the wind, and her eyes glistened as she stared at the box. Brother Fox, the Baptist preacher, with his coattails flapping stood among the tombstones that stuck out like decayed teeth and read from the Bible, but the wind blew his words away.

Scott's heart went into his throat. For a moment he thought it was Bobby in the box. But his parents were

219

not there, and the box was too big. He recognized the old woman as Aunt Hattie Springfield, who never missed a white funeral.

"It must be Old Man Sheed," Jimmy whispered.

Brother Fox closed the Bible, and the other two men, Negroes, grabbed both ends of the box and lowered it into a deep hole. Scott gripped the iron fence tight, his knuckles white. A drop of rain struck his cheek.

"C'mon," Jimmy urged. "We're gonna get soaked." Scott hardly heard him.

The Negroes stepped away from the hole. Brother Fox crumbled a handful of dirt into it and so did Aunt Hattie Springfield. They looked up at the black clouds flying overhead and hurried away, leaving the gravediggers to spade the red earth back into the hole.

Scott took a deep breath. Tomorrow would be Bobby's turn. The kids said he was over at Paxton's Funeral Home. He knew he would not come to see Bobby lowered into the ground and earth spaded on top of him.

He turned away and looked at Jimmy. They stared at one another in silence, each knowing the other's thoughts. Thunder cracked. Big drops of rain spattered around them. They turned their backs on the cemetery and began walking quickly away. With the flash of lightning over the water tower half-a-mile away, they broke into a run. Knees and elbows pumping, they ran abreast through the tall weeds.

The wind at their back skimmed them along as they left the graveyard far behind and, side by side, raced toward home.

THE END